THE SEA WITCH

A WICKED VILLAINS NOVEL

KATEE ROBERT

TRINKETS AND TALES LLC

ALSO BY KATEE ROBERT

Wicked Villains
Book 1: Desperate Measures
Book 2: Learn My Lesson
Book 3: A Worthy Opponent
Book 4: The Beast
Book 5: The Sea Witch
Book 6: Queen Takes Rose

A Touch of Taboo
Book 1: Your Dad Will Do
Book 2: Gifting Me To His Best Friend

The Island of Ys
Book 1: His Forbidden Desire
Book 2: Her Rival's Touch
Book 3: His Tormented Heart
Book 4: Her Vengeful Embrace

The Thalanian Dynasty Series (MMF)
Book 1: Theirs for the Night
Book 2: Forever Theirs
Book 3: Theirs Ever After
Book 4: Their Second Chance

The Kings Series
Book 1: The Last King

Book 2: The Fearless King

The Hidden Sins Series
Book 1: The Devil's Daughter
Book 2: The Hunting Grounds
Book 3: The Surviving Girls

The Make Me Series
Book 1: Make Me Want
Book 2: Make Me Crave
Book 3: Make Me Yours
Book 4: Make Me Need

The O'Malley Series
Book 1: The Marriage Contract
Book 2: The Wedding Pact
Book 3: An Indecent Proposal
Book 4: Forbidden Promises
Book 5: Undercover Attraction
Book 6: The Bastard's Bargain

The Hot in Hollywood Series
Book 1: Ties that Bind
Book 2: Animal Attraction

The Foolproof Love Series
Book 1: A Foolproof Love
Book 2: Fool Me Once
Book 3: A Fool for You

Out of Uniform Series

Book 1: In Bed with Mr. Wrong

Book 1.5: His to Keep

Book 2: Falling for His Best Friend

Book 3: His Lover to Protect

Book 3.5: His to Take

Serve Series

Book 1: Mistaken by Fate

Book 2: Betting on Fate

Book 3: Protecting Fate

Come Undone Series

Book 1: Wrong Bed, Right Guy

Book 2: Chasing Mrs. Right

Book 3: Two Wrongs, One Right

Book 3.5: Seducing Mr. Right

Other Books

Seducing the Bridesmaid

Meeting His Match

Prom Queen

The Siren's Curse

CHAPTER 1

ZURIELLE

Three simple rules have been ingrained into me from birth:

1. Never leave Olympus.

2. My family members are the only people who value my safety and well-being, and as such, my loyalty to them should be my first priority at all times.

3. Never trust the Sea Witch.

Tonight, I'm breaking all three.

There might be time for regrets later, but as I watch Olympus disappear into the horizon behind me, I can't dredge them up now. My sisters will be fine. They've never felt the city borders quite as acutely as I have. They're happy in a way I can't replicate. Maybe I could have settled before I met Alaric, but that possibility is long gone.

Now, I only have one path available.

I try very hard not to think about my father during the long bus ride to Carver City. I'm his youngest, the baby to be protected at all costs, for all that I'm twenty-three and lost my innocence right around the time my mother lost her life. Even if she were still among the living, no one stays sheltered in Olympus for long. Not when they move in the circles my father does.

I push the thought away and close my eyes. The future. The future is all that matters. My father will forgive me eventually, especially once he realizes I did it for love. Is there any more honorable motivation?

And I *do* love Alaric. Those weeks I spent with him over the winter were the happiest I've ever had. He's kind and sweet and so incredibly respectful. What father wouldn't want his daughter with a man like that?

I allow myself to sink into the warm memories to pass the time. It feels like between one blink and the next the bus shudders to a stop and the driver announces that we've reached the station. I move with the others to file out the doors and collect my bag.

Carver City looks much the same as Olympus. Tall buildings that threaten to block out the sky. People who go about their own business and spend their lives happily ignorant of what goes on in the shadows. Of the power players who hopscotch between what's right and what's wrong, because the only thing that matters is what they want. They posture and perform for friends and enemies alike.

It makes me tired just thinking about it.

I pull my phone out and bring up the address. It took me several long weeks to dredge up the courage to respond to the Sea Witch. Ursa, that's her name. Somehow it doesn't make her seem any less intimidating than the other. She's not to be trusted. It doesn't matter now. She's only a woman, albeit a powerful and dangerous one. I am capable of taking her help without giving her anything priceless in return.

I hope.

As I stop at the curb, debating whether to call a cab or use an app to get a ride, a shiny black car melts out of the traffic and pulls to a stop in front of me. I stare at it blankly before giving myself a shake. Coincidence. That's all it is. I'm sure it's waiting for someone else.

The window rolls down, and the first thing I see is red—red lips curved in a sinful smile. Then the woman emerges from the shadows inside the car. She's Black and curvy and has a mass of locs that go from dark brown to a crimson at the ends that I envy. My father never let me color my hair "unnatural" colors, even after I turned eighteen, and so though my hair is technically red, it's a deep red that's almost brown.

I know who this woman is even before she speaks. "Ursa."

"The very one." I don't know much about her beyond what my father's ranted about when he drinks too much. A woman who threatened everything he held dear. One who tried to kill him and take his place as Poseidon's second-in-command. A witch who likes to drown her victims to boost her reputation; someone who tried to drown *him* before he managed to win the war and drive her out of Olympus.

She must be my father's age—somewhere in her late-forties to mid-fifties, but she looks younger than I expect. Or rather, she has the kind of ageless beauty that could put her anywhere from thirty to sixty. Her smile widens, though it doesn't reach her dark eyes. "You're looking for me, I presume."

I am, but I haven't quite caught up with the fact that she's *here*. I expected her to wait for me in her home, to set the tone for me to be the powerless woman begging for aid and her as the only one who can give it to me. I didn't expect *this*.

Then again, what is this but setting the tone in a different kind of way? She knew what bus I'd be on. Knew I'd be here at exactly this time and place. She must be watching me.

Getting in cars with strangers is a very basic rule that I've never had a problem following, but it's silly to reject the ride

3

KATEE ROBERT

when this is the woman I've traveled to see. The only one who can help me.

I lift my chin. "Yes, I'm looking for you."

"Very good." She leans back and rolls the window up.

I blink at my own reflection distorted back at me. I look impossibly young and naive, and I'm pretty sure there's a crease on my face from where I had myself propped up against the window on the bus ride. I'd hoped to clean up before meeting her, because first impressions matter. Oh well. One works with what one has.

The driver's side door opens up and a tall Black woman with short cropped hair emerges. She gives me a once-over and shakes her head, but she doesn't say a word as she puts my bag into the trunk, and opens the door for me. It's too late to back out now. I've come too far.

I climb into the backseat.

When I was small, my sisters used to threaten me with the Sea Witch whenever they decided I was being annoying. *If you don't act right, the Sea Witch will come and take you away.* It used to terrify me as a child. Now she terrifies me for other reasons. A woman doesn't come by a reputation like hers without some kind of truth behind it. But she *is* only a woman, flesh and blood just like me. Or that's what I tell myself as I try to shake the feeling I'm a mouse who's just cuddled up to a cat.

Her presence fills the space, squeezing my chest even though she's retreated to the other side of the seat and isn't touching me. In the dim interior, I can see that she's wearing a wrap dress with a dark pattern almost like bubbles on it. It's pretty and obviously expensive, but a printed dress should make her more approachable.

It doesn't.

She's studying me the same way I'm looking at her. I don't want to know what verdict she comes up with. I'm not at my best. I dressed for comfort instead of making an impression, wearing my favorite faded jeans, a tank top, and knitted cardigan that's fraying a bit in spots.

The silence spins out between us, strangely loaded. Even knowing better, I can't stop myself from breaking it first. "I don't trust you."

"You shouldn't." She shrugs a shoulder. The move draws my attention to her impressive cleavage, and I immediately jerk my eyes back to her face. Ursa is attractive, but it's more complicated than beautiful. She's *powerful*. She's not even doing anything other than looking at me, and I'm fighting to draw each breath.

All the lessons I've spent a lifetime learning go right out the window. "What do you want with me?"

"I want to help you." There it is again, her wicked smile that does nothing to reassure me. "I have something of a soft spot for Alaric. This is a favor to him."

She isn't telling the truth. Ursa is *the Sea Witch*. Even if she were madly in love with Alaric, she wouldn't give him to me. She certainly wouldn't do something to undermine her own power and territory as a favor. She's also very clearly not going to tell me the truth.

I narrow my eyes. "Then why not pay his debt and free him?"

"It's complicated." She doesn't look away from me as the car slides back into traffic. "I can see you don't believe me, so I'll lay it out for you. Hades's neutral territory is too valuable to risk; as such, he won't allow anyone in Carver City to interfere with his precious deals. Alaric made a deal, and I pay his debt, it might look like I'm using Alaric's bargain as a way to bribe Hades, which impacts his interactions with the other territory leaders. It's messy and that man abhors a mess. You, my dear, are a very convenient loophole."

It seems reasonable enough, but she's very pointedly not

mentioning her history with my father, which is the very definition of *mess*, even if I don't know the specific details. "Very convenient indeed."

"Now, before we begin, I have to ask." Ursa sits back, somehow looking every inch a queen in the vaguely cramped backseat. "How far are you willing to go?"

I don't even have to think about it. "As far as it takes." I've never experienced what I feel for Alaric with anyone else. If that's not love, what is? And if it *is* love, it's worth fighting for. It's worth sacrificing for.

She nods as if she expects no less. "And what do you have to bargain with?"

I flush. I have a trust fund, but I won't have access to it until I'm thirty. I've never wanted for anything, but all my credit cards and bank accounts are linked to my father. My liquid assets are minimal. Except… I touch my necklace. "I have this."

Ursa motions with impatient fingers, each topped with bloodred polish to match her lips. "Let's see."

I lift it, intending to take it off, but she snags it and tugs, drawing me closer. My breath stalls in my chest. I don't know if I'm imagining it, but I swear I can feel the warmth coming off her body, and it has something coiling low in my stomach in response. I shiver and watch her run her fingers over my mother's necklace. Sapphires, diamonds and emeralds depict the depths of the ocean around a stylized ruby seahorse. It's worth a small fortune, but it's priceless to me.

Ursa lays it back against my chest, her knuckles dragging over my sternum through my tank top. An accidental touch, maybe, but it has me jerking back. I don't understand my reaction to her, but I'm loyal to Alaric, even if he's not able to give me the same currently.

I'm still regaining my equilibrium when she shakes her head. "It won't be enough."

I blink. "Surely he doesn't owe Hades so much?" I still don't know the circumstances of Alaric's deal with Hades, what he needed such a large sum of money for. All I know is that Hades provided it and Alaric has been paying off that debt ever since. He's assured me that it's not a bad life, as such things go, but he's not free, either.

"He does." Ursa finally releases me from her gaze, turning her face to the window. "He still owes Hades a quarter of a million dollars."

Helplessness rises in my chest, clawing at my throat. She's right. The necklace is worth a lot, but not that much. Especially if I'm forced to pawn it. "You promised a way to free him."

"I didn't promise that you'd like it." She gives another of those shrugs that mean absolutely nothing. "You have the pretty necklace, but it's not enough."

"I don't have anything else!"

"Don't you?"

I shake my head, trying to concentrate past the hopelessness welling up inside me. "What are you talking about? Don't you think if I had anything of value, I'd willingly bargain it for him? I would in a heartbeat."

"If you had anything of value?" She finally looks at me again almost pitying. "Come now, little girl. Surely you're not that naive. You must know you possess the one thing guaranteed to be valuable enough to free Alaric."

"I don't understand." Except, as her gaze sweeps over my body, I'm starting to. I shake my head. "If I make a deal with Hades, that only reverses our positions. It doesn't solve the problem."

"No, making a deal wouldn't solve anything." Her lips curve up like she's telling a joke, except nothing is funny. "I'm talking about your body. Would you give a single night to free him?"

Sex.

She's talking about sex.

I fight not to tense, and I'm not entirely successful. I could brazen my way through this, but... "I've never had sex before."

"That only makes what you're offering more valuable in the eyes of people willing to pay for it."

A small, foolish part of me thought I'd give my virginity to Alaric. During our time together, we'd never had the opportunity to decide if I was ready one way or another, not when we could only meet in public places. Am I willing to sacrifice the romantic notion of him being my first for his freedom?

Yes. Of course. It's barely even a question.

What are a hymen and a single night when weighed against forever?

It's only sex. If I have no experience with it, at least I'll have no expectations going in. Maybe it'd actually be better to get it out of the way with someone else first. From most of what I've read on the subject, the first time isn't anything to look forward to. Better to rip off the bandage and then move on to the good stuff with Alaric afterward.

Even if none of that were true, my answer would be the same.

"I'll do it."

CHAPTER 2

*S*omehow, it surprises me that Ursa takes us directly to the Underworld. From the outside, the building looks much like the others around it, though I almost thought it'd be taller. I squint up at it and then have to scramble to keep up with Ursa's long strides.

I thought she'd be taller, too.

It's such a strange expectation, but she felt larger than life on our way over here, and discovering that she's maybe six inches taller than my five-three is disconcerting for some reason. Out of the car, her presence should be dispelled. It's not. Despite the other people on the sidewalk, she is in a class all her own, a shark swimming with minnows. Like minnows, people flit out of her way as if sensing danger.

The sunlight plays across her body the same way the shadows of the car did, drawing my gaze to the way her dress hugs her curves with each stride. She's large and powerful and confident, and she makes me feel tiny and breakable and brittle by comparison. I don't think I like it.

But then, that's my problem, isn't it? I have a feeling she'd walk the exact same way even if I weren't here.

I follow her through the doors and into the warmth of the building. The reality of my situation cascades over me as we step into an elevator and it ascends.

A virginity auction.

That's what she wants me to do. Sell myself to the highest bidder.

Two days ago, the possibility would have made me laugh. Me, Triton's youngest daughter, stepping onto a stage and embracing the humiliation of a bidding war? Never going to happen. Except it's what I'm agreeing to, and the knowledge sits like shards of glass in my throat.

"You don't have to do this, you know." Ursa sounds almost kind. A quick glance at her gives no lie to the first impression. Her eyes are still cold, but I have a feeling they don't warm often, so I don't take it personally. But she's smiling at me as if trying to be reassuring.

I turn back to face the shiny elevator doors. "Yes, I do. As you pointed out in the car, I have nothing else to bargain with."

"Is he worth it? I've found that men rarely are."

Is she closer? I'm not sure, but I'm suddenly achingly aware of how the cut of her dress gives the faintest tease of cleavage. I jerk my gaze away from her reflection, but it doesn't help. Even though there are a polite twelve inches between us, she's everywhere in this small space. My face is flaming and I can't make it stop. "He's worth it," I finally manage.

"I think you're wrong." She shrugs. "But I suppose young love conquers all. Even if that's not how most of the stories go." Her laugh is deep and sensual, and my skin prickles with something like need in response.

I close my eyes, but even that doesn't help. I can *feel* her there, just out of reach. I have the strangest desire to sink to my knees and beg her to stroke her nails along my skin. What is she *doing* to me? "Stories aren't real life."

"No, but they contain a multitude of lessons that a clever person heeds."

The doors slide open before I can formulate a response, but what response is there? I've decided to do this, so I'm going to do this. It's such a small sacrifice to make for Alaric's freedom. People have sex for money all the time. It's the world's oldest trade, or near to it. There is no shame in making this choice.

The room we enter is nearly empty, except a desk in the center and a bold black door behind it. Behind the desk sits a beautiful Black man who smiles when he catches sight of Ursa. "Good afternoon."

"Don't stand on formality on my account, Adem." She moves around the desk, and he rises so they can exchange air kisses on each cheek. When she leans back, she's smiling. Not just smiling. Her eyes are warm with fondness, and she grips his shoulders as if she genuinely cares about him.

I don't expect the jab of envy. I don't know what to do with the strange response. Ursa is not a friend. She might not be an enemy—though my father would argue otherwise—but she's a stranger. What should I care that she obviously likes this beautiful man with his perfect skin and perfect laugh that seems to fill the empty room?

He turns that perfect smile on me, and it's everything I can do not to lean forward in response. The man is *magnetic*. He shifts fully to face me as Ursa releases him. "And who might you be?"

Ursa laughs, a low and melodious sound. "Tell Hades I have a delightful little surprise for him."

My gaze swings to her. Somehow, it didn't occur to me that I'd be meeting *Hades*. The man responsible for Alaric's situation.

But then, that's not entirely accurate, is it? Hades only offered the terms of the deal. Alaric made the choice to take it. It was something else that drove him to those lengths. Some*one* else.

Maybe someday he'll trust me enough to tell me the full truth of it.

Adem instantly goes back to his professional mask, his smile fading to something practiced, the warmth in his eyes shifting to polite interest. "Of course."

Ursa drifts in my direction as he picks up the phone. She ends up between me and the desk, hiding my view. "You have nothing to fear here."

I almost laugh. "I'm about to sell my virginity. There's a lot to fear here."

Her expression is almost kind as she lifts a hand to curl a length of my hair around her fingers. I go stock-still, not sure if I want to pull away or move closer. Ursa drops her hand before I reach a conclusion. "Consent is everything, darling. Nothing will be done to you that you don't want to happen."

The unexpected kindness in her voice staggers me. "You can't honestly think that I'll enjoy giving myself to a stranger."

Another of her shrugs. "You'd be surprised what you might enjoy now that you're in Carver City. There's no one here to tell you what to think, what to feel. The only way to figure out what you enjoy is to try it."

I stare. How could she possibly dismantle my entire life with a few choice words? I am twenty-three, but there are sixteen-year-olds out there with more life experience. After my mother died, my father locked down our household. Fear and love drive him in equal measures, but knowing that doesn't make living under his iron fist any more enjoyable. Not when nearly every minute from waking to sleep is spent under the watchful eyes of tutors and guards and people all too willing to report anything they consider *dangerous*.

The number one thing on that list? Curiosity. The very trait I can't seem to scrub from my existence. I can't help that I want to know more about everything, that the walls built high for my safety are the same ones that suffocate me when I'm not lost in a book.

I know my father loves me. I might doubt countless things in Olympus, but never that. It doesn't change the fact that he's done everything in his power to prevent me from leaving his household. It doesn't alter the truth that his love has been slowly smothering me since I was old enough to dream of a normal life.

"Would you like it?" I don't mean to voice the question, but it's there all the same, taking up space between us.

"A virginity auction?" She laughs again. "Darling, I'm going to *love* it." Before I can ask what she means, she continues. "But no, I don't enjoy being on the submissive side of the power balance. I like to give orders, not take them."

"Oh." Nothing else to say to that, because Adem is off the phone and ushering us to the door behind him.

He spares another smile for Ursa. "Be good."

"It'll never happen."

The words contain a flavor of ritual, as if they're repeated often between these two. Again, that stab of envy. Surely it's not because she seems to genuinely like this man? Surely it's because I envy the freedom they both have, the ability to do what they want, when they want. Surely.

The door leads into a dim bar area, but Ursa doesn't check her stride to allow me to look my fill. I get the impression of a large sculpture and booths lining the walls, and then we're in a hallway, heading back to another door—this one a more normal size. It spits us into a tastefully decorated office that lacks any hint of color. Gray on gray on gray, which should make it as soulless as the entrance, but somehow doesn't.

I almost miss the man sitting behind the desk.

My gaze snags on him on my second pass over the room, and I frown. He's sitting back in the shadows, and another quick look around confirms that it's intentional. Most of the space is lit well enough. Theatrics, but effective ones.

The nerves that Ursa temporarily tamed flare to life in response. I've skirted the edge of power enough to know it when I see it, and Hades *drips* power even while bathed in darkness. "What have you brought me, Ursa?"

Ursa presses a hand to the center of my back, urging me forward. I stagger a few steps, my legs suddenly not working correctly, and am grateful when she doesn't drop her hand. She smiles at Hades, but it contains none of the warmth she gave Adem. "An opportunity."

"What makes you think I'm interested?"

I'm not sure, but I don't think he's done more than glance at me since we walked into the room. I press my lips together and let Ursa take the lead. I'm not sure I can speak at this point. I'm out of my depth and sinking fast.

"An auction. You haven't hosted one of those in ages."

He shifts ever so slightly. "With good reason. They're messy, and you know as well as I do that without a good draw, they're not worth the headache."

"We have the draw."

"Do tell."

She moves her hand to stroke over my hair, her nails prickling my scalp. "An Olympian princess." A pause. "A *virgin* Olympian princess."

Hades leans forward, the light kissing his features for the first time since I walked into the room. He's a handsome older white guy with salt-and-pepper hair. Not particularly large, but only a fool believes all strength is physical. "I'm listening."

"I'm willing to give you ten percent."

His lips curve up the tiniest bit. "You'll give me thirty."

"Hades, now you're just being greedy. The girl is doing ninety percent of the work. She deserves ninety percent of the money."

They go back and forth, bargaining over the percentage of money Hades will profit off my auction. I have to bite my tongue to not tell him it will all go to him anyways. Ursa hasn't offered up that information, and I know enough not to give it freely. I'm already at enough of a disadvantage; no reason to add to the scales being tipped against me.

They finally settle on giving Hades twenty percent, leaving me with the remaining eighty.

The amount of money I had to earn was already astronomical. With that added twenty percent on top of it, it feels impossible.

Once again, Hades turns his attention on me. "You may change your mind at any point with no repercussions. Once the auction is finished, the money will be put in a holding account until the terms are met, and then your percentage will be distributed to the account of your choosing."

It takes me two tries to speak. "Okay."

His eyes narrow. "There is some paperwork. Sit a moment while my partner retrieves it. Ursa, a word."

"You know, they still talk about you in Olympus. Or at least they still whisper your name." I don't mean to blurt it out, but I can't seem to help myself. Hades turns those cold eyes on me, and I just keep talking. "You're something of a boogieman."

"I know." He tilts his head. "Ursa."

I nearly topple over when her hand disappears. I had barely realized she was still touching me, hadn't noticed how hard I was leaning on that for strength. I manage to keep my feet as Hades rises and ushers Ursa out the door.

Then there's nothing to do but wait.

I sink into one of the leather chairs across from the desk and do my best not to fidget. Things are in motion; no going back now. I thought I'd have more relief once Hades agreed to it, but all I feel are nerves leaping in my stomach.

I nearly startle out of my skin when the door opens again and a white man walks into the room, but my fear disappears as recognition takes hold. I shoot to my feet. *"Hercules?"*

"Zuri." He crosses toward me slowly, and I can't help comparing and contrasting this man with the one I knew in passing back in Olympus. He's been gone for well over a year now, and there were rumors that he'd taken up with someone in Carver City, but I didn't expect him *here*.

He looks good. There's a confidence to his walk and the way he holds his broad shoulders that wasn't there a year ago. His blond hair is a little shaggier, but it looks intentional and almost roguish. The kindness in his blue eyes is the same, though.

He takes my hands and hesitates. "I have to ask several uncomfortable questions."

Somehow, I didn't expect this, either. That Hades would send in the one person in Carver City who's familiar enough with Olympus that he's capable of getting to the truth of things.

"I'll answer them as best I can." I lift my chin. I can tell the truth without giving him *all* of it. Hades called him a partner. The might mean professional partner or it might mean romantic partner—or both—but the one thing it definitely means is that I can't really trust Hercules.

"Let's sit." He urges me back into the chair I just left and takes the one next to it. "First and most importantly, are you here of your own free will?"

"Yes, of course."

He gives me a look like there's no *of course* about this situation. "You walked in here with Ursa, so forgive the need for more information."

"She's helping me."

"Ursa doesn't help anyone but herself."

I give a bitter laugh. "Says the man *Hades* calls *partner*."

Hercules opens his mouth and then shakes his head. "Okay, fair. But she's not blackmailing or manipulating or forcing you into this?"

"No. I need the money, and she suggested this as a solution."

He looks like he really, really wants to ask me what I need the money for. "Does your father know you're here?"

"You knew my father back in Olympus. What do you think?"

"I think he's going to try to tear Carver City to pieces once he figures out where you've gone." He grimaces. "I think you're making a mistake, Zuri. If you need money…"

"No." I'm already shaking my head. "Thank you, but no. You won't have enough, and even if you did, I need this free and clear. I can't take out a loan I have no hope of repaying. I'll just end up back here again." Without my virginity as a bargaining chip.

"If you're in trouble—"

"I've got it covered. I promise." I'm lying through my teeth, but if I raise enough money with this auction, I *will* have it covered.

Hercules hesitates for so long, I'm sure he plans to send me away. But he finally sighs. "In that case, let's go through it." He rounds the desk and rifles through the drawers with the ease of someone who's done it before. A few moments later, he hands me a stack of papers. "You'll need to fill this out before we can continue."

I expect a contract, something to tie me in legal knots to ensure my compliance. I don't expect the several-page list of preferences. I scan them, my eyebrows inching up. "What is this?"

"This is for your protection and the protection of the person who has the winning bid. Only mark what you're interested in. There will still be a safe word to stop things if you need to, but this cuts down on the possibility of crossing lines."

Some of these things, I've never even heard of. I can't take my gaze from the list. "And if I only want sex in the, um, vanilla way?"

Again, that hesitation, like he doesn't want to answer truthfully. "I've only seen one auction in the last year, though it was with several people and set up differently. From that experience, the more interests marked, the higher the starting asking price. If you're serious about needing money, I'd consider putting as much on the list as you're comfortable with."

As much on the list as I'm comfortable with. The very idea is laughable.

But he's right. If I'm doing this, I have to make it count.

"Okay." I accept the pen he offers. "This may take a bit."

Hercules looks like he wants to bundle me into a hug until I feel less shaky. "Take as long as you need."

I take a deep breath and settle in to read.

CHAPTER 3

URSA

"*W*hat game are you playing, Ursa?"

I lean against the bar and smile at Hades. "Darling, you're going soft. It's not like you to be so protective of strangers who are more than eager to make you money."

He ignores the drink that Tisiphone set at his elbow and stares at me. It's a good look, firm and icy. One I've seen bring even the most dominant and dangerous people in Carver City to their knees. I've been playing in deep waters for nearly as long as he has. I'm old enough to remember when Hades was betrayed by Zeus and driven out of Olympus, though I was less than a year into my position under Poseidon at the time. I lasted another year before being driven out as well. He should really know better than to try to intimidate me.

"You brought her here. It would lead a man to believe you have a vested interest in the girl. I'm not interested in playing pawn in your games, Ursa. I'm neutral territory for a reason."

He's also developed a soft spot since he and Megaera took up with their precious golden boy, Hercules. Zurielle needs help, and he's in a position to give her that help—and make a profit in the process. It's only my presence that has alarms blaring for him. Ah well. I can throw him a bone. I pick up my drink and swirl it a little, enjoying the way the ice clinks against the glass. "You know the circumstances surrounding my leaving Olympus."

"I know Triton was behind it."

Even hearing my old enemy's name sends fire simmering through me. He was a friend until he wasn't, until I reached too high and he decided I was a threat to his position as Poseidon's favorite. It's his fault I can never go home again, his fault I wasn't able to see my parents again before their deaths. His fault that I had to come to a strange city and start over with nothing. If I were another woman, that exile would have spelled my death, and Triton still orchestrated it. It doesn't matter that I've climbed higher in Carver City than I ever could have in Olympus. That betrayal still stings despite the years that have passed. I take a slow breath and shove my anger down. It has no place here, and I can't afford to do anything but put Hades at ease. "Zurielle is Triton's youngest daughter. His favorite."

Hades sighs. "And you expect me to believe it's merely coincidence that she's here with you, about to agree to something that's sure to infuriate her father?"

"Of course not." I laugh a little, keeping my tone light. "But I am only guilty of baiting the hook. She wanted freedom, so she jumped at it. If this auction angers her father, all the better."

He studies me for a long moment and finally shakes his head. "I'll agree to this auction on one further condition."

I already know I won't like it, just like I know I don't have a choice but to agree. "I'm listening."

"We will hold it tomorrow night." He barely pauses. "And she'll stay here in the meantime."

"You really *are* going soft." I smooth a hand over my hip and lean in. "Hades, darling, you're underestimating the girl. She's already set her course. Whether it happens this morning or in thirty-six hours won't make a difference."

"All the same."

I shrug. She was already committed the second she snuck out of her father's house and boarded a bus to Carver City. Another day or so won't make a bit of difference, not when I hold the leash to the one thing she wants. "Whatever you think is best. It's your show."

He narrows his eyes. "Remember that."

"She'll need the full treatment."

"I expected no less." He waves that away. "Hercules will take care of it."

"And no doubt spend the entire time attempting to change her course."

His lips curve the tiniest amount. "If she's as set on her path as you claim, you have nothing to fear."

"Regardless of her choices, *I* have nothing to fear." I tap my nails on the shiny wood bar. "I would like a private playroom to keep me occupied while Zurielle wades through the paperwork."

"Your usual?"

"Of course."

He nods slowly. "Aurora will take you back when it's ready."

"You're a gem, Hades." I sip my drink and watch him walk away. He's gone soft in the last year, but not soft enough to cross. It's just as well. I have no interest in ruling the Underworld. Neutral territory is useful, but being the one to enforce it would be tedious in the extreme. Hades might irritate me, but he's good at what he does.

I've barely finished my drink when Aurora appears. She's been in the Underworld for years now, a pretty Black girl

21

who started as a virginal plaything and who now has stepped into the role as Megaera's second-in-command. Today, Aurora's wearing a blue dress that flounces around her upper thighs. It practically begs someone to bend her over their knee, flip it up, and spank her. Her hair is nearly the same deep blue, having now fully transitioned from the pink it was last season. "Aurora."

"Ursa." She dips into a cute little curtsy. "You're here early."

"You know how it is, darling. Business waits for no one."

She gives an impish smile. "Should I be hurt that you don't want to play with me tonight?"

"Aurora, I *always* want to play with you." I tap her under the chin. "But tonight I have other pursuits."

She arches a brow. "And here I thought it was because Malone's warned you off."

That surprises a laugh out of me. There was a time when this girl wouldn't dare mouth off like this. She's not entirely wrong, though. For all that Malone hasn't touched her since that first time, my friend gets tight around the mouth whenever I play with Aurora. Which means I do it often enough to irritate her, but not so often as to damage our friendship irreparably. We're complicated like that.

I lightly drag my nails down Aurora's neck, enjoying the way she shivers in response. "Another time."

"Promise?" She's breathy just from this touch. Gods, I don't know what game Malone is playing with this girl, but she should get off her ass and do stop wasting time. Aurora is a gift of a submissive and Malone's too smart to let something so priceless escape her.

"Promise." I squeeze her shoulder. "But not tonight."

Aurora pouts a little, but it's mostly for show. When push comes to shove, she can have anyone she wants in Carver City—with the exception of Malone. She leads me through the lounge to the door into the public playroom. The escort is purely for show. I know my way around the Underworld as well as any of the regulars. At this time of evening, the public playroom is empty and dim.

Aurora opens a door and stands back. "Enjoy yourself."

"I always do."

I step into the room and close the door softly behind me. It's designed to look like a bedroom that could be found in any high-end penthouse in the city. A thick rug beneath my feet, tastefully dark colors, a dresser with a large mirror positioned to see the bed and two nightstands on either side of the bedframe. A fireplace is already lit, combating the customary chill of the room.

Alaric kneels in the middle of the space, his head bowed.

I take my time walking toward him, allowing the anticipation to build. We've played this game before, time and time again. He's wearing a pair of slacks and nothing else, and his lean muscles tense as I move to his back. His skin is paler than normal, a testament to his need to get out in the sun more. Another day, I'd play this out until he shakes with the need to look up, to be touched. I don't have the patience for it at the moment. Not with the heady feelings of being *so close* to getting my revenge on Triton.

I sift my fingers through his dark hair and give a light tug, lifting his head until he can meet my gaze. Even after years of fucking him, his beauty leaves me a little breathless. It's more than just pleasing features, though. He's got a magnetism that draws people to him without effort. And when he smiles and turns on the charm? No one can resist.

Not even me.

I give his hair another light tug. "Tell me your safe word."

"Mermaid."

"Good boy." I release him and move back to sit on the edge of the mattress. Alaric watches me warily, a hunger in

23

his blue eyes. I often wonder how others in the Underworld miss that hunger. Maybe they mistake it for lust—an easy mistake to make when he's smiling and playing the part of Prince Charming. Still, it's not like Hades to miss an opportunity to use a person's ambition to further his own goals.

His mistake is my gain, however.

Or that's how this started. A mutually beneficial arrangement in which we're both getting our needs met. Sexually, yes, but once we realized we had a common enemy in Triton, the beginnings of a friendship formed. Friendship. The thought might make me laugh if I had less control. Our relationship is far more complicated than friendship. I *like* this man with his wicked charm and eager submission. I even like his flaws despite myself. He's a danger I've never been able to turn away from. Now, I don't have to.

I crook my finger and lean back to brace my hands on the mattress behind me. Alaric crawls across the floor toward me, and the sight thrills me just as much as the knowledge of how close we are to revenge against Triton. Layers upon layers, all of them working in our favor.

Alaric stops just short of touching me and brushes his fingers against the hem of my dress. "May I?"

"Do you think you deserve it?"

He gives me a quicksilver grin, one that says he knows I'm going to say yes. "I know I do."

"Mmm." I spread my legs just a bit, all the invitation he needs to start sliding his hands up my legs, bringing my dress with him. I wait until he reaches my thighs to speak. "I should thank you."

"Oh?" Alaric's question is distracted, his gaze following his hands as he shifts my dress up and strokes my thighs. "Are you thanking me in advance for orgasms?"

"Darling, you know those orgasms are mine by right. It's *your* reward to give them to me."

He flashes another grin. "I better get started then."

"You'll want to hear this first."

He hesitates, but finally presses his palms to my thighs and gives my face his full attention. "Okay, I'm listening."

"She's here."

It takes three long seconds for comprehension to settle over his features, quickly followed by a cascade of emotions. Guilt. Lust. Hope. More guilt. Alaric clears his throat. "That took longer than you thought it would."

That, right there, is why I can never trust him fully. For as much as he cleaves to his internal image of the selfish playboy, Alaric has a conscience. It's not enough of one to stop him from doing what it takes to further his own goals, but it raises its head at the most inopportune of times.

His hands pulse on my thighs. "Are you sure you want to go through with this?"

Here we are.

I've been waiting for this moment from the second Alaric got back from Olympus. He'd done what was necessary, but he'd lost that fierce joy at the thought of revenge. I hoped time might smooth out that guilt, but I'm not surprised it didn't. I sift my fingers through his hair. "How long have you worked in the Underworld?"

His expression closes down. "Eight years."

"Who's responsible for that?"

He holds my gaze, some of the guilt clearing. "Triton."

"That's right. He was going to take out your debt on your pretty face, your beautiful body, and when you were too broken to do anything but give up, he would have killed you." I stroke his cheekbones with my thumbs. "You did the only thing you could and made a deal with Hades, but it wouldn't have been necessary if Triton hadn't painted you into a corner."

Alaric finally meets my eyes. "Maybe we should have found a way to get revenge that doesn't include Zuri."

I laugh in his face. "Lie to yourself if you must, but don't lie to me. You wanted that girl from the moment you laid eyes on her, and you didn't bother to look for another path forward." I lean down a little. "You don't care what the fallout will be for her, darling. You want her pretty virgin pussy, and I'm more than happy to provide it to you." He could have taken her and run. She was ripe for it during the weeks he spent in Olympus. All he had to do was crook his finger and he could have had her.

He chose not to. He *chose* to play out this revenge scheme.

He chose *me*.

Some days, I can hardly believe it. I don't truly trust this man, but it's difficult to remember to keep him at a distance when he's looking at me like he is now. Like I'm a goddess he's only too happy to spend his life worshipping. If I was a different woman, I'd let down my guard with him after all this time.

I can't. I've built my walls too high and too strong to protect myself, and it didn't occur to me that I might want a door or window to let someone in. Who can I trust? My people pledge their loyalty, but they're benefitting from it as long as I'm territory leader. Alaric submits to me so perfectly, but he's a caged bird. I can't guarantee what he'll do when the door is blasted open and the entire sky is at his disposal.

"Ursa."

I give myself a little shake. I hadn't meant to let my thoughts get away from me. "Mmm?"

"Where did you go just now?"

I am so fucking *tired*. Most days, I wear my armor as a second skin and barely notice its weight. Or at least that's what I tell myself to get through my days. It's even the truth, but there are moments like this, moments when I can't shake the deep desire to lean on another person. To let Alaric in like he seems to want. It's really a shame I can't trust him enough to try.

Instead of answering, I crook my finger at him. "Give me a kiss, love."

Alaric hesitates the barest moment, and I almost imagine I see hurt in those pretty blue eyes. He surges up and catches my mouth before I can be sure. Alaric kisses me like he wants to forget everything that brought him to this place, everything he'll do to escape it. I love this moment with him. It comes in every scene, when he drops the charming routine and shows his true colors.

In this moment, he's mine and mine alone.

CHAPTER 4

ALARIC

I pull Ursa's dress over her head even as I bear us down to the mattress. I learned a long time ago that sex and submission are the only comfort she'll allow me to offer, and so I push away any dissatisfaction that she's shutting me out once again. How can I be unhappy when I have this woman naked in my arms?

The rest will come later. Once I'm out of the Underworld, out from under Hades's thumb. Once I'm Ursa's in truth, once we've enacted our revenge and set the past firmly in the past. *Then* she'll let me in. I'm sure of it.

Until that moment, we still have this, and I'll never pass up an opportunity to provide us with the escape we both need right now.

I move down her body, stroking her curves, spreading her thick thighs. She's one of the toughest territory leaders in Carver City, but when it's just us, she gives me glimpses of the woman behind the impressive walls she shows the rest of the world.

It's a heady thing to kneel between the thighs of the Sea

Witch. She's the Dominant in this scene, in our relationship, but sometimes I wonder if she realizes how much trust she displays in moments like this. When she lets me close, when she allows me to bring her pleasure.

I dip down and drag my tongue over her pussy. I fucking *love* how she watches me when I go down on her. She doesn't lose control, not until the very end, and I crave those little slices of vulnerability more than I want to admit.

I let go of my guilt over what comes next. It doesn't matter. Not here, not now, not with us right on the cusp of a future I've barely let myself contemplate. Instead, I give myself over to the taste of Ursa, the feel of her, the sound of her breathing picking up. She indulges me for a few minutes before she digs her fingers into my hair and pulls me up to her clit. "Stop teasing, Alaric."

I almost test her. Almost disobey and see what she'll come up with as punishment. In the end, I need this too much to play. I lick Ursa's clit just like she loves, adjusting a little as her thighs tense against my hands. I know exactly what touch she likes, and as much as I want to drag this out, I'm intensely aware that she could stop me at any moment. I don't want to stop. Not until I've made her come all over my face.

Ursa orgasms with a low moan that's almost my name. She lets me ease her down, and then her fingers tighten in my hair and tug me upward. I rise eagerly and she takes my mouth. She let me guide the first kiss. This one is a reminder of who truly has control. Ursa. Always Ursa. Just the way we both like it.

She bears me down to the floor and straddles me, all without breaking the kiss. By the time she lifts her head, I'm breathing hard and struggling to stay still. Ursa's brows pull together. "I owe you a beating."

29

"I don't care. I need you." I love the pain she gives me, but feeling her wet pussy slide against my cock is enough to shelve the desire for anything but sinking deep inside her. Her little smile tells me she knows it, too. I fight for control. "Please."

"You're so pretty when you beg." She snakes a hand down my stomach and wraps it around my cock. "I'm inclined to give you what you want this time, love. You deserve it after you've pleased me so greatly." She guides my cock inside her and then takes my wrists and pin them on either side of my head.

I could get free if I wanted. That's not what this is about. I choose submission time and time again, but it's different with Ursa. She's not holding me down. She's anchoring me. Keeping me tethered to this place, this moment, as she rides my cock in agonizingly slow strokes. Letting me feel every inch of her, reminding me that every inch of *me* belongs to her.

Time ceases to have meaning. Every nerve in my body is focused on the tight squeeze of her pussy, on the even tighter grip she keeps on my wrists, on the slow slide of her skin against mine. A preview to the moment when we can have this any time we want, when it doesn't require a set schedule approved by Hades and his people.

I dig my heels into the carpet, fighting not to thrust up into her. "I'm close," I grind out.

"Come for me, lover."

At her low command, I stop fighting the pleasure coursing through me. One stroke. Two. On the third, I curse and orgasm, driving up into her and emptying myself. She leans down, pressing her breasts to my chest, and kisses me. "Good boy."

It takes a few moments to drift down from coming, but

she eventually climbs off me and we both end up on the bed, Ursa tucked against my side. It's a token of how far we've come that she allows this. When we first used to scene, she would get dressed and wrap me up in a blanket, only holding me until I was steady enough to leave. Now, the aftercare lasts almost as long as the scene does.

I lay there for a long time as she traces patterns on my chest with her nails. Gentle. So fucking gentle when she wants to be. It doesn't make her any less devastating.

I should keep silent, but I can't quite manage it. "She's actually going through with it?"

Ursa smiles. "Of course she is, darling." I know what's coming even before she sits up and reaches for her dress. "She thinks she's in love with you."

Guilt rises again, gaining teeth and claws. I made my decision when I went to Olympus and effectively seduced Zurielle Rosi without ever fucking her. There's no going back now. The die is cast. All that matters is riding this to the bitter end. It doesn't matter that I already know the outcome of the auction, that Ursa is setting this up with only one end result. Something could go sideways. No matter how powerful she is, she can't tell the future. If someone comes in and blows the plan out of the water, we could be putting Zuri in actual danger. "She needs to be safe."

"Safe is not the word I'd use." She takes one look at my face and lifts an eyebrow. "Are you having an attack of conscience?"

"No, of course not." It's almost the truth. We've worked long months to get this into place, to irk Triton even as we pave the way for me to pay of the remainder of my bargain with Hades. If Zuri is the one to ultimately pay the price? Well, the worst she'll deal with is a blow to her fragile heart. Really, I'm doing her a favor. Anyone else would throw her to the wolves for their freedom instead of ensuring the auction has the proper end result.

Or at least that's the narrative I've spun.

I've always been good at lying to myself to get what I want.

Still. I swallow down the uncomfortable feeling in my throat. "She's an innocent."

"Please. She's from Olympus. Her father might not be one of the Thirteen, but he's close enough. Or do I have to remind you what he's done to both of us?"

"You don't have to remind me." Triton would have killed me if I wasn't able to pay that debt, and he wouldn't have lost any sleep over it. Fucking his favorite daughter is the *least* I could do for revenge. "She's a good girl."

"Mmhmm." Ursa taps my under the chin with one blood-red nail. "And after the auction, she'll be *our* good girl."

Heat surges through me at the thought of Zuri here, in bed with us. If I was a better man, I'd have found another way. I'm not. I want my freedom. I want Ursa. And, yeah, I want Zuri, too. Not forever, but the idea of playing with her hot little body? I'm selfish enough to want it all. "You really think she'll be into it?" The Zuri I spent time with in Olympus was painfully sweet. I can't imagine her *wanting* what's coming. I'm not sure what it says about me that I'm not sure if I care. She's agreeing to it. That's enough.

"I think you underestimate her, but then you're a man. Of course you do." She taps my chin one last time and stands. Even as I tell myself not to, I watch her get dressed. I love these moments when I get to see her like few other people do. It feels like a secret, and there's nothing so addicting as a vulnerable moment shared with someone who is otherwise so fucking untouchable.

Ursa finishes pulling on her dress and smooths down the

skirt. She catches me watching and shakes her head. "Stop that. We don't have time for another round."

"You sure about that?"

"Alaric." Even after several years, I still can't quite tell if the fondness in her voice when she says my name is feigned or truth. I kind of enjoy that I can't tell.

I stand and give her a mocking bow. "Yes, Mistress."

Ursa shakes her head and moves to the door. "She'll be in the Underworld until the auction tomorrow night. Do what you need to do." She's gone before her words fully penetrate.

When they do, I sink back onto the bed.

She's in the Underworld.

Zuri is *here*.

She'll be here until the auction. In the same building I live in.

If I'm smart, I'll stay away from her. One conversation, that's all it will take to cement her motivation to go through with this. Seeing her more than that is tempting fate— tempting my self-control. No matter what Zuri thinks, I'm no Prince Charming. I want her. I've wanted her since I set eyes on her, wearing that cute little sundress and walking through the gardens like she'd never seen anything so beautiful as flowers. I didn't realize then that she looks at all new experiences that way, soaking them in and memorizing them as if she'll never get another chance.

Will she look at sex the same way?

I'm dying to find out.

And that's the crux of the matter. If I were any less selfish, I'd get Zuri out and find a different way to enact my vengeance. But I want her, and Ursa has paved the way for me to have her. For both of us to have her.

I manage to keep my shit locked down for the rest of the night, spending most of my time in the lounge with a short reprieve to play out a scene with Hook and Tink.

As much as I want my freedom, I really do love my job. Who wouldn't? I get to fuck and scene with the most powerful people in Carver City. It's a dream—or it would be if I didn't have my debt to Hades hanging over my head. The man might not ever force me to do something I don't want to do, but knowing that I owe him is a festering wound I can't treat until I'm free of it.

By the time the club closes and it's time for our nightly round up, I'm weaving on my feet. I peel off my slacks in the employee locker room and take my third shower of the night. Around me, the rest of the employees on shift are doing the same. As I dry off and pull on jeans and a T-shirt, it strikes me that most of the faces are new. Aurora is the only employee who's been here as long as me—longer, even. She's also the only one with a deal with Hades that hasn't wrapped up yet. The rest of them are actual employees, people who came here for a job and go home at the end of their shifts.

We gather in the room off the locker room and rattle off any interesting information we picked up while Aurora takes notes. There's been plenty of power shifts in Carver City in the last couple years, but it seems to have stabilized a bit recently. There's nothing of note, with the exception of the rumor of another auction coming in a few days. A *virginity* auction.

But then, I already knew that.

Aurora finishes her last note and looks up. "That's everything. Good work tonight." She beams at us. I don't know the terms of her bargain any more than she knows mine, but I don't have to in order to recognize that it's different. Rumor has it that Aurora came to the Underworld seeking safety for herself and protection for her comatose mother. Regardless of what price Hades asked of her, it's different than my situation.

My bargain isn't driven by anything as noble as keeping someone I love safe.

No, it was pure selfish greed that drove me to be one hell of a thief in Olympus, and it was an equally selfish need to keep my skin intact that had me bargaining with Hades. Now, it will be selfish desire that drags Zuri down into the depths with me.

I'm nothing if not consistent.

CHAPTER 5

ZURIELLE

I don't expect to sleep once Hercules sets me up in a suite a few floors down from the club, but the next thing I know, I'm opening my eyes to a pounding on my door. I stumble out of bed and shove my hair from my eyes, still discombobulated from strange dreams. Reality hits me in the ten feet between my bed and the door.

I'm in the Underworld.

I'm going to auction off myself tomorrow night.

It still hasn't quite sunk in as I open the door to find Hercules standing there. He gives me a soft smile. "You managed to get some sleep last night. Good."

"Yes." I'm relieved it's him who seems to be in charge of handling this whole thing, though a small part of me wishes Ursa hadn't abandoned me. It doesn't seem like she had much choice, but as disconcerting as I find her presence, it's reassuring all the same. She has a vested interest in seeing me follow through on this, so she'll protect me in the meantime. Or she would if she were here.

It's getting all tangled up in my head.

I can't trust her. I *know* I can't trust her. But that doesn't stop the flicker of disappointment I can't quite extinguish.

I step back and let Hercules into the room. It's so strange. This isn't *my* room. Not really. I suspect he has a key to it just like he seems to have a key to every other door in this place. For all that I slept here last night, I'm not the host; *he* is.

He stops in the middle of the room and turns to me. "I know it might be a little weird, but there's a protocol for this. Think of it like a very niche spa package."

I try for a smile but can't quite manage it. "Have to get the product looking as expensive as possible."

"Something like that." He sighs. "I don't suppose you've changed your mind?"

"No." That, at least, I'm sure of. I tilt my head to the side. "Why are you so determined to talk me out of this? I'm sure you're being paid for your time."

Hercules waves that away. "I get a percentage of the final total, but I don't care about the money."

It strikes me that money *is* something I'm going to have to care about, and soon. I've never had a job. One of Triton's daughters working? Unthinkable. My trust fund is enough money to keep me for the rest of my life if I'm not foolish, but I won't have access to it for another seven years.

Gods, what am I going to do?

"Zuri?" Hercules takes a step forward, his hands outstretched like he's going to catch me. "Are you okay?"

I shake my head. "It's nothing." I'll figure it out one way or another. Better yet, once Alaric is free, we'll figure it out together. Right now, I just need to focus on getting through the next few days, the auction, and the resulting sex. That's it. "I'm not changing my mind."

"I figured you'd say that." He huffs out a breath. "In that case, let's get started."

I'm not sure what I expected, but it's almost exactly as Hercules said; a spa day. I'm waxed and moisturized. And then it's on to manicures, pedicures, and my hair. I almost ask for brightly colored hair, Ursa's red lingering in my mind, but chicken out at last moment. Instead, they refresh my deeper auburn and give me a trim. My clothes disappear during my skin treatments, and I'm given a robe that feels so decadent, it has to be astronomically expensive.

Hercules leads me several floors up. I don't realize where we're headed until he opens a door and I see the lounge I only got a glimpse of last night. There are no windows in this room, so it might be any hour of the day or night, but the lights are a little brighter than they were when Ursa hustled me through this room. The only testament to the Underworld being closed, aside from the obvious lack of people.

"I'm going to walk you through how it'll go tonight. All business of this sort is set up in the public playroom because it's the only space big enough to pull it off." He opens the door on the other side of the lounge and motions for me to precede him.

The room is as large as our ballroom back home. There are a number of couches and chairs arranged for people to congregate in small groups, with plenty of room around them for walking with ease. There are also…things. I move toward one, Hercules silently shadowing my steps.

He speaks as I stop before it. "That's a St. Andrew's Cross."

"I'm familiar with it." Even if I hadn't done some research once I realized the role Alaric plays in the Underworld, I'd be able to understand its purpose from the straps at the top and bottom of each part of the skinny X shape. Someone is strapped to it. I turn and look out at the room.

Someone is strapped to it *in front of an audience.*

A fissure of heat goes through me at the realization. I

move from piece to piece, and let Hercules explain them despite my research. There's no telling what new information I could pick up, but everything he says lines up with what I expect. I think he's trying to scare me into changing my mind. It's only partially working. I *am* scared. But the longer the knowledge of what comes next has to settle, the more a deep, dark part of me is almost looking forward to it.

I have been cosseted and protected and smothered my entire life, living by rules that aren't my making. My sisters would expire on the spot if they knew I was going to have sex for money. The thought sends a delicious thrill through me. Dangerous to give in to that impulse. Following the tug in my stomach only leads to disappointing my father and hurting those I love.

I don't care.

"Where will the stage be?"

Hercules's jaw tightens, but he leads me to the center of the room. "We'll move the furniture around to accommodate it so everyone can get a good view."

A good view of *me*.

I turn slowly in place, my bare feet on the cool floor, and try to picture it. "Lights?" He points up. There are lines on the ceiling that seem to indicate part of it can shift open. "Clever."

"Only the best in the Underworld." He gives a grim smile. "Someone will act as auctioneer, and another will assist them and help you display yourself to the best advantage. Do you have a preference on whether it's a man or woman?"

I frown. "No. Why would that matter?"

"Because they're going to touch you, Zuri." He says it almost gently. "You'll stand there naked, and they'll expose you and touch you and do what it takes to rile up the crowd to get the price going."

The blood rushes from my head, and I weave on my feet a little. "Oh."

Hercules shakes his head. "That's it. I'm calling this off. This is a fucking mistake."

"It's fine," I manage. "Even with the touching, I don't have a preference on men or women. I like both."

"That doesn't change the fact that you're clutching your robe to your chest like it's a shield and *I'm* the only one standing here. What are you going to do when the room is filled?"

"I can do this."

"No, you can't."

"Yes, I can!" I don't know what possesses me to drop my robe. I don't know what I'm trying to prove. I just react, letting the silky fabric slide from my shoulders and pool at my feet. "I'm not shy, and I have to do this."

"That's not a good enough reason." Hercules glances at my body as if he can't help himself and then jerks his gaze back to my face. "Your first time should be—"

"Don't you dare spout that virginity nonsense at me, Hercules. It's just sex, and people have sex for a lot crappier reasons than money, so you really don't get to take that high-and-mighty tone with me. I'm choosing this, which is more than some people are able to do. It's only as important as I let it be."

I don't realize we're not alone until Hercules looks over my shoulder and his eyebrows rise. "Hello, Alaric."

Oh gods.

I knew I'd have to face him eventually, but this is the worst case scenario—with the possible exception of seeing him tonight during the auction. Pride and frustration have gotten me this far. If I scramble to pick up my robe, I'll just be proving Hercules right that I'm not ready to do this. So I brace myself, lift my chin, and turn to face the man I'm doing this for.

It's been months since I've seen him. Somehow he looks better than ever. He's wearing slacks and a gray button-down shirt, and his black hair is a little longer than when I saw him last. But those blue eyes are the same, hot and hungry and ready to devour me whole.

Alaric stalks across the room, and I'm helpless to do anything but watch him approach. He snatches up my robe and yanks it around me. "What are you doing here, Zuri?"

"Exactly what it looks like." For the first time since I arrived here, Hercules sounds downright amused. "Zuri is going to auction herself off tomorrow night."

Alaric flinches, but he drops his eyes before I can read the emotion in them. He glances at Hercules. "Can we have a minute?"

"No, I don't think you can." Hercules gives Alaric's hands, still fisted in the front of my robe, a significant look. "If you want to talk, I'm going to walk over there and wait." His expression goes hard. "But you manhandle her again, and we're going to have a long fucking talk."

Alaric slowly releases my robe. I have to grab the slick fabric to keep it from falling off my shoulders again. We both watch Hercules walk to the next group of couches over and sit down. It's not quite far enough to be out of hearing range, but he's affording us the illusion of privacy, which is better than I expected. I waste no time righting the robe and getting my arms into the appropriate places. "Hello, Alaric."

"Hello, Alaric? That's all you have to say to me right now?"

No, I have a whole lot more than that, but as sheltered as I've been, I don't think declaring my love and then promptly selling my virginity to someone else is the best route forward. I tighten the belt at my waist. "I'm going to help you. I said I would, and now I'm here."

He clenches his jaw. "You don't have to do this."

"Yes, everyone keeps insisting on telling me that." Even Ursa, though at least she only said it once. I appreciate that she actually took me at my word instead of questioning me every step of the way.

"You're never going to forgive me if you do this."

That surprises a laugh out of me. It sounds nothing like my usual laugh, bitterness coloring the tones. "I could say the same to you." I hold up my hand before he can speak. "I'm doing it. If it means I lose you, at least you'll be free. What's one night compared to that?"

His dark brows draw together. "One night? They didn't tell you?"

Something like fear opens up in the pit of my stomach. "They didn't tell me what?"

"The contract you'll sign is for seven days."

Seven days.

I steel myself even as I'm reeling internally. I thought I read the sample contract so closely, but apparently I missed that little bit in the midst of my exhaustion. "Fine. What's your freedom compared to a week? Even a month? It will be okay, Alaric. I've completed the list, and Hercules has assured me it will be honored."

He doesn't look reassured in the least. There's still that strange look in his eye, but I can't quite define it. Finally, he looks away. "Are you sure this is what you want to do?"

Frustration boils up. I'll admit that this situation is hardly ideal, but this is the first conversation we've had in months and it's not going anything like I've imagined. "Hi, Alaric. Yes, it's so good to see you again. I've missed you terribly. I'm so happy I was able to slip my father's leash and come here.

You're so incredibly welcome that you'll be free in a little over a week."

Just like that, his expression softens. "I'm being a jackass, aren't I?"

"Yes."

His lips curve, a sensual line that has my stomach leaping in response. "I've missed you, Zuri. Terribly." He glances at Hercules. "If we didn't have an audience, I'd kiss you right now."

"Kiss me anyways."

Surprise widens his eyes the tiniest bit. "If you're sure."

I don't remind him that I'm going to be naked and on display on this stage tonight. What's a kiss compared to that? Instead, I just nod. "I'm sure."

He steps closer and cups my face between his hands. Alaric is built lean, but he's tall. He has to bend down quite a bit to take my mouth, a soft kiss that starts with the barest brush of his lips against mine and then deepens in slow strokes. He teases my mouth open and then he's kissing me fully. My entire body comes alive under that single point of contact, as if his tongue stroking mine is touching me elsewhere, too. I shiver and arch toward him, needing more, but the clearing of a throat freezes us both.

I step back, my skin flushed. Alaric looks at me like he wants to consume me whole, but he increases the distance between us.

Hercules walks up, his expression carefully neutral. "I think it'd be best if you made yourself scarce until after the auction."

"Yeah, you're probably right." Alaric smiles, but it's a faint echo of his normal charming one. "I'll see you soon, Zuri."

Just like that, the nerves I've been trying so hard to quell rise up to flutter in my throat. "Okay." Soon. After the auction. After the week I'll have spent with someone else. Do we even have a chance together after I go through with this?

We have absolutely no chance if I don't.

In the end, it's still the only option.

He reaches out and strokes his thumb down my neck. I feel that possessive touch all the way to my bones. "We'll get through this."

"Yes. We will." I have to believe that. I *have* to.

CHAPTER 6

*A*n hour before the auction starts, I'm back in Hades's office. This time, we're joined by Hercules and two women. One is white with brown hair and features sharp enough to cut the unwary. From the way she casually touches both Hercules and Hades, this is the Meg I keep hearing about. The other woman is around my age and Black with a head of blue hair that I envy. She's so pretty, it takes my breath away, and when she smiles, I find myself getting a little dizzy.

Hades folds his hands. "Hercules has assured me that you're committed to this."

I've come to expect Hercules questioning me at least once an hour with the hopes that I'll change my mind. I didn't expect it from this cold man. "I am."

He nods. "Meg."

The sharp-featured woman steps forward. "I'm going to handle the bidding. Aurora will be the one displaying you." She motions at the blue-haired woman, who smiles again. "Do you have any issues with orgasming in front of an audience?"

I blink. "No?"

Meg gives a small smile. "Was that an answer or a question?"

My skin goes hot and tight, but I fight for focus. Honesty is important right now, and I don't want to promise something that I can't deliver on. "I'm not sure I can."

Her dark brows rise. "You're not sure you can orgasm?"

Is it possible for a person to die of mortification? I fight to keep my spine straight and not melt into my chair. "I can orgasm," I manage. "I mean I'm not sure I can with another person and in front of an audience."

Meg tilts her head to the side. "Does being on the stage bother you?"

"Not as much as it probably should."

She chuckles. "And Aurora?"

I look at the woman in question and, again, answer honestly. "She's one of the most beautiful people I've ever seen."

Aurora beams. "Thank you."

"Do you have any issue with her touching you? Being intimate?"

I should. I really, really should. I have deep feelings for Alaric, and that means I shouldn't look at this woman and have things low in my stomach clench. I shouldn't wonder what she tastes like. I lick my lips. "No, I don't have any issues with that."

A small, dark part of me doesn't feel guilty in the least. Alaric has been with countless people before I met him and who knows how many since. I don't hold that against him. Not really. He's not indebted to Hades entirely by choice, but before coming to the Underworld, I was under the impression that he'd been pressured into the sex work. After meeting Hercules and brushing against others who work here, I don't think I can believe that any more. They're too concerned with consent to force someone to do anything, bargain or no. Even *Hades* is checking in with me, which boggles the mind.

I wonder what else I was wrong about?

Meg nods. "Up. Let's see how Hercules did."

I stand slowly. Aurora moves behind me to help me out of the silk robe. Beneath it, I wear a deceptively complicated lingerie set. Thigh highs and a garter belt. Panties and bra. Even an underbust faux corset. All in a creamy ivory that makes me think this might be something a bride wears on her wedding night.

Meg whistles softly. Hades nods once. "Well done, little Hercules."

For his part, Hercules is blushing in a really sweet way. He picks up a length of fabric and walks to me. "You'll start in this."

I take it from him, and it unfurls into a dress. I raise my brows. "Isn't this a little redundant? Why not just walk out there naked like you said?"

"I didn't say you'd walk out there naked. You'll end up naked."

Meg moves up and presses a quick kiss to his mouth before turning to me. "It's about a show, honey. The more we rile the crowd, the more money you walk away with. You start in that sweet little dress, and they're going to be howling by the time Aurora gets you out of your panties."

It makes sense when she puts it like that. "Okay." I step into the dress and pull it up my body. It's a loose sheath dress that covers me from shoulders to the tops of my knees, but when I eye the fabric, it's nearly sheer. Depending on how they have the lights on the stage, the audience will be able to catch glimpses of my body through it, even if it hangs loosely around me.

"I'm placing bets on Malone."

For a second, I think Meg's talking to me, but she looks at Hades. "She really goes for the innocent thing."

"So do you." Hades gives a small smile. "Maybe I'll bid on her for you, love."

Meg arches her brows. "You give the best gifts, Hades."

My jaw drops as he rises and ushers a muttering Hercules out of the room. I turn back to Meg. "Isn't there some rule against the host bidding?"

"It's the Underworld. The only real rules here are Hades's, and he does what he wants." She shrugs. "Besides, if he wins the bidding, it will reassure Hercules that you aren't going to be whisked off to be ravaged by someone else for the next seven days. He's been driving us both up the wall worrying about you."

Something relaxes in my chest. I don't know how I feel about being shared amongst three people, but I like Hercules, and neither Meg nor Hades seems that bad. Maybe this really will be okay. "I don't think I'd complain about being in your bed."

"Honey, I know you wouldn't." She grins. "Let's go. We'll be getting started soon."

I jump when Aurora takes my hand, lacing her fingers through mine. She smiles. "It's normal to be nervous, but it will be okay. Hades runs a tight ship."

The walk to the public playroom seems to take no time at all. One moment Aurora is leading me out the door of Hades's office and the next we're following Meg into the darkened room. As promised, there's a stage set up in the middle, complete with lights pointed right at it.

Meg steps up easily and spins in a slow circle. "You're in for a treat tonight." She was arresting before, but it's like she's amped everything up. She commands the stage, commands every eye in the room. "We have a true treasure in our midst—and she's just for you. A *virgin*." She motions with an imperial flick of her fingers, and Aurora tugs me up onto the stage. Meg gives the crowd a slow smile. "Not just any virgin, though. An *Olympus* virgin."

Buzzing fills my ears, and I can't tell if it's my panicked thoughts or a murmur going through the room. Lean arms go around my waist, and Aurora's whisper sounds in my ear. "Relax, Zurielle. You're safe. I have you."

I close my eyes for a moment and exhale slowly, doing my best to release my tension. I chose this. I am actively *choosing* it.

"Give her a spin, Aurora."

Her arms slip away, and she takes my hand again, lifting my arm above my head and spinning me like we're dancing in slow motion. My dress flares out around my thighs, and Aurora brings me back against her chest. She's about my height and built petite like I am, but she feels strong enough to hold me up when my legs shake. "Here comes the fun part," she murmurs.

Meg chuckles, low and husky. "We start the bidding at twenty-five thousand."

It's nowhere near enough. I need ten times that much to pay off the rest of Alaric's loan, more when I add in Hades's percentage. I start to look at Meg, but Aurora gives my hips a squeeze. "Trust us."

Movement in the crowd. Meg laughs. "Twenty-five to my dearest Hades. You treat me too well." Her gaze sweeps the room. "But I think we can do better than that."

The only warning I get is Aurora's nimble fingers at the back of my dress and then it's fluttering down around my feet. I'm still clothed in more than a swimsuit, but it *feels* different. Especially when Aurora starts skating her hands over my sides. She's not really touching me anywhere untoward, but it feels good. Really, really good. I shiver as her thumbs skate along the undersides of my small breasts.

"Look at that tight little body." Meg's voice has gone husky, as if she didn't see me in this exact outfit less than an hour ago. "Untouched. Unbreached. I know you, friends. Tell me you wouldn't get off on being her first, on being the one who introduces her to how good it feels to be filled, to come around fingers and cock and tongue."

"Fifty thousand," someone calls.

"Fifty thousand to Malone."

"Sixty."

She laughs. "Now we're talking. Sixty thousand to our new friend in the back."

Aurora gives me a squeeze. "Ready?"

"Yes," I whisper. I'm not sure if it's a lie or not. Things are moving too quickly. There's too much to focus on, so I choose to focus on Aurora instead of the rest of the room. She's my pillar in the midst of this, the one thing keeping the panic at bay.

She teases my bra straps over my shoulders, tugging them until she *almost* exposes me, and lifts her voice. "Seventy-five to see her pretty breasts."

Meg shoots her an amused look but doesn't contradict her. Especially when the woman from before—Malone—confirms seventy-five. "Stop teasing the nice bidders, Aurora."

Aurora's laugh is light and sweet even as she unhooks my bra and eases it down my arms. She presses a kiss to my shoulder, her voice going low. "Tell me if you want me to stop."

I manage a nod and then her hands are on my breasts, cupping them and pressing up as if offering me to the audience. She tugs lightly on my nipples, and I can't stop a gasp.

"Ninety."

"One hundred."

"One-oh-five."

I lose track of who's bidding. All I can focus on is Aurora's clever fingers playing with my nipples. I arch back against her, just a little, and she skates one hand down my stomach to cup me between my legs. Aurora makes a sound that's damn near a purr. "She's so wet, friends. I can feel her through the lace."

Meg laughs. "Now you're just teasing us."

"How about a taste?"

Meg's brows arch up. "That's not a terrible idea." She turns back to the audience. "How much is a taste of that virgin pussy worth? A little enticement of things to come."

"One-twenty."

She crooks her finger at the crowd. "Give me two hundred and you can lick her off Aurora's fingers."

My whole body clenches at the words. I've felt desire. Of course I have. Desire and need and sheer lust. It's never been anything like this before. It feels good and it's uncomfortable and Aurora's barely touching me, but I have pleasure coursing through my body all the same.

I feel…wicked. Really and truly wicked.

"Two hundred."

The white woman who appears at the edge of the stage is a study in icy perfection. Her short blond hair is styled back from her face, and she's wearing high-waisted fitted black pants with suspenders and an off-the-shoulder white blouse.

Aurora goes tense behind me for the barest moment, and then she tugs my panties to the side and drags two fingers through my folds, holding them up so everyone can see the way they glisten with my need. She leans us forward and the blond woman holds *her* gaze as she sucks both fingers between her dark-red lips. It's horribly intimate, a little filthy, and I can't tell if the heat in her gaze is aimed at my taste or the fact that it's Aurora's fingers in her mouth.

"Two-twenty." Comes from the back of the room. I think it might be Hades, but I can't be sure.

The blond moves back, throwing casually over her shoulder, "Two-fifty."

"Two-seventy-five."

Holy crap. It's enough. I've made enough to free Alaric. I look at Meg, but she's studying the room like a predator scenting prey. "We can do better than this. The panties, Aurora. Let's see how pretty our little virgin is when she comes."

Aurora drags them down my legs slowly, teasingly. I'm still wearing the underbust faux corset and the garter belt and thigh-highs, but I'm exposed in every way that counts. Aurora presses another kiss to my shoulder. "Do you see the way they're looking at you?"

I can't see anything but vague impressions of people. Heads and shoulders, occasionally hands lifting drinks to mouths. "No."

"I can." Her fingers trace the garter belt where it presses against my lower stomach, framing my pussy. "They want you, Zurielle. They're practically panting after you." She laughs softly as the bidding continues. "They're so damn jealous of the fact I get to touch you right now, they're willing to drop insane amounts of money to be next. That, my girl, is *power*."

My skin feels too tight for my body. I shift against her, not entirely sure if I'm trying to shift toward her hand or away from it. "It doesn't feel like power." I can't quite catch my breath. "It feels like hunger."

"Yes." Another of those surprisingly sweet kisses to my skin. "I'm going to stroke your clit now." She barely waits for me to nod before her fingers are between my legs. Not entering me, but sliding through slick folds, gathering my wetness to trace playful circles around my clit. I tense. I can't help it.

Aurora's free hand comes up to lightly cup my throat, bending me back against her body. "Close your eyes, pretty girl. It's just you and me up here. Nothing matters but how good this feels." She drags her thumb over my clit again. "It does feel good, doesn't it, Zurielle?"

"Yes," I gasp.

I'm vaguely aware of the room going deathly silent, but I push it from my mind. Aurora is right. It's easier to close my eyes and let her touch me. I...*want* her to touch me. But she doesn't go after my pussy like she's on a mission. Aurora strokes me like she's enjoying this as much as I suddenly am, her breath shuddering against my neck. "I might pay two hundred grand for a taste of you, too," she murmurs.

I don't mean to roll my hips to rub myself against her fingers. I don't mean to do anything but submit. But pleasure coils through me, tighter and tighter, all slippery touches and the heavy feeling of so many eyes on my skin. I thought I couldn't come like this, but now I think I might die if I don't. "Aurora," I moan.

"Show me."

I grab her hand and press her palm hard against my pussy, grinding wildly against her. I bite my lip, trying to hold in another moan, but she shifts her grip on my throat to tug at my chin. "No. Don't hold it in. Let me hear you."

It's as if her words unlock that last bit of resistance. I orgasm, a whimpering high sound emerging from my lips. Aurora coaxes me through wave after wave, until I'm a boneless mess of a person in her arms.

"One million dollars."

I blink slowly. Surely I just heard wrong. Surely someone didn't just bid a million dollars on me, and *surely* that voice isn't as familiar as I think.

I look at Meg, but she's giving nothing away. "One million dollars to Ursa. Would anyone like to bid higher?"

Silence.

I lean forward, trying to see into the shadows of the crowd. Not Ursa. Accepting her help to set this up is one thing. Giving myself to her sexually for an entire week? Unforgivable doesn't begin to cover it. My father will hear about this. He has spies in her territory even now. He'll...

It's too late.

I know it's too late the second Meg nods almost to herself and says, "Sold to the Sea Witch for one million dollars." She spreads her arms, every inch an entertainer. "Thank you so much for playing, my friends. You may not have bought yourself a virgin tonight, but the Underworld has the best Dominants and submissives on staff. Please avail yourself of them."

Aurora shifts to hold my hand, steadying me as the lights shift, the room brightening and the stage dimming a little bit. I blink rapidly. "I...I can't do this."

"What?"

"Ursa wasn't supposed to bid. She wasn't supposed to *win*."

Aurora turns me to face her and clasps my shoulders. One look at my face, and she glances at Meg. "I think she needs a drink."

"Take her back to the office."

They're talking about me like I'm not here—again—but I can't hold it against them. I feel like I'm not here at all. Like I'm floating and this is a dream or a nightmare or some twisted combination of both. Aurora guides me through the room and into what looks like an employee locker room. Another door. Another hallway. Then I'm back in Hades's office and she's tucking a blanket around me. "Just keep breathing. It will be okay." She tries for a smile. "Ursa's really not that bad."

"My father would kill her if he could."

She blinks. "I'm going to get you that drink now."

"Seriously, Aurora. If I do this, I can't go home. Not ever. He'll never forgive me."

She pours a healthy splash of amber liquid into a glass and brings it back to me. "I know a little something about never being able to go home again. Sometimes it's true. Sometimes it's all in your head." She waits for me to take the glass before she continues. "You chose to do this auction for a reason. Is it a good enough reason to go forward with this?"

Alaric.

I almost forgot about him in the midst of this. I take a sip of the alcohol and wheeze a little as it burns a path down to my stomach. I told Alaric that his freedom was worth the price of seven days. How is it less true because Ursa's the person who won? Easy answer. It's not. "Yes. It's still a good enough reason to move forward with this."

"Then you have your answer." Her smile falters. "Hades will go over everything, and I suspect Hercules will be checking in on you, but if you've changed your mind, it's not too late to back out."

"I haven't," I respond before I can think too hard about it. I *haven't* changed my mind. I knew the risks when I accepted the Sea Witch's help. I just never expected this.

I'm swimming with the sharks now.

It'll be everything I can do not to drown.

CHAPTER 7

I can barely keep my satisfied smile off my face as I walk through the public playroom. This has all gone according to plan. The price went higher than I expected, but with the show Zurielle put on... I lick my lips.

It's going to be *such* fun to have Triton's daughter playing my sinful games. It'll be even better that all evidence points to her enjoying them despite herself. Preferable that way. Alaric promised that she wasn't the good girl her father believes, but men have a habit of seeing what they want and ignoring all evidence to the contrary. What man doesn't believe that every virgin is a little slut waiting to happen? Only for him, of course. Only ever for him.

Fools, all of them.

Malone strides up like a great slinking cat. She narrows her eyes at me. "Did you drop a million on her solely to spite me?"

"Of course not, darling." I grin. "It was only the icing on the cake. It's good for you to be acquainted with disappointment from time to time, instead of getting everything you want without a fight. It keeps that pretty head on your shoulders instead of in the clouds."

Malone smirks. "And here I thought it was because you wanted to give your little boyfriend a toy."

"I'm sure I don't know what you're speaking of." I'd hardly call Alaric my boyfriend. It's such a mundane title and implies a trust I don't have in him. Alaric is the kind of man skilled in telling others what they want to hear in order to pave his way forward. If I have a fondness for him, I would have paid his debt myself if not for that tricky little caveat in Hades's bargain.

Well, it's not something I'm going to get into here in the Underworld.

She raises her brows. "Uh-huh."

I can't quite resist ribbing her in return. "Don't think I missed the way you licked every bit of our virgin off Aurora's fingers. Was that all for the taste or the pretty submissive offering it?"

"Bite your tongue, Ursa," she snaps. "You know better."

Yes, I do. But the advantage of friendship is that sometimes we dance over each other's lines without apology. "You should take her, darling. She's primed for it, and maybe it'll put you in a better mood."

Malone gives a delicate sneer. "Worry about your own household." She shakes her head. "I suppose you'll be too busy with that virgin pussy for drinks this week."

A slow heat has been building in me since I placed the winning bid. "Call me in a few days. I might be in a mood to share."

Her green eyes light up, though her voice stays dry as always. "You truly are a friend cut above the rest."

"I'm *everything* cut above the rest." I catch sight of Hades across the room, and he tilts his head, indicating I should follow him. "I have to go. Duty calls."

"Enjoy your night." She loads enough innuendo into the sentence to sink a fleet.

"You, too. Find some pretty submissive to take out all that frustration on." I walk away to her soft cursing, my smile widening. It's a good night. There are still factors in play, but things are going my way. I just need to be patient enough to let the final few dominos fall.

I find Hades in the lounge, leaning against the bar. Some of the other territory leaders have made their way back here as well. I catch sight of Jasmine and Jafar tucked in what's become their booth. Those two are always so lost in each other, it's tempting to test them to see if their distraction expands past their time in the club. I know better than to give in to that impulse. In the year or so since Jasmine's taken over her father's territory, she's proven herself to be a capable leader. That and the fact we don't share a border is enough to keep me on my best behavior.

For now.

I stop next to Hades and prop my hip against the bar. He doesn't seem overly keen on breaking the silence, but that's a simple negotiation tactic. We already settled this yesterday. He won't interfere, even if he doesn't like this.

Tisiphone appears behind the bar. She's a tall Dominican woman, and one-third of Hades's Furies. I've never seen her anywhere except behind this bar, but that doesn't mean I'm foolish enough to believe all she does is sling drinks. She nods to me warily and pours Scotch for him and gin and tonic for me.

I pick up the drink. "Hades, darling, you look tired. Are you getting enough sleep between those two randy partners of yours?"

His brows inch up. "I won't bother to ask what game you're playing by bidding on that girl."

"Good. It's none of your business." No matter what most

of the other territory leaders believe, I have no real interest in war. It's messy and expensive and even if you win, you lose. Better to be subtle in my revenge. I might want Triton dead, but I know better than to bring all of Olympus down upon our heads.

What better way to enact my revenge than taking his daughter?

Easy. Having her come to me willingly, entrapping herself in my net of her own choice. It only took the right bait, and she leaped without checking for predators in the water. I might pity her if I were the type of woman to pity fools.

Hades takes a sip of his drink. "If she changes her mind anytime in the next seven days, I'll take her from you and return her to her father."

I let my smile slide free. "She won't." *That*, I'm sure of. The trap is too well baited. My plan is too perfectly balanced. "And she's an adult, Hades. You'd have to be a monster to hand her back to her father against her will."

"Ursa..." He shakes his head. "This won't end the way you want it to."

I laugh a little. "Give me some credit. I'm not in danger of falling for the mode of my revenge. You're the one who let emotions get tangled up in your goals."

He gives me a long look. "The girl watches you with lust in those big brown eyes."

I know. Impossible not to notice when Zurielle hasn't learned to mask her expressions nearly as well as she should by now. How she survived Olympus is more a testament to her father's overprotectiveness than any survival instincts she possesses. Really, her lust makes her easier to manipulate, ensures that my end goal is simple enough to obtain. No matter what my reputation, I have no interest in forcing the girl. Revenge is all the sweeter when it's walked into willingly. It gives Triton no place to stand and cry foul if Zurielle loves every depraved thing I'm going to do to her little body. Every depraved thing *we* are going to do to her little body.

Now, I get to have my cake and eat her, too.

"Shall I have the amount wired to you?"

He shakes his head slowly. "My office."

I allow him to lead the way. We find Aurora and Zurielle already there. The latter has her clothing back in place, the tease of a dress making me want to rip it off. She looks nothing like her father, a big burly white man with red hair and a full beard. No, Zurielle is like a replica of his dead wife, the pretty, petite Vietnamese woman he brought back to Olympus with him after one of his business trips at Poseidon's behest. She lasted long enough to bear him five daughters before she died. The official story is a car accident, but rumor has it that Zeus was responsible. Knowing what I do of Zeus, it could be anything from her rejecting his unwanted advances to him deciding that Triton was focused too much on his lovely wife and not enough on Olympus business. Who can say?

I've only seen his wife in pictures, but Zurielle has the same delicate bone structure and warm beige skin. Everything about her screams breakable in a way that makes my mouth water. The only difference between her and her dead mother is that her long hair has been dyed a deep auburn color and her mother's was a more natural dark brown. They even have the same sweet smile and foolish hope in their brown eyes.

Watching Zurielle up on that stage with Aurora touching her, playing with her nipples, delving a hand between her thighs… It was sexy and strangely sweet, and I wanted to stride up there and put my mark on her for everyone to see. She is the mode of *my* revenge, and I fully intend to use her until I balance the scales skewed by her father.

All in good time. A patient hunter is a successful one, and I haven't come this far to let lust derail me.

I take the seat next to Zurielle and wait for Hades to rifle through the paperwork. He flips around two pages and slides them across the desk to us. "These are the terms. Once Ursa signs, the money will be transferred into a holding account to be paid out upon the end of the seven days. My twenty percent will be taken off the top."

Zurielle nibbles her bottom lip. "I can't have the money now?"

Hades raises his brows. "Are you often paid before doing the promised work?"

"Hades." I laugh. "What I have in mind is hardly *work*."

He doesn't look at me, his attention narrowing on Zurielle. "If Ursa is in agreement, I'll release up to thirty-three percent of the total tonight."

I have to fight down my smile. Zurielle couldn't be more predictable if I'd laid out the steps for her ahead of time. "Of course. I suspect her word is good."

She glances at me, finally wary for the first time since I picked her up two days ago. "It is."

"There you have it." I wave casually at Hades. "Make the necessary changes."

"I want to pay off Alaric's debt," Zurielle blurts. "So it's going to you anyways. There's no real need for moving the money around. Just take the remainder of what he's owed."

Shock flashes across Hades's face. It's quickly concealed, but I see it. In all my years in Carver City, I've never managed to see him surprised. Not like he is right now. He gives me a sharp look and then studies Zurielle. "Are you sure?"

"I'm not from Carver City, so there should be no issue with my paying his debt." Her voice wavers a little, but she doesn't drop her gaze. I might be impressed if I wasn't down-right giddy with victory. Zurielle lifts her chin. "I'm sure."

Hades hesitates a beat but finally nods. "Consider it done." He motions to the papers. "Sign here."

She reads it over carefully and finally signs with a flourish. I do the same. It's a contract more for the money than for the sexual bits. Selling one's virginity isn't exactly on the up-and-up legally, and something like this would never hold up in court. It doesn't have to, though. I've already gotten my way. It's just a matter of tipping the last domino.

Hades glances at the signatures and nods again. "I'll see the funds transferred tonight and Alaric's amount paid in full." His dark eyes go almost pitying. "I hope he's worth it."

"He is." Zurielle sounds so pure, so determined.

I'm going to take great delight in cutting her knees out from beneath her. "If that's everything?"

He flicks his fingers. "Go. Expect Hercules at some point in the next week, and remember what I said about the conse-quences of not honoring your part of the contract." His expression freezes over. "Don't make me have to act on it, Ursa. No one in Carver City will like it if I do."

"Darling, I wouldn't dream of it." I may have flirted with war when the Man in Black died, but I have no intention of letting something as petty as political squabbles derail my current trajectory. Zurielle is mine for the next seven days, and no one will take her from me. Not even Hades.

I push slowly to my feet. "Come along. Hades will have your luggage delivered in the morning." I should leave it at that, should avoid feeding the unease in her pretty, dark eyes. I can't quite resist. "You won't need it tonight."

Zurielle flinches but rises to her feet without hesitation. Does she realize she's responding to the snap in my voice? I don't think so. Virginity doesn't mean innocence. It doesn't really mean anything at all. But this girl is *innocent*.

If I were a virtuous person, I wouldn't find that so delicious. But then, I've never shied away from *my* desires, and dirtying up a girl who's done barely more than kiss makes me feel like Christmas has come early. All the better that she looks at me like she can't decide if she wants to crawl at my feet or run screaming.

I stay silent while we leave the Underworld. She's practically vibrating with nerves and questions, and she lasts longer than I expect, managing to wait until we're settled in the back of my town car to speak. "If you were going to give me the money, why not just do it yesterday when we talked?"

I twist to look at her, finally—*finally*—releasing my mask for the barest few seconds. I let her see my hunger, my anger, my lust. Then I wrap it up in a warm smile that I'm all too aware doesn't reach my eyes. "I want you, Zurielle. Now I have you for the next seven days. It's as simple as that."

As simple and as complicated as that.

CHAPTER 8

ZURIELLE

 rsa wanted me, so she bid on me. It seems simple enough, but there's nothing simple about this situation. I may be naive at times, but I'm not foolish enough to ignore the connection between her and my father nor to pretend it has nothing to do with her winning the bid on me. Maybe she wants me, but having me for the next week will be a strike at my father and that has to be more attractive to her.

I push the worry from my mind. It's something to deal with at the end of this week, and maybe not even then. With Alaric free, we can leave Carver City, leave Olympus, just *leave* and go somewhere my father's anger will never touch us, move to a city where no one knows the names Triton or Ursa. The thought makes me smile a little, but I let it drift away as the car pulls into a parking garage that looks like any other.

Ursa barely waits for the car to stop before she's out, motioning for me to follow her. The same Black woman from before climbs out of the driver's seat. Ursa waves a hand at her. "This is Monica. You won't see her much this week, but as my head of security, if she tells you to do something for your safety, do it."

I swallow hard. "Okay."

Monica gives me a once-over and shakes her head. "You're going to regret this."

For a moment, I think she's talking to me, but then Ursa's laugh booms through the echoing space of the parking garage. "You know me, darling. I make a habit of regretting nothing. I'm *certainly* not going to regret this week."

"Sure." Monica rolls her eyes. "Whatever you say, *darling.*"

I half expect Ursa to slap her down over the blatant familiarity, but she surprises me by laughing again. "You missed dinner. Go get something to eat after you check in with our people."

"Bossy."

"I am your boss, yes."

Monica gives a slim smile, but it dies when she turns to me. "I take Ursa's safety seriously. You fuck with her, and I'll toss you off a balcony without a second thought."

I blink. "Um." I really, really want to believe she's joking, but her expression is deadly serious. "I'm not going to fuck with her." As if I would, when doing so would risk violating our agreement. As if I *could*.

Ursa raises her brows. "If that's all?"

"Yeah, yeah. Get out of here." Monica waves us away.

I don't realize that she's not following us into the elevator until Ursa pushes the button and the doors slide shut. *That's* when my nerves begin to get the best of me. My heartbeat kicks up, slamming against my ribcage. I'm at this woman's mercy, and I should be preparing to do whatever she asks and bear whatever she wants to do to me. Simply survive it.

I am afraid. But I'm not only afraid.

The thought of her dragging those nails over my skin? Of watching her strip out of that dress and seeing what she has on—or doesn't—beneath it? Of kissing her and kneeling before her spread thighs...

I shiver.

No, I'm not only afraid. Or even primarily afraid.

I should be. Wanting Ursa might be the worst mistake I've made yet, but I can't help how drawn I am to her.

The doors open, and she steps out. I follow but stop short. I don't know what I expected. Something minimalist and chic, maybe. That's all the rage right now, and it seems like everyone with money in Olympus has jumped on the trend.

Ursa's penthouse feels like a home. The front door leads into a lavish living room with a thick patterned blue rug over the cool-gray marble floors. The couches are a paler gray with blue and gray patterned pillows. A large white stone fireplace sits in one wall and in the corner opposite is a deceptively delicate fountain that stretches nearly to the ceiling. The windows overlook the city, spanning the breadth of the wall opposite the door. It's remarkably cozy.

Ursa props a hand on her hip and looks at me. "Strip."

"Excuse me?" The question is out before I remember why I'm here, what the next seven days will entail.

"Strip, Zurielle. One item after another until I tell you to stop."

I reach for the back of my dress without another thought, responding to the command in her voice. I should be questioning this, should still be demanding answers, but I *want* to obey. Still... I unclasp the top of my dress and pause. "I thought you and Alaric are friends."

Ursa's red lips curve. "We are."

"You don't think he's going to have a problem with you and I having seven days' worth of sex?" It was one thing when I was giving myself to a stranger. Ursa *is* a stranger, technically—but only to me. Alaric knows her. He's *known* her in the most biblical of senses.

66

"Alaric understands how things work in Carver City." Her expression doesn't change. "Sex is only sex, until it's not."

I frown. "That doesn't make any sense."

"The dress, Zurielle."

I release it and let it flutter to my feet. I was more naked than this on stage, but I can't help holding my breath as Ursa drinks in the sight of me. She peruses me from the top of my head, down the length of my body, pausing on my feet before retracing the same path upward. By the time she reaches my face again, I'm trembling.

She licks her lips. "First things first. Hercules explained to you how safe words work?"

A word that's an emergency failsafe if something happens that I don't want. A way to make everything stop, even in games where "no" doesn't really mean "no." It seems strange and almost too good to be true to trust someone to honor a single word, but Ursa's expression is deadly serious as she waits for my answer. "Yes, he explained it to me."

"Pick one. Something you won't use in casual conversation on accident."

I swallow hard, this entire situation suddenly becoming that much realer. "Hurricane."

Ursa considers me for a moment and nods. "Very well. Did you like being on stage with Aurora?"

I flush hot. "I think everyone could tell that I did."

"That's not an answer." She snaps her fingers. "Kneel."

I obey. The rug cushions my knees, the floor catching me even as the room seems to spin. It's so *solid*. A strange thought, but I can't help it as I look up at Ursa. She seems larger than life, a goddess to be worshiped with words and actions. *I* want to worship her.

"Did you like being on stage with Aurora?" she asks again.

This time, I don't try to dodge the question. "Yes. I loved it when she touched me. I loved how she whispered in my ear that everyone was getting off on it, and I really loved it when she stroked my clit. I wanted more."

She nods and moves closer until the hem of her dress brushes my knees. Ursa sifts her fingers through my hair, petting me in an almost innocent way. I'm still trembling, poised on the verge of something I don't understand. This is pleasure, yes, but it's something beyond that. Kneeling at her feet, knowing that I'll obey any command she gives right now, having her touch me… It all combines into a need that takes my breath away. "Please."

"Please what?" She still sounds warm, welcoming, completely at odds with the look in her dark eyes. I don't know why the contrast pulls at my chest—lower—but it does.

I want the warmth.

I want the bite.

I want it all.

"I feel…" I'm not sure how to put it into words. "I need."

"Ah." She twines my hair around her fist and tugs sharply. She inhales as I gasp, as if she can taste the sound on my lips despite the distance between our faces. Using that hold on my hair, she urges me to my feet. It hurts a little, but the pain does something funny to my head. I feel floaty and warm, warm, warm, my pulse throbbing in my pussy until I'm shaking.

Ursa releases me. "Take off everything. I want to see what my million dollars purchased."

A million dollars.

She paid *a million dollars* for me. Or, more likely, for some kind of revenge, but it's hard to remember that with her staring at me like I'm a dessert she's about to sample. It takes me several tries to get my bra undone, and even longer to work the clasps on my faux corset. As I slide my panties down my legs, she turns and walks away. I pause. "Um?"

"Did I say stop?" She doesn't look at me.

"No."

"No, Mistress," she corrects.

"No, Mistress." I listen to her heels click down the hallway and then keep stripping. It's tempting to just shuck off the garter belt and thigh highs, but I make myself undo them first and take them off properly. I'm removing the last stocking as she reappears with a glass of red wine in her hand.

Ursa says nothing as she circles me slowly, but I can *feel* her gaze on my bare skin. I'm achingly aware of how lacking I must be. She's lush and full of curves and soft in the very sexiest of ways. I'm a string bean by comparison, narrow hips and small breasts. I've never wanted another body as much as I do in the moment when she's at my back.

At least until she finally comes to stand in front of me and I see the hunger in her eyes again. As if she can't decide which part of me she wants to devour first. "You're very beautiful."

"*You're* beautiful," I blurt.

"I know." She sips her wine slowly. "Sit on the couch. Spread your legs."

I stumble to the couch and sit on the center cushion. She follows and perches on the heavy marble coffee table in front of me. I hesitate but finally spread my legs, inch by inch, until I can feel cool air against my heated flesh. It takes everything I have not to slam my knees shut as she studies me there just as thoroughly as she studied the rest of my body.

Another slow sip of wine. "You're very wet, little Zurielle."

"Zuri," I whisper. When Ursa arches her eyebrows, I explain. "My friends call me Zuri."

"We aren't friends." She says it almost kindly. "I'm going to fuck you until you come so many times, it's my face you see when you think of god. But we are not, and never will be, friends."

I can't quite catch my breath. "Oh."

"I'm going to touch you now." She doesn't wait for me to answer before she coasts one hand up my thigh to use her thumb to part my pussy. "So wet and pink. I think you like being on your knees."

"I—"

"You will not speak until I give you permission." The sentence comes out absently as she keeps up that slow exploration with her fingers, circling her thumb gently over my clit. "You will not speak, and you will not move, and you will not come. Do you understand me, little Zurielle?" Her gaze flicks to my face. "You may answer."

Now I truly am gasping. How can she strike to the very heart of my dark desires with a few short words? "Yes, Mistress."

Another sip of her wine and she sets the glass aside. "The next time you speak, it will be to request my permission to come." She lightly drags her fingers up my thighs to my hips and then yanks me to the very edge of the couch, my legs on either side of hers. "Better." She takes my hands and guides them to the backs of my thighs, pulling my legs up and out, exposing me in a way there's no hiding from. "Hold just like this."

It's uncomfortable and embarrassing, and I forget both those things as she resumes touching my pussy. Slow strokes of her fingers as she explores me, circling my clit, tracing my entrance, dipping down to press her thumb against my ass. I jump at the last, but then quiver as I force myself to hold still. Ursa doesn't press inside, but she watches me, cataloguing every reaction.

She presses one hand to my lower stomach, holding me perfectly still as she goes back to playing with my clit. "Look how eager you are. You sold yourself for love, and you're so wet for my fingers, you're practically shaking with the need for more." She licks her lips. "Would you beg for my mouth, I wonder?"

Humiliation and shame lance me, but somehow they combine to a greater desire. I am suddenly sure I *will* beg for her mouth. I press my lips together hard, determined to obey and keep the words inside. She's wrong. She must be wrong. I love Alaric. My body might be confused right now beneath her expert touch, but it's just sex. It doesn't mean anything.

It can't mean anything.

"So unfaithful, little Zurielle. Such a little slut." She smiles slowly. "Would you like my mouth? You may answer." I open my mouth to deny her, but she cuts me off before I can spill the lie. "If you're going to speak, you do it honestly."

I don't want to. We're barely an hour into the seven days and I'm already dancing across lines I thought were set in stone. I had thought to merely endure, but Ursa is forcing me to be an active participant, forcing my betrayal with both word and action.

All the same, I can't lie.

"Yes." I sound like another person, someone needy and desperate, someone on the verge of breaking. "Yes, Mistress, I want your mouth."

"So eager," she murmurs, her gaze dropping back to where she hasn't stopped stroking me. "I suppose a little appetizer won't hurt."

The words don't make sense, but then they don't matter at all as she dips down, her locs sliding against my thighs, to drag her tongue over me. Her mouth on the most private part of me is slippery and sinful, and I dig my fingers into my thighs to keep from reaching for her. It feels so good, so much better than I could have dreamed. She licks my pussy

71

like I'm her favorite flavor of candy, like she wants to taste every inch of me.

Pleasure swarms me, buzzing through my veins and making me shake with need. I never want this to stop, but I'm devastatingly aware that I'm on the verge of disobeying her already. "Ursa," I gasp. "Mistress."

She barely lifts her head. "Mmm?"

"May I come?"

Her dark eyes flick over me, pausing at my breasts before settling on my bottom lip. It stings from where I've been biting it in an effort to keep silent. "Yes." And then she lowers her head and resumes eating me out.

My toes are curling with pleasure, the room spinning around me. I'm *so close*.

I barely register an unfamiliar sound in the distance. I'm too focused on my pleasure. Ursa sucks hard on my clit and then I'm coming, the orgasm bowing my back and drawing a cry from my lips. I fight to keep my eyes open, a dark, dirty part of me loving that there's red lipstick smeared on my pussy from her mouth. A mark that she's given me, for all that it's temporary. I don't know why it's so hot, only that I don't want her to stop.

She doesn't.

The elevator doors slide open as Ursa slips her tongue inside me. I look up and blink, sure that I'm hallucinating. *Sure* that I'm not splayed out on this couch, Ursa's mouth all over me, as Alaric walks into the penthouse.

Except he doesn't disappear. I blink rapidly, but he's still there, something like shock written across his features as he takes in the scene before him.

The man I love is watching another woman eat my pussy.

Oh my god, what have I done?

CHAPTER 9

URSA

urielle goes tense beneath me, and I smile against her pussy. Really, this was too easy. That doesn't stop me from licking my lips as I lift my head. I expected to win the bidding. Expected Alaric to show up and interrupt us.

I didn't expect to enjoy Zurielle's responsiveness so much.

Even now, with her eyes wide from horror and guilt, she's still silent and holding herself open for me. She's still *obeying*.

I press my hand to her lower stomach, as much to keep her in place as to feel the delightful little shakes from the orgasm she just had. Only then do I look over my shoulder at Alaric.

He stands just inside the elevator, looking every inch the Prince Charming he plays for everyone else. Gray slacks, black button-down, black hair styled in a careless sort of way that's just shy of being rakish. And those eyes. He's able to lie with his eyes better than anyone I've ever known. Right now he's a blank slate, waiting for me to take the lead.

I love a man who knows his place.

I crook the fingers of my free hand. "Come here, lover."

There. The tone is set. He doesn't have to lie anymore, though I'd be a fool to trust Alaric to pursue anything but his own interests. Everyone in this town is selfish; he's just a little more upfront about it. At least to me. The other patrons of the Underworld think he's something else altogether.

Alaric crosses slowly, his gaze sliding over me, lingering on my mouth, and then giving Zurielle a similar treatment. She opens her mouth, no doubt to blurt some kind of explanation, and I shoot her a look. She clamps her lips shut, expression miserable. I shouldn't be warmed by that instant obedience. I truly shouldn't. It doesn't matter. She's such a *delicious* little subbie.

Alaric reaches us and slides his hands into his pockets. "What do we have here?"

"Darling, you're being mean. You can stop pretending. She's mine for the week. There's no going back now." I won't *allow* us to go back. Just like I won't allow him to continue the façade that he's not an active participant in this. I allow a slow smile.

His lips quirk. "Then I suppose the cat's out of the bag."

"It is." I lift my chin. "Give me a kiss."

If Alaric were truly the nice guy he pretends to be, he'd brush a quick kiss to my mouth and make a hasty retreat. He's not. He never was.

He cups my chin and kisses me like it's been years since we've seen each other, like I wasn't riding his cock a little over twenty-four hours ago. He licks the inside of my mouth and I know without a shadow of a doubt that he's soaking up every bit of Zurielle's taste he can. Wicked boy. I allow it, just like I allowed him to stand over me. Alaric kisses me with all the expertise of someone with his history. But it's more than sheer skill. For as calculated as he is, he gets lost in it. He tempts me to do the same.

When he finally lifts his head, I'm fighting not to lean into him. I raise my brows. "Go wash the Underworld off you. You're free now."

Another quick kiss to my lips and he's gone, walking away without a single look at Zurielle. I narrow my eyes. That was too cold. He can be calculated and manipulative, but Alaric has a heart beneath all that scar tissue of his past. And no one with a heart would be able to remain unaffected by the slow tears tracking down Zurielle's cheeks right now. Even *I'm* not completely unencumbered by her watching her rose-tinted future slide down the drain.

The only reason to be so cold is to avoid showing his hand. His *guilt*.

Interesting.

I tuck the knowledge away to test out later and turn back to Zurielle. She's even pretty when she cries. Of course she is. She's like a living fantasy created solely to entice me to play with her. Even if she wasn't Triton's daughter, I'd be sorely tempted simply because of how her lower lip quivers.

Still, she obeys.

I lightly stroke her lower stomach with my nails. "You may speak."

Her breath shudders out. "You and Alaric..."

"Mmm?" Best to let her get it out now.

"You're together."

"Yes. We have been for some time." Or as together as two people can be with our respective circumstances. I can't help adding a qualifier every time my mind skirts too closely to what *together* might look like now that he's free. It's entirely possible that he's been using me as much as I'm using Zurielle. Only time will tell, and I'm not foolish enough to let him closer than he already is in the meantime. Or that's what I tell myself as I look down at this woman who fancied herself in love with Alaric. I'm not nearly so naïve. Truly, I'm not.

She blinks those big eyes at me. "You *tricked* me."

She may be naive, but she's intelligent enough to connect the dots quickly. Good. Still, I'm inclined to play this out a little longer. "Did we?"

"Did you send him to Olympus for me?" She shakes her head. "Of course you did. Gods, I am so *stupid*."

"That's about enough of that." I tap her hands where they still hold her thighs. "You were outplayed, darling. Nothing more, nothing less. Sit up."

She sits up, still obedient even as another tear slides down her cheeks. Have I ever cried so freely as this girl does? No. Never. There is a time and place for emotions to take the forefront, but they are never, ever in front of an audience. Even if I weren't the leader of an entire territory, I am a Black woman. Extreme emotions in front of others will never result in the outcome I need. Better to craft a face to give the world. What weakness I have is restrained to those moments alone, and even then I don't let them escape all that often. Not when doing so will undermine everything I've worked so hard to accomplish.

Zurielle obviously hasn't learned a similar lesson or she's been protected enough not to feel the negative results. Either way, I enjoy her tears far more than I should.

She wipes angrily at her face. "I didn't know we were playing a game."

"Now you do." I don't sit back, don't give her space. "Life is a game, darling. The faster you learn that, the better time you'll have of things."

She narrows her eyes. "I don't understand you. You're so cruel and so kind at the same time."

"One does not negate the other." The best cruelty lashes unexpectedly, the sweetest kindness can hurt so acutely. I've learned to wield them interchangeably. I *like* it. I lick my lips, tasting the combination of Zurielle and Alaric. With the end result all but guaranteed, I can allow myself to fully enjoy the next seven days. "I'm in a good mood, so I'll give you a choice, little Zurielle."

Her lip is still quivering, but she's managed to get her tears under control. "What choice? I don't have a choice. I'm here. It's too late."

I give her thigh a light smack. "Don't be dramatic. You have your safe word, and it will be honored. Do you want to use it?"

"I should." Her gaze skates to the doorway Alaric disappeared through, expression bleak.

I'm silent, letting her work through it. If she calls this whole thing off, it would be a bit of a wrench in my plans, but she would lose the money. More, *Alaric* would lose the money to pay off the remainder of his debt. She's too soft to make that decision, not nearly angry enough. It's only a matter of waiting for her to come to the same conclusion.

Finally, she shakes her head. "What choice?" she repeats.

"Tonight, I can fuck you." I intentionally keep my tone light, my language crass. "Or Alaric can fuck you."

She presses her lips together for a long moment. "And after tonight?"

"Darling, I'm going to get at that pussy until we're sick of each other. And Alaric wants you, so I'm inclined to give you to him until he works out all that frustrated lust on your pretty little body. That's not up for negotiation. Tonight is."

Zurielle frowns, her brows drawing together. "Are you two..." She seems to sift through possible options to finish that sentence. "Dating?"

"We enjoy each other. We haven't put anything resembling a label on it." It's as simple and complicated as that. I'm the territory leader. The person who shares my bed with regularity is granted a level of power as a result. I have to be careful because of that. And before Zurielle paid Alaric's debt, he was effectively owned by Hades. *Dating* one of Hades's people is as good as saying that I'm allowing a spy into my inner circle, and that would be unforgivably weak and foolish.

A weak and foolish territory leader is one living on borrowed time.

Zurielle doesn't seem content with that. "But he's here. You orchestrated this so he'd be freed."

"Not only that."

She shakes her head. "Not only that, but you could have found a different way to get revenge on my father. You chose *this* way because of Alaric."

She's not wrong, but I'm also not inclined to dig into my complicated relationship with that man for her benefit. "All you need to know is that we're happy to share you between us, and we plan on doing exactly that." Something we've never done before. Oh, we've participated in group play in a number of ways, but this is different. We aren't in the Underworld right now. *I* am topping both of them. The next seven days are for fucking and enjoying ourselves. After, we'll cut this little fish loose and figure out what comes next for us.

"I thought I loved him." She says it so quietly, I don't think she intends for me to hear.

Too bad. "A lot of people fall in love with Alaric. It's a special skill of his. Don't beat yourself up over it."

Zurielle shakes her head. "Kind and cruel."

"It's a gift." I smile, but give my next word some bite. "Choose."

"I want him." She closes her eyes as if the truth pains her.

"I shouldn't. I should hate him, but I can't help wanting him still."

I suspected as much. "Very well." I push to my feet and offer her my hand. No matter how smart this girl is, she's still harboring romantic notions about Alaric. Given half a chance, she'll convince herself that he's really a noble prince who was somehow forced into this situation, instead of a man with a habit of getting what he wants, when he wants it. Even laboring under Hades's deal hasn't been a hardship for Alaric, not with the power players in Carver City lining up to fuck him and play with him and spoil him. He wasn't free, but one would have to look far and wide to find a more enjoyable cage.

Zurielle takes my hand, and I'm struck again by how delicate she is. Not just physically. A rough touch, a harsh word and she might crumple.

She's no use to me broken.

Maybe that's why I stroke my thumb over her wrist and tug her closer. I dislike being required to baby submissives, but she's got a shell-shocked look on her face that bothers me. "Zurielle."

She blinks up at me. "Yes, Mistress."

Gods, she's sweet. Even swaying on her feet from going round after round tonight, she's still obeying my initial commands. I don't think she realizes she's doing it, either, which makes it all the more enjoyable.

I catch her throat lightly with my free hand, letting my nails prick at her sensitive skin. She instantly closes her eyes and parts her lips in a little gasp. My pussy clenches at that sound. She's not scared. No, she *likes* me holding her like this as much as I like doing it. My voice comes out tighter than I intend. "For the next seven days, you belong to me. I do what pleases *me*, and tonight it pleases me to watch him fuck your virgin pussy. But make no mistake, it's at *my* command. Do you understand?"

She swallows hard, a movement I can feel against my palm. "Yes, Mistress."

"Good. We may begin."

CHAPTER 10

ALARIC

$\mathcal{I}$t takes me nearly my entire shower to successfully label the heavy feeling in my chest. Guilt. I feel fucking guilty. I shake my head and turn off the water. Ursa will laugh when she figures out I'm having second thoughts *now*, when everything is already in motion. The time for changing my mind was at any point during the countless hours I spent with Zuri over those weeks in Olympus. Or during the months since I came back to Carver City.

Or, here's a thought, I could have told her the truth when I saw her in the public playroom yesterday.

I didn't. I made my choice, and feeling guilty about it now is just self-indulgent. I'm a bastard and a half for letting Zuri pay the price of my decisions, but it's too late to change my mind. Truth be told, I was never going to. I'm finally, *finally* out from under powerful men. First Triton. Then Hades. Now, the only person I answer to is myself.

And Ursa.

I'm still drying off when I hear the bedroom door open. I wrap the deep-blue towel around my waist and walk over to lean on the door frame. Ursa looks just as decadent as ever,

81

her generous curves wrapped in a printed dress I want to take off with my teeth. Zuri is still naked, padding behind the other woman and looking a little dazed.

Ursa sees me first. Her gaze rakes over my bare chest and, fuck, the promises she makes with that single look. It makes me want to hit my knees, to give way to the sheer dominance this woman wields. Any other night, I'd do that and happily crawl to her. Tonight isn't about us, though. Not entirely. Not when Zuri is standing there, still flushed from the orgasm Ursa licked out of her.

And fuck if *that* wasn't the hottest thing I've ever seen. I could have stood there all night and watched Ursa make Zuri come again and again. If there's a flicker of jealousy there, I'm used to it. Nothing in this world is ever entirely *mine*. Not a home. Not a possession. Certainly not a romantic partner.

Even Ursa, whom I care about far more than is wise, will never be mine in truth. I might be hers, but that's hardly the same thing at all. She's got walls upon walls, and she's spent most of her life making sure no one comes near. I'm closer than most, close enough to recognize the distance she maintains between us, close enough to be stung by it.

She's still watching me, amusement flickering through her dark eyes. "You're thinking too hard, Alaric."

I force myself to shrug. There's no point in letting my circling thoughts take precedence. Tonight is about action, about the culmination of months and months' worth of plans. I won't be the one to ruin it. "It's a habit."

"And a poor one at that." She crooks a finger at me, her red nail gleaming in the low light. "Come here, lover. Come take a look at the present I got for you."

A bolt of sheer lust strikes me. "You always give the best gifts," I murmur. I keep my attention on her, trying to read how this scene will go. Because this is a scene. During my time in the Underworld, I've played both Dominant and submissive, but there is only one role for me here. Submit to Ursa. It's only the flavor of it that is left to be determined.

Luckily, she likes group play nearly as much as I do.

I stop just short of touching her, and she reaches up to sift her fingers through my hair. Times like these always surprise me. Ursa has such a big personality, I sometimes forget that she's a good six inches shorter than me. She smiles up at me, as warm as standing in the late July sun that's long since disappeared below the horizon. "Would you like to play with your gift, Alaric?"

I resist the urge to look over her shoulder at Zuri. Ursa's mean enough to tempt me with this and take it away. I *love* that she's mean like that. "Would *you* like me to play with my gift?"

"Clever boy." She gives my hair a tug and steps back. "How many nights did you leave Zurielle untouched? Walk away with a painfully hard cock without doing all the things you wanted to her?"

Answering a definitive number is out of the question. Ursa's just as likely to deny me that many orgasms again out of perversity. I manage a smile. "More than a few."

She snaps her fingers. "Zurielle. Stand before the bed. Don't move or speak."

I watch Zuri obey without protest, submitting so sweetly that my mouth waters. *A gift, indeed.* I'd suspected she had submissive tendencies, but I couldn't be sure, not when we were never alone enough to follow through on anything. Not when doing so would jeopardize this entire plan. But suspecting and seeing it in action are two very different things.

Zuri looks so small in this room of deep blues and blacks, a minnow who's lost herself to the dark. A treat for the first predator that comes along.

I let Ursa nudge me to sit on the edge of the massive bed. The mattress gives as she climbs up to kneel behind me and clasps my shoulder. Her lips brush my ear, her voice just loud enough to carry to Zuri. "How many times have you imagined this? Her naked and flushed with need?"

"More than a few," I repeat. If I were a better man, I'd put a stop to this. Hell, if I were a better man, I wouldn't have acted the part of bait for this innocent woman. I'm not. She's here and I want her, and Ursa is offering to give her to me.

Still… "Safe word?"

"Please. Give me an ounce of credit. I'm a villain, not a monster." She laughs, deep and sinful. "Tell him your safe word, darling. Alaric will respect it the same way I will."

Zuri's small frame shakes, and she watches us with wide eyes. "Hurricane."

"Good girl." Ursa squeezes my shoulders, and her lips brush my ear. "I won't apologize for unwrapping her before you got here. She's too delicious to resist."

"I liked seeing it," I murmur.

"Tell me something." She gives my shoulders another squeeze. "Those agonizing nights, what did you think about when you wrapped your hand around your cock? Give us all the details."

There's no hiding from this. No lying. It's almost a relief to let that version of myself go. The fake innocent who's been fucked over by the world. I got in over my head, yes, but I have no one to blame but myself. I made the choices that put me here, every step of the way. The bad ones. The good ones. All of them.

Now I don't have to pretend to be anything other than what I am. "I thought about her sweet mouth wrapped around my cock."

Ursa presses her breasts to my back and gives a hum of approval. "And?"

"Not just her sucking my cock. I want to fuck her mouth." My voice hardly sounds like my own. I can't stop staring at Zuri, a perverse part of me reveling in her shock. Because shock isn't the only thing she's showing me right now. Her warm beige skin is flushed, and her breath is coming faster now. "I want to fuck *her*."

"I know." She smoothes her hands down my arms and back up again. "Come closer, little Zurielle."

Zuri takes several hesitant steps, finally stopping with her knees almost touching mine. I drink in the sight of her, her small breasts, the flare of her hips, her bare pussy still marked with Ursa's lipstick. Finally, I let myself meet her eyes. I expect... Fuck, I don't know.

There's hurt there, lingering in the dark depths, but she's staring at me just as intently as I studied her, her gaze on my chest and lower to where my cock presses against the towel around my hips. Zuri licks her lips, and I nearly growl.

"I think our little darling has a confession of her own." Ursa's just as tempting as a devil on my shoulder. "Did you touch yourself while you thought of our Alaric?"

Zuri's face goes crimson. She opens her mouth but pauses and looks to Ursa.

"You are a *delight*." Ursa makes a pleased hum that I've only ever heard when I'm inside her. "You may answer when I ask you a direct question."

"Yes." The word is barely audible. Zuri clears her throat and tries again. "Yes, I touched myself."

"So honest. So sweet." Ursa settles in behind me, her thighs on either side of my hips, her body pressed fully against my back. The position makes her dress ride up, and I stroke her bare knees, enjoying how soft her skin is even as I can't quite take my attention from the woman standing before us. Ursa shifts to wrap her arms around me, idly running her fingers over my chest. "Touch her, Alaric. You know you want to."

I do. I really, really do.

I check Zuri's expression, but she doesn't appear to be particularly terrified. "I'm going to touch you now." I don't play Dom nearly as much as I play submissive these days, but communication is key. Especially with a new submissive. *Especially* with a virgin who hasn't done much more than kiss another person, the earlier scene in the living room excepted.

Zuri gives a jerky nod and seems to hold her breath. I can't tell if she's bracing herself or shaking with need as I grasp her hips. I hate that I can't tell. I open my mouth, but Ursa beats me there. "I like the look of his hands on you, darling. Do they feel good?"

"Yes," she whispers. She's trembling so violently, I might have to catch her if her legs give out. Fuck, it's sexy and overwhelming at the same time.

"Do you want more?" Ursa keeps stroking my chest, but her words are all for Zuri.

She hesitates, almost as if she's at war with herself, and finally nods. "Yes, Mistress."

"See how easy it is to tell me what you need, darling?" I don't have to see her face to feel her smile. "Touch her properly, Alaric."

I skate my hands up her sides until my thumbs brush the undersides of her breasts. Zuri sucks in a breath, and I nearly come right then and there. "Fuck."

"Alaric." A note of warning in Ursa's voice, a reminder to obey.

I use the barest pressure to guide Zuri closer, until she's standing between my thighs. The towel restricts her ability to get closer for now, but she's near enough that I am able to lean forward and suck one of her pebbled nipples into my mouth. This time she gasps aloud, and her hands flutter to my chest. To *Ursa's* hands.

I switch breasts, savoring the way she whimpers. I've barely gotten started. I have months of pent up lust for this woman, and one taste isn't anywhere near enough to slake my desire. I look up to find her watching me with a tormented expression on her face. Lust and anger and hurt. It stings, but I push my conscience down deep. It's never gotten me into anything but trouble, and right now the only thing I want to get into is Zuri.

Ursa releases Zuri's hands and reaches around me to stroke her fingers down the other woman's stomach and cup her pussy. "She's so wet, Alaric." She pulls her fingers away, and I have to move back so she can lift them between us. "Would you like a taste?"

I want my mouth all over Zuri, but I know better than to push Ursa. She's likely to deny me out of spite. Another night, it'd be fun to try. Tonight, I'm determined to be on my best behavior. "Yes, Mistress."

"How polite you are when you want something." She laughs and touches her fingers to my lips. I suck them deep, running my tongue over her and soaking up Zuri's taste. "Good, yes?" She withdraws her fingers.

"Yes," I manage.

She presses her hand to Zuri's chest and urges her back a step. "On your knees, Alaric."

I slide off the bed and onto my knees. There are people I've submitted to in the past that I chafed at, but with Ursa it feels as natural as breathing. She commands, I obey. Simple as that. There's freedom in that submission, freedom in trusting her to get us where we need to be. I don't know if I trust her entirely outside the bedroom, but in here? She's my Mistress, my queen, my goddess.

"Behind her." She moves to take the same position I just

vacated, sitting at the edge of the bed. Ursa tugs on Zuri's hands until the other woman bends at the waist and lays her head in Ursa's lap. The position leaves her ass in the air, and as I move to kneel behind her, her pretty pink pussy is on full display.

"Don't play coy, lover. Have a taste." Ursa sounds as regal as if inviting me to sample a dish her cook whipped together.

I lick my lips. "I think I will." I run my hands up Zuri's legs and urge her to widen her stance. I should go slow, should work up to things, but having her so close after being denied for so long...

My control snaps at the first drag of my tongue over her pussy. I grab her hips and jerk her back against my mouth. I'm vaguely aware of Zuri crying out, of Ursa's sinful laughter, but I can't bring myself to care. Not with Zuri's taste on my tongue. Not with the way her legs shake on either side of my head.

Fuck, I never want to stop.

CHAPTER 11

*A*laric's mouth on me feels completely different than Ursa's did. She teased and tasted. He's...feasting. I don't know another word for it. Each possessive stroke of his tongue winds me up tighter, his big hands holding me in place even as I try to squirm.

I can't move my lower half, but I can move the rest of me.

I rub my face on Ursa's thighs and cling to her hips. The desire is building and building, until it feels too big for my skin. "Please."

She sifts her fingers through my hair, devastatingly gentle against the harshness of Alaric's grip on my hips. "Please what?"

I rub my face against her thighs again. I don't know what I'm doing, just that I need more. Ursa shifts back a little and spreads her legs, making room for me. I'm flying on instinct alone, driven wild by the feeling of Alaric pushing his tongue inside me. "Oh gods."

Ursa gives my hair a sharp tug. "Obey my rules, darling. Unless you're begging or asking permission, don't speak."

I'm not sure I can obey her, not unless I do something

drastic. I don't mean to start kissing her through the thin fabric of her dress, but it keeps my mouth busy. And she feels good, almost as good as what Alaric is doing to me.

I drag my hands over her thighs, taking her dress with me. I need, need, need. I want to be good, to obey her simple commands. Or that's what I tell myself as I kiss her soft thighs. Her laugh makes me shiver, and she tugs her dress up, baring herself from the waist down. "If you're that eager, don't let me stop you."

Alaric moves upward, licking my pussy and then... *Oh gods.* I shove my face between Ursa's thighs and muffle my moan against her skin. I should slow down, should ask permission, but she tugs my hair again, guiding me to her pussy, and apparently we don't really need words at all. I can't stop my moan at the first taste of her. She's earthy and slick, and as she guides me up to her clit, I give up the last bit of resistance.

I may hate myself at the end of this—I *will* hate myself at the end of this—but it feels too good to stop.

And what choice do I have?

I signed the contract. I made the deal. I bargained away a bit of myself that I'm sure I won't miss. I consented. I've gone too far to change my mind now.

Alaric's fingers shift down to grip my thighs, holding me open for him. Desire coils through me, tighter and tighter. The closer I get to the edge, the more desperate I am to consume what little bit of Ursa she'll allow me. I moan against her pussy and suck hard on her clit. Her fingers dig into my hair, and she lets loose a low laugh that has me shivering right down to my core. Her thighs tighten around me, every move designed to hold me in place as her hips roll to ride out the rhythm of my mouth.

Holy crap, I just made Ursa come.

She uses my hair to pull me off her and leans down to

press a surprisingly soft kiss to my lips. I'm still perched on the edge, though Alaric's tongue has slowed, as if he's teasing me, as if he wanted to ensure I finished pleasuring Ursa before he took me to the point of no return.

She grips my throat in that casually possessive way of hers. I don't understand why the feeling of her palm pressed to my vulnerable skin, her nails pricking me, settles me. In the presence of her approval, I don't care enough to wonder. "Good girl." She gives my throat a little squeeze and nudges me back. "For that, I won't make Alaric tease you for hours before he finally fucks you."

I can't quite catch my breath. "Thank you?"

"It's a reward, yes." She shifts me back enough that she can fix her dress. "Alaric, stop playing and give her that orgasm you've been promising."

He growls against me and then he's tonguing my clit in a devastatingly good rhythm. I whimper, and her fingers tighten the tiniest bit on my throat. I'm caught between them, a piece of flotsam in the middle of a storm. Ursa holds me steady, but she's not doing it for comfort. She's exposing me just as thoroughly as Alaric is with his mouth, stripping me down to my base parts. I don't know what she'll find. I truly don't.

My eyes start to slide shut and she pricks me with her nails. "Ah ah. Eyes on me, darling. He may be giving you this orgasm, but it's at my command."

She looks almost as perfectly put together as she did during the auction. The only evidence that we've been up to no good is the faint sheen of sweat on her medium-brown skin and an equally faint smudging of her lipstick. The reminder of where she left evidence of that same vivid red shade is enough to make the pleasure Alaric deals coil almost painfully tight. I gasp and then I'm coming. I try to writhe, but they hold me immobile, and somehow that only makes my pleasure spike higher, last longer.

My legs give out, and together Alaric and Ursa get me onto the bed. Being between them shouldn't feel so good, not when there are a thousand things I am very intentionally not unpacking right now. The fact that Alaric is *here*… The fact that he *tricked me*… So much of what I thought was truth is actually a lie.

I shove the thought away.

Better to tell myself that I don't have a choice, that I have seven days in this strange limbo. Easier to convince myself that I *must* consent.

Anything is easier than admitting I want them both too much to poke holes in the betrayal lingering just out of reach. Alaric seduced me and made me believe that he might love me, when all the while he was kneeling at the feet of Ursa. He *lied* to me.

Ursa and I couldn't be more different. I'm a mere shadow of everything she is. A ghost. A half-formed thought. A faded memory when she's blazing with life and personality and charm.

How could I really believe that he'd want me when he has *her*?

Ursa ends up lounging next to me, looking perfect and touchable, while Alaric kneels between my spread thighs. She traces a single finger down the center of my chest, over my left breast to circle my nipple. "Have you used toys, darling?"

I blink, my mind sluggish to divine her meaning. Once I realize what she's talking about, I blush so fiercely, it's a wonder my skin doesn't burst into flames. "No."

"Why not?"

I have to fight not to squirm. "I didn't want to have to sneak it into the house or explain its presence if it was found." Once, my older sister Jael offered to smuggle me in a sex toy, but I was too worried that someone would find it. My father has a staff of cleaning people, and I'm certain that half their job is simply reporting on what they find in his unmarried daughters' rooms. How Jael managed to keep a secret like a dildo is a mystery.

Alaric's frowning down at me, but it's Ursa who says, "And they call me a monster." She glances at him. "Slowly. When she hurts, it will be on purpose, not because we're careless."

I'm still trying to decode *that* statement when Alaric wedges a single finger into me. The intrusion has me lifting off the bed and writhing, though I can't begin to say if it's because I'm trying to get away or trying to get closer.

Instantly, Ursa catches my throat. "Relax." Her melodic voice courses through me as Alaric presses his finger a little deeper.

"She's so fucking tight," he mutters. He sounds almost in pain.

Ursa chuckles. "Don't pretend you aren't about to come just from knowing that you're the first person to finger her pretty pussy."

The pressure of his finger eases a little as he slowly strokes me, the tension turning liquid and scalding. "*Oh.*"

"Does that feel good, darling?" She has a smile in her voice, like she already knows the answer.

"Yes, Mistress." Every time I swallow, my throat presses against her palm. Her touch anchors me, even as Alaric's threatens to send me to the moon.

"Another."

For a moment, I think she's talking to me, but then Alaric presses a second finger into me. I hiss out a breath. It doesn't exactly hurt, but I have never been so aware of my body the way I am right now. He still has the towel wrapped around his waist, but I can clearly see the imprint of his dick. It's *much* larger than two fingers.

Even as I tell myself not to, I look up at Alaric. There's no pretending this is some stranger who means nothing to me, no pretending that this doesn't hurt me in a way that has nothing to do with the physical.

He's never looked at me the way he is now. Always before, he was sweet and restrained, and if there was heat in his deep blue eyes, it was carefully banked. I didn't realize how *safe* he was until this moment, when he's kneeling between my thighs, staring at the spot where his fingers enter me as if tormented. As if he's barely restraining himself.

As if the only thing holding him back from ravishing me is the woman lying next to me and idly stroking my throat.

Ursa watches Alaric fuck me with his fingers. "Really, lover? You can do better than that."

He makes a sound suspiciously like a growl and twists his wrist. Suddenly, he's not just fucking me with his fingers. He's stretching me. Exploring me. He finds and strokes a spot inside me that has my bones melting. I gasp. "Oh, gods."

"I'll allow that one since he just discovered your G-spot." Ursa lifts her free hand and presses her fingers into Alaric's mouth. He watches me as he sucks them deep, wets them, and then she drops her hand to stroke my clit. What he was doing felt amazing before. Now it feels like I might just come right out of my body. Both their hands on me...

I orgasm harder than I have previously tonight. The wave racks my body, bowing my back, pressing my neck hard enough into Ursa's palm that I lose my breath. Or I would if I could remember how to breathe. I think I'm sobbing. I think I might be dying.

Alaric withdraws his fingers, but Ursa keeps up light teasing strokes to my pussy as he gets rid of the towel and fists his cock. He starts to lean forward but hesitates. "Are you on birth control?"

I takes me too long to answer, to remember how to speak. "No."

He curses long and hard even as Ursa laughs. "Condoms are in the nightstand."

He moves away for a few moments and then it's just Ursa and me. She gives my neck another of those faint squeezes that settles me and drives my desire higher at the same time, but her expression is contemplative. "I knew he was positively rabid to keep his daughters under lock and key, but I had no idea it went so far."

I don't really want to talk about my father while I'm here in this position, but I can't deny the unspoken command in her statement that isn't quite a question. "He's overprotective."

"Controlling," she corrects gently. "One could almost argue abusive. You're an adult, Zurielle. The only person in charge of your body should be you." She smiles slowly. "And me for the next week."

I frown. "Ursa—" I clamp my mouth shut. I forgot about her command to be silent.

"Speak."

Alaric climbs back onto the bed with a silver packet in his hand. I watch him rip it open and roll the condom down his length. I can't tell if I'm shaking from Ursa stroking me or from a sick combination of fear and anticipation. "I should hate you. Both of you." I don't mean to speak, but once I do, it's impossible to stop. "I think I do."

"I can live with that." He notches his cock at my entrance and looks me in the eye as he slides into me in a single stroke.

I cry out. It's too much, he's too big, it's too foreign a

feeling even after his fingers. It feels like my lower half is on fire, and my confused nerves don't know if they like it or not.

Alaric braces his hands on either side of my ribs, holding perfectly still. His expression is a thousand times more tormented than it was earlier. "Fuck."

Ursa's low laugh makes my toes curl despite the nearly overwhelming urge to cry. She gives my clit a slow circle. "Don't embarrass yourself by coming on the first stroke, lover."

"You're not helping," he grinds out.

Her smile is warm and mean, all at the same time. "Am I making it difficult on you? Does she clench around your cock every time I do this?" She circles my clit again. Indeed, my entire body tightens in response.

"*Ursa.*"

He's saying *her* name while he's inside *me.*

Ursa's voice goes harder than I've heard it. "Fuck her. You know it's what you want to do, selfish boy. Chase your pleasure at her expense. Now."

I barely have time to register the command before Alaric obeys. He pulls almost all the way out of me and shoves deep, drawing a cry from my lips. It's too much, but Ursa keeps stroking my clit and my body is already beginning to accommodate him. It still burns, but pleasure begins to drown out the pain almost immediately. Maybe because of all the earlier orgasms.

He drives into me hard enough that my body starts to move up the mattress. Ursa's grip on my throat tightens, and Alaric grabs my hips, holding me in place. They consume me. Her hands. His cock. The way they look at each other while he's fucking me. I should hate it, should resent it, should feel anything but another orgasm building in my core.

Each time he drives into me, each time she circles my clit,

each time their hands hold me forcibly in place, I get closer to another, more powerful, orgasm.

"Stop holding back," Ursa commands.

For a moment, I think she's talking to me, but then Alaric picks up his pace. He wedges his hands beneath my ass and lifts my hips off the mattress, yanking me onto his cock as he shoves forward. I swear I can feel him in the back of my throat. Once. Twice. A third time.

A high keening noise erupts from my lips and then I'm coming so hard, I think I black out. I vaguely register Alaric's strokes losing their smoothness and him cursing as he drives into me one last time.

Stillness descends.

I'm achingly aware of his cock still inside me, of the breath filling my lungs, of Ursa's grip on my throat. Alaric finally pulls out of me and moves off the bed, walking quickly into the bathroom. I stare at the ceiling. Should I say something? I don't have words right now. The reality of this situation is soaking into me one wave at a time.

I sold my virginity tonight.

Alaric tricked me into doing it.

Ursa orchestrated the entire thing.

I belong to her—to them—for another six nights.

She releases my throat, and I start to sit up. She touches my chest. "Not yet." She disappears into the bathroom and comes back a few seconds later with a washcloth. I wince as she presses it between my thighs. She's back to the kind version of herself, the warm smile that shields the cruelty. "You did well."

"I lay there and took it." I swallow hard. "You commanded he fuck me selfishly."

"Mmm. I did." She finishes wiping me up and urges me to sit. "If I were more merciful, I'd give you tomorrow to recover, but every one of these days belongs to me, and as such I'm going to use them to their full capacity."

I look up at her and shiver. I want to reject what she's saying, to be able to truthfully say that I want nothing of what she's offering me. I hate her for being part of this, for witnessing my humiliation. What kind of person is foolish enough to walk into the trap and then refuse to walk back out again? What kind of person craves their betrayers' touch?

Apparently the kind of person I am.

CHAPTER 12

ALARIC

I barely get three steps back into the room when Ursa cuts through my plans for the rest of the night with a few short words. "Take Zurielle to the spare bedroom and get her situated."

"The spare bedroom?" I stop short. "Why is she going there?"

"Because I want her to."

I start to argue, but there's no point. Ursa has given a command and I won't change her mind, not when we're apparently playing out a particular scene in her head. It was fun fucking Zuri. *Really* fun. But I want to be on my knees in front of Ursa on my first night free of the Underworld. More, the thought of wading through emotional conversations with Zuri sounds about as fun as throwing myself headfirst into a wood chipper.

Arguing won't work, but maybe another tactic will.

"Ursa. Mistress." I give her my best charming smile. "I thought I'd keep you company tonight." I thought we'd *talk*, too. Maybe not tonight, but soon.

She rises slowly from the bed. Normal people would look

awkward doing the same motions, but with Ursa it's pure grace and deadly power. She smooths down her dress. "Alaric, you can go sleep in the spare bedroom with Zurielle, or you can go outside and sleep on the balcony like a disobedient pup. It's your choice, lover."

I clench my jaw even as part of me responds to the sweet poison of her words. Everything about this woman draws me in: her beauty, her power, her deceptively sweet meanness. Even now, the threat makes my body go tight.

But that desire will only last about five minutes in the cold night.

I finally nod. "I'll take her now, Mistress."

"Good boy. I knew you'd see things my way." She crosses to me and presses a light kiss to my lips. "Start with aftercare. You may do anything she consents to—except fuck her pussy with your cock. Do you understand?"

I frown down at her. I don't understand this. *We* were supposed to be the endgame, and now she's essentially giving me to Zuri. Or giving Zuri to me, depending on how one looks at this. Either way, the equation doesn't include Ursa, which is the one component I crave above all others.

I like Zuri. I do. But she's so sweet, I feel like I'll bruise her with a harsh word. She has her entire heart pinned to her chest, just ready to give it to the first person who offers her a tiny bit of kindness, fake or not. Being around her makes me feel guilty, and I fucking hate it.

"Do you understand?"

"Yes," I grind out.

Ursa doesn't move, a deadly stillness stealing over her. "If you harm her, it will displease me." If Zuri has a problem with us talking about her like she isn't there, she doesn't say a word from her spot on the bed. Ursa reaches up and gives my chin a light flick. "Go." No negotiation. No bargaining. A simple command with the illusion of a choice.

There's no point in arguing further. She's not bluffing about making me sleep outside, which might amuse me in different circumstances. Not tonight. Not with everything riding so close to the surface.

I turn to Zuri. "Let's go."

She gives Ursa a wounded look but climbs off the bed on clearly shaking legs. I'm moving before I make a decision to do so, closing the distance between us and scooping her into my arms. If she takes a nose dive, it'll just be more work for me to scrape her off the ground. Or that's what I tell myself as I walk out of Ursa's room and down the hall to the spare bedroom that's been mine the few nights I've been able to slip my leash long enough to stay over.

I kick the door shut with my foot, which is right around the time Zuri seems to register that I'm carrying her. She squirms in my arms. "Put me down."

"Can you stand without falling on your ass?"

She goes rigid. "I never knew you were such a *dick*."

I set her carefully on her feet. "You never knew me." I'm irritated at being banished from Ursa's bedroom, at being forced into this conversation. The idea of revenge against Triton sounded like a good plan when she first proposed it to me. A way to bring that bastard down a few notches, even if ultimately we have no power in Olympus. It took some doing to be able to meet Zuri "by accident" when Triton would kill me before he'd let me touch one of his precious daughters, but it was all for the sake of revenge and freedom.

That plan feels so distant now with her standing in my room, naked and still flushed from our fucking. She seems to realize it at the same moment and moves to cover herself. "Turn around."

I burst out laughing. "Zuri, there is nothing that you're covering that I didn't have my mouth all over back in Ursa's room. No point in playing the coy virgin when you aren't one anymore."

I don't even try to dodge her slap. The force of it turns my face to the side and sends pain blossoming over my cheek. It's nothing more than I deserve for being such a goddamn bastard.

Zuri's big eyes are furious and filled to the brim with hurt and betrayal. "Don't act like you took something special from me. It's just sex, Alaric. Whether it's my first, hundredth, or thousandth time." Her lower lip quivers, but she makes an obvious effort to still it. "And when this week is finished, I'm going to fuck as many people as it takes to forget all about you and Ursa."

Jealousy sinks its barbs into me. It doesn't matter that I have no right to it, that I want to get rid of her as much as she wants to be rid of me. I take a step forward, a part of me delighting when she stands her ground. She wouldn't have done it a few months ago. I lean down. "That's your mistake, Zuri. There *is* no one better than me and Ursa. You could fuck your way through Carver City, Olympus, *and* Sabine Valley, and you'd still feel the imprint of us on your skin."

"Whatever you have to tell yourself to sleep at night." She smooths her hair back, regaining her composure bit by bit despite the fact she's still standing there completely naked. "I might not be experienced, but even I can tell that your technique could use some work."

"You weren't complaining when you were coming all over my cock."

Her eyes flash. "Because *Ursa* was touching me."

A perverse kind of joy fills me. She never would have gone toe to toe with me when she lived in her father's house. A few days in Carver City and little Zuri thinks she can play with the big dogs. She might even be right.

That's not going to stop me from putting her in her place right now, tonight. "Tell me your safe word."

"We're not doing this."

I don't back down. "Your safe word, Zuri."

She stops short, finally registering that I'm not fucking around. "Hurricane." A little meekness filters back into her tone, but nowhere near the sweet submission she gave Ursa. I take a step forward, and she stops me with her hand on my chest. "I *hate* you, Alaric. All the sex in the world isn't going to cover up the fact that you lied to me and betrayed me and fully intend to ruin my life because of something that has nothing to do with me."

"You're right." I enjoy her shock at my agreement. "But that doesn't change a damn thing. I want you. So I'm going to take you. Again."

"Better ask for permission first. You wouldn't want to be banished to sleep on the balcony like a dog." The venom in her tone only delights me more. She didn't show Ursa a damn bit of this steel, but she's giving it to me. It doesn't matter that it's because she loathes me. I like it. Fuck, it makes the sparks between us burn hotter.

I lean down until my lips nearly brush her ear. "There are a thousand things I could do to you tonight that don't involve you on my cock."

"I'm not interested."

"Liar." I skate my hand down the center of her chest, over her stomach, to cup her pussy. She hisses out a breath at the touch, and her hands come to rest on my biceps. I explore her gently, tauntingly. "You feel awful wet for someone not interested."

"Maybe I'm thinking of *her*."

Ursa is magic, and if it's the magic that comes with sacrifice and shadows, it's all the more addictive because of it. That said, I can't stop the jealousy that makes me want to shove Zuri's desire in her face and rub her nose in it. She might be caught in Ursa's spell, but before she met the Sea Witch, Zuri was *mine*.

I crowd her back toward the bed. Where Ursa's bedroom reminds me of the dark depths of the sea, this is a lighter room, leaning more toward grays and tonal blues that make me think of a storm coming in. It's not here yet, but soon.

Or maybe the storm is inside me. Some days it feels that way, wind and rain and thunder violent enough to shake my very bones. It's always been like this. Nothing is enough. There's always something just beyond my reach that I want, regardless of whether I deserve it or not. The only time I don't feel that devastating hunger is when I'm fucking, or when I'm kneeling at Ursa's feet.

One of those options isn't available to me tonight. The other will have to do.

I give Zuri's pussy a light squeeze. "Get on the bed and spread your legs."

She glares like she might challenge me, but I keep stroking her until that delicate little whimper slips free. No matter what Zuri thinks of me, she's getting a taste of what true pleasure at another's hands—at *my* hands—can feel like. She's got a bit of a little slut in her, because she shoves off my chest and climbs onto the bed and does as I command, spreading her legs. "I'm going to think of her."

Her words spur me forward, following her onto the mattress and gripping her thighs, spreading her wider yet. "No, you're not."

Zuri lifts her arms over her head, baring her body to me completely. Does she understand how sexy she looks right now? How sweet this tiny vulnerability is? It means she trusts me, at least a little, no matter how much she hates me at the moment. No matter how hedonistic she's turning out to be, Zuri isn't a complete fool. She wouldn't put herself in danger for the sake of orgasms.

Except that's exactly what she's doing right now.

I coast my hands up her thighs until my thumbs brush her pussy. I part her. "You're a silly girl for agreeing to this. You came to this penthouse and we can do anything we want to you. *I* can do anything I want to you."

"I have my safe word."

"Mmm." I brush her clit. "And you're trusting us to respect it. Some would say that just proves what a fool you are."

She props herself up on her elbows and gives me a long look. "Do you know that Hades is the one who will enforce the contract?"

That makes sense. I can see where she's going with this, but I'm too stubborn to admit it. "Is that supposed to mean something?"

"If the deal isn't honored, it will be a violation of the contract both Ursa and I signed." Her eyes are a little hazy with pleasure from my touching her, but her voice is clear. "The penalty for breaking the contract is harsh, Alaric. If Hades turns against Ursa, there's a good chance the rest of the territory leaders will as well, if only to stay on his good side. So, you see, I *am* protected. You'd know that if you read a contract in your life instead of jumping into deals recklessly."

I should stop this, should slow us down. She just had sex for the first time in a situation that is hardly ideal for emotional stability. But, damn it, I can't help stepping to the line she's drawn in the sand. "Now we're going to throw stones, Zuri? Don't act like you had a plan when you came here." I press two fingers into her.

She makes that delicious whimpering sound, but she's still glaring at me. "*You* don't get to be mad. *You* got what you wanted. So climb down off that high horse, Alaric. It's not a good look for you."

I shift forward, bracing myself over her shoulder with my free hand as I continue the slow fucking with my fingers. "You like the way I look."

"A pretty face..." Her breath gets a little choppy. "It doesn't mean anything. I don't know you. I thought I did, but I was wrong." Abruptly, she shoves at my chest. "I can't do this. Not like this."

"Zuri—"

"Hurricane."

The word falls between us like the calm before a storm. I stare down at her, my exhale damn near a gasp. When did I start breathing hard? "You just safed out."

Zuri inches away from me slowly, like she's not sure I'll really stop. That, more than anything, sends reality slamming into me. I told her I could do anything to her, and now she's not sure what to believe. I am an unbelievable asshole.

I move back, giving her space. "I'm sorry."

"No, you're not. Stop lying to me." She only stops putting distance between us when her back presses to the headboard. "Please leave."

"Zuri—"

"You don't get to call me that anymore! Only my friends call me that." A tear trails down her pretty face, that single piece of evidence of her hurt striking me more than her slap did earlier. "Please leave."

She won't accept aftercare from me, and I have no one to blame but myself. Ursa paved the way for us to figure out shit out. Except... Maybe she knew it would end like this, a chasm opening up between us that is destined never to be crossed. Ursa doesn't like loose ends, and my conflicted feelings for Zuri are exactly that. It would be just like her to ensure that there's nothing left unsaid between us, no matter how venomous the words.

That blasted guilt pricks me again, except it doesn't feel like a vague pain. It feels like it has me by the throat. I swallow hard, but it does nothing to dispel the sensation of having my airway closed off. I always fuck up the things that matter. I just didn't realize Zuri might number among them until this moment.

And now it's too late.

CHAPTER 13

URSA

*I*t takes all of thirty minutes for Alaric to return to my room, slouching through the door like a whipped dog. He hesitates, his gaze firmly on the wood floor. "She kicked me out."

I almost laugh at how perfectly these two are playing to my tune. It's really too simple. I wind them up and set them on a collision course and they are only too happy to perform to expectation. "I gave you an order, lover."

His brows lower, the first indication that I'm pushing him past the point of caution. "We need to talk."

He's not wrong, but talking can wait until Zurielle is no longer in my home. We've waited this long; waiting a week more requires a pittance of patience. That's *logical*. It's not procrastinating a hard conversation. I simply...

I fight back a sigh. It doesn't matter what my motivations for holding things off is. Right now I have an angry Alaric in my room and he's not going anywhere, regardless of my commands. The man might be submissive in most of his interactions with me, but one glance at the stubborn expression on his face tells me everything I need to know.

If I try to send him away again, he'll dig in his heels and we'll have a fight on our hands.

He stalks toward me. He takes in my wardrobe change with a sweep of his gaze, lingering on the deep V of my robe before he finally lands on my face. "We need to talk," Alaric repeats.

I'm not ready. I don't have the framework for this conversation laid out. For the first time in a very long time, I am not sure what he's going to say. "Talk."

"What happens now?"

I raise an eyebrow, striving to keep my faintly amused mask in place. "Now we spend the next seven days fucking Zurielle."

His jaw tightens. "That's not what I meant."

"Isn't it?" I step closer. "Are you looking for permission or forgiveness? If you want the former, you have it. The latter, you might as well seek out a priest."

"It's not that simple."

"It's exactly that simple." I'm already tired of this conversation. Alaric is beautiful and savage beneath his polished exterior, but he's nowhere near cold enough to survive this world without someone watching over him. He's so incredibly lucky that Hades offered him a bargain—and subsequently the Underworld became his caretaker for the last few years. The guilt he's carting around over allowing Zurielle to walk into this situation of her own will is ridiculous.

Unless...

I tilt my head to the side, considering him. "Did you start to believe the lie, lover?"

"What?" He closes down his expression, which is a tell all its own.

I run my hands up his bare chest. "You spent several weeks in Olympus playing Romeo to her Juliet. Did you start to see a different version of yourself reflected in the stars in her eyes?" I reach his shoulders and skate my nails down his arms. "One where you really are Prince Charming, or at least a knight in shining armor? One where you have *honor*?"

Alaric drops his gaze. "I know better."

"Yes, you do." I lace my fingers through his long enough to give his hands a squeeze and then force myself step back. No matter what else I am, I'm not in the business of tying people to me who don't want to be here. Not in any kind of long-term way. Better that he leaves now and makes a clean break for both of us. "If you don't have the stomach for this, leave. It was meant to be a reward after months of hard work, but I'm hardly going to force you to fuck the girl."

"Ursa, that's not what I meant."

This time, I can't stop my sigh. Alaric is wonderful. Truly, he is. But sometimes I am so godsdamn *tired* of having to play the dominant party so he can dodge his guilt. Up until this point, he's been a fun partner, but this hesitance just proves what I already suspected. I can't trust him enough to lean on him. My frustration gets the best of me and adds some ire to my tone. "Then what *did* you mean?"

"I just..." He hesitates. "I need you to help me stop thinking."

I try not to resent him for not asking what *I* need. I'm the one who's established the rules in this relationship, and expecting him to guess what I can't quite make myself put into words isn't fair. Then again, I'm not feeling particularly fair right now. He wants to be punished? Fine. "Kneel."

His mouth goes flat. "That's not—"

"Get on your knees, Alaric." I inject enough bite into my tone to make him respond instinctively. He kneels in a smooth move, and he's glaring at the floor because he knows better than to glare at *me*. I sift my fingers through his dark hair. "You came to me to meet your needs."

"I came to you hoping I could convince you to let me stay the night in your bed."

"No." My bed is fine for fucking, but it's my sanctuary at night, a place I can let down my walls completely and rest a little bit before I have to don my armor and go back out into the world. If he stays, there will be no rest, not when he's too focused on his internal conflict to worry about *my* needs. "You are going back into that room tonight. Would you like a beating or a fucking before you do?"

He tenses and then relaxes on his exhale. "A beating."

I suspected as much. "Tell me your safe word."

"Mermaid."

I am tired and irritated, but I push it away. I knew Alaric would let his guilt get the best of him. I didn't think it'd happen quite so fast, but one learns to adapt when they're in a position of power. A good beating will purge some of the messier emotions he's nursing, at least for now. "Stand at the foot of the bed. You know your place."

He rises gracefully and moves to one of the columns of the four-poster bed. The strap is artfully concealed within the fabric there, but Alaric and I have done this before. He frees it and loops it around his hands. It's capable of tightening enough to bind, but he's choosing this, and if I allow him some fantasies, this isn't one. He's choosing this. Choosing *me*.

I walk to the cabinet next to my armoire and pick through the options there. Crops and a wide range of floggers and even a whip, though I don't use the latter often. It's dramatic and really gets a point across, but not practical for regular use. I finally settle on one of my favorite floggers, a heavy leather one that will bruise him, but won't cut his pretty skin.

One heavy enough to tire me out so that I can get some sleep tonight.

I walk back toward Alaric, enjoying the way he looks standing naked by my bed. I take my time studying the way his broad shoulders create a V down to his ass. He's not huge, but he spends a lot of time on his body and it shows.

I swing the flogger, warming up my arm and shoulder. It takes effort and practice to become as good as I am—not to mention a whole lot of stamina. I'll never admit as much, but I've had to work on my upper body strength since I started playing with Alaric regularly. He can take a much longer and harsher beating than someone like Aurora can, though she's a little pain slut, too.

I beat Alaric until my entire arm and shoulder are on fire and his pale skin is a dark pink that promises he'll wear my marks by morning. Until he's leaning against the column for support and his body is loose and pliant. Until I've beaten all the guilt right out of him, at least for now. Until I'm so tired, I'm practically weaving on my feet.

I toss the flogger aside and walk to press against his back, relishing his hissed exhale at the contact. "Do you feel better, lover?"

"Yes, Mistress." His voice has gone dreamy and low.

My irritation has long since passed. Maybe we needed this, a touchstone before the week begins in earnest. I move back enough to untie my robe and let it fall to the ground. When I press against him again, it's skin to skin. I reach around and laugh a little when I find his cock hard. "Get on the bed, Alaric."

He moves slowly, as if in a daze. I'll have to bring him back down to earth before I send him back to the spare bedroom. I wait for him to lie down on his back and then climb up to straddle his hips. I press my hands to his chest, press his aching back more firmly against the mattress. "Did you like fucking that virgin pussy?"

He cries out and writhes beneath me. "Yes, Mistress."

"It wasn't enough for you, though, was it? Once is never enough for you." I reach between us and guide his cock into me. I have to close my eyes for a moment. This never gets old. No matter where Alaric and I misstep in other areas, we are consistent here. Our needs fit each other's too well to give up. I work myself down his cock and then open my eyes to find him watching me with a dazed expression on his handsome face.

"You're so fucking beautiful," he gasps. He tentatively reaches out. "Can I—"

"Touch me." Another time I'd make him lie there perfectly still while I fuck him slowly, coming over and over again while he's denied that final pleasure. Not tonight. I want it quick and dirty. I ride him as he palms my breasts, his expression rapturous. Pleasure rises in steady waves, driven by how good he feels inside me, by the worshipful way he watches me fuck him. I press two fingers into his mouth. He opens eagerly, sucking me deep and stroking me with his tongue. This man really is a joy, even if he's high maintenance as hell.

I withdraw my fingers and begin stroking my clit, intent on my pleasure. "Don't you dare come first."

"Wouldn't dream of it," he grinds out, the hoarseness of his words giving lie to them. He's dancing on the edge.

I slow down, torturing us both as I lift myself and sink down his length. "You feel good inside me, lover. You feel like *mine*."

"I am." His whole body is one long line of tension as he struggles to obey my command not to orgasm. "I'm yours, Mistress."

I come hard, and as I begin to lose control, Alaric grabs my hips and keeps me fucking his cock, drawing out my orgasm even as he fights his own. I half collapse, catching myself on his chest. "Now you have permission to come."

He drives up into me, his expression agonized as he follows me over the edge. I roll my hips a little, enjoying the feeling of him softening inside me, enjoying how possessive it makes me. My cock, my Alaric, *mine*. It doesn't matter that I'm sending him back to Zurielle in a few moments because in this moment he is undeniably mine.

I press a kiss to his lips and climb off him. "Do you feel better?"

"Yes." It comes out as a sigh.

It's so tempting to tell him to stay. To finish getting ready for bed and tuck him in next to me and spend the night with his comforting weight against my body. To just...let down the barriers for a little while, set down the weight I've carried for so long. To let myself rest.

I can't do it.

I care about Alaric, but I don't trust him. Not entirely. He's too wrapped up in himself and now in Zurielle. The entire time I've known him, he's been essentially owned by Hades because of the reckless decision he made in Olympus. Even throwing in his support with me is reckless. *Alaric* is reckless.

I have sacrificed too much and done too many terrible things to put my territory at risk for something as mundane as love.

If I let Alaric in, if I allow him to be a full partner, he won't stop being reckless. And then I will have to manage his decisions in addition to everything else already on my plate. There may come a time when I'm willing to take that risk, but not now, not when I'm finally on the verge of bringing Triton down a few notches.

So I turn away, even though it hurts to do it, and grab my robe off the floor. "Your choices for the night remain the same. Your bedroom or the balcony." I force steel into my spine despite the exhaustion threatening to bow my shoulders. "Don't be here when I get back." I walk into the bathroom and shut the door.

As tempting as it is to stand there and listen to ensure he obeys, I busy myself with getting ready for bed. It doesn't take long to wash my face, brush my teeth, and lotion up my body. I wrap my hair and take a deep breath. If he tries to challenge me on this, I'll be forced to punish him, which means my night will have just gotten longer.

But when I walk out of the bathroom, my room is empty.

I waste no time walking to the door and locking it. When I deal with Zurielle and Alaric tomorrow, it will be on *my* terms. I'm heading to the bed when my phone rings.

I stare at it, allowing myself to actually consider not answering. It's not really an option, but the fantasy is pretty all the same. The name scrolling across my screen is a familiar one, though. I'm smiling as swipe to accept the call. "You're so nosy, Malone."

"I gave you an appropriate amount of time before I called. Not even you can give a virgin enough endurance to last all night." There's a thread of amusement in her cold tone, something very few people ever get to witness.

"You're underestimating me."

"Obviously I'm not or you wouldn't be answering right now."

I snort and climb into bed. "And *your* night ended early if you're calling *me*."

Malone's silent for a few moments. "It just doesn't hold the same attraction at the moment."

It's as close to a confession as she'll ever get. Up until recently, Malone and I were the only women territory leaders in Carver City. Now we had two more—Jasmine Sarraf and Cordelia Belmonte—but they're both young and green and focused on solidifying their power base as new leaders. Malone and I went through those steps at nearly the same time well over a decade ago. That sort of thing bonds a person, and we've created a solid friendship as a result.

I grin. "If you'd just take her, you wouldn't have to brood about everyone else who is."

"I don't know what you're talking about." But the snap in her tone belies her words.

I glance at my door, sparing a thought to wondering if Alaric and Zurielle are fighting again or if they've managed to ice each other out enough to get some sleep. Either way, they'll be primed and ready for me tomorrow. "I know a thing or two about taking what you want, Malone. If you're concerned about it becoming messy, just put an external timer on it."

She chuckles drily. "You be sure to tell me how un-messy things are at the end of this week."

"I have a plan. It's not changing for the gods or Zeus."

"I hope it doesn't. A million dollars for that girl." I don't have to see her to know she's shaking her head. "I hope you know what you're doing."

"As I said—I have a plan. Speaking of, I need to go."

"Yeah, me too." The thread of exhaustion is back in her tone, but she sounds like she's smiling. "Have fun with your little pets, Ursa. You deserve a little pleasure after all the sacrifices you've made."

"You do, too."

Naturally, she doesn't respond to that. "Good night." Malone hangs up.

I set my phone down and sigh. The next seven days are for pleasure, yes, but they're also serving a purpose. I can't afford to forget that truth, no matter how much fun I'm having toying with Zurielle and Alaric.

One misstep, and this will all end in ruin.

CHAPTER 14

ZURIELLE

*T*he sound of the door opening has me sitting up and clutching the sheet to my chest. Alaric walks in with his hands up as if warding off an attack. "I'm just following orders."

Just following orders.

Does he understand how those words cut me to the quick? They're yet another reminder that he never wanted me, was never the nice guy I believed when I met him back in Olympus. I have never felt so young and foolish as I do now, and I *hate* it. I want to keep lashing out with my words until he hurts as much as I am right now. Until he doubts his very instincts and questions everything.

Too bad my words bounce off him as if from impenetrable stone. He'd have to care what I think in order to be hurt by me.

Somehow, that stings more than anything else so far.

I point at him. "If you climb into this bed, I will smother you in your sleep."

He stops at the edge of the mattress. He's still as naked as I am, and even as much fury surges through me, I can't help noticing how perfectly formed he is. All chiseled lines and hard planes, a body made for *doing*. If I let myself, I can still feel his broad hands on my hips. On other parts of me.

He's been gone for a long time, and there's a new tiredness on his face and present in the line of his shoulders that wasn't there before. "I'm not sleeping on the floor." Alaric shakes his head. "Look, I don't know if Ursa wants us to fight or fuck, but I don't have energy for either right now."

I should fight until we're at a standstill and then keep silent for the rest of the week. I've already been so foolish, and wanting answers from him sets me up to prove I haven't learned anything from this. Better to just ride this week out and then walk away, taking my absurd amount of money with me. It's more than enough to set me up anywhere I want to go, to start a new life away from Olympus and Carver City and this entire corner of the country.

But as I stare at Alaric while he awaits my response, I can't build up my walls fast enough. "I just want to know why." My voice breaks on the last word. "I deserve that much."

He sighs and drags his hand through his dark hair. "Yeah, I know."

"Then tell me."

One corner of his mouth kicks up. "Promise you won't kick me out of bed again."

"No." I hesitate. "But I won't do it tonight unless you give me reason to."

"Guess that's as good as I can ask for." He climbs onto the mattress, moving slowly as if in pain.

It's not until he turns to adjust the blanket that I see his back. "Alaric, what happened?"

His soft smile is completely at odds with the marks on his back that are already darkening to bruises. "I had a good beating. That's all."

"Ursa did this."

"Yes." He gives himself a shake and seems to zero back in on me. "Because I asked her to."

I swallow my next words, ones that make all sorts of assumptions, and try to *think*. I know about kink, at least in theory. When Alaric went back to the Underworld, I spent a lot of time researching what exactly goes on in a place like that. There's nothing about the actual Underworld on the internet, of course, but there are other more public places that cater to similar clientele and tastes.

Not to mention I saw the things on the list I filled out before the auction. I am aware that some people enjoy pain the same way others enjoy a fine wine. Layers upon layers depending on the instruments used and the game being played out.

It just never occurred to me that *Alaric* might be one of those people.

"Is she going to beat me?"

"Do you want her to?"

I don't know. A few days ago, I would have conclusively said no, but now I'm not sure of anything. "May I see?"

Alaric considers me for a few moments and then shrugs. "If you want to." He rolls over and settles himself face-down on the bed.

I should be asking questions right now, demanding answers, but I shift closer and tug the blanket down to bare his back. Just like I suspected from my glimpse, he'll be sporting quite an array of bruises by morning. It spreads down his back and farther, disappearing beneath the blanket. "What did she use?"

"A flogger."

She's been very careful, I think. There are welts, but no cuts mar his skin. "Does she ever make you bleed?"

Alaric shifts restlessly. "Sometimes."

My body flushes hot, but I can't quite quantify my reaction. Am I jealous that he got this part of Ursa after I was sent away? Am I afraid that I'll be asked to submit to the same thing? Do I *want* to submit to the same thing?

I don't know. I just don't know.

I move away. None of this changes anything. I can't let myself get distracted by curiosity. "Tell me why."

He sighs and turns his face toward me. "I wasn't lying when I told you how I ended up at the Underworld."

"But you weren't telling the full truth either."

"No, I wasn't telling the full truth, either." He looks at me, really looks at me. "Do you know what your father does for Poseidon?"

"He's the second-in-command."

"Yes, but do you know what that really means?"

I search for the answer he's obviously looking for. "He handles a lot of the day-to-day stuff at the marina, the imports and export schedule and the like."

Alaric's mouth twists. "Yes, half of which is illegal."

I blink. "What? But why would he do something illegal? Olympus is a port city. It has an incredible economy." Olympus is dangerous. I know that, even if I sometimes believe my father exaggerates the danger to keep me and my sisters under lock and key. The Thirteen rule and they're all but above the law. It takes something as simple as catching Zeus's eye or pissing off Aphrodite and an entire person's world can come crashing down around them. But my father? A *criminal?*

"Zuri." He clears his throat. "Zurielle. That's incredibly naive. The illegal shit funds just as much of Olympus as the legal stuff, if not more. Poseidon and your father have their hands on all of it."

My father is involved in illegal activity? I'm already

shaking my head even as I try to wrap my mind around what he's saying. "Impossible."

"Hardly."

"My father is one of the most uptight and overprotective people in existence. He has rules upon rules upon rules. A person like that doesn't break the law. He worships the law."

"You know better. Those rules apply to his daughters—to you. Not to him." He sighs. "But all this is to say that I, ah, misplaced one of the shipments."

Easy enough to read between *those* lines. "You stole."

His lips quirk. "Yes, I stole, though it was already stolen goods, so it wasn't like he had a leg to stand on when it came to morals. Your father didn't see things that way."

I shake my head. "I don't understand."

"He tracked me down, but I'd already, uh, found the item a new home. So he offered me a choice—reimburse the amount owed or he'd take out payment in broken bones. If I chose the latter option, I'd run out of bones before the debt was fulfilled."

It's so brutal, I don't want to believe it. But Alaric says it drily, as if it's barely worth noting that my father apparently was willing to use deadly force as a form of punishment. "He wouldn't." But then, what do I know of my father's work, *really?* I've already proven woefully inadequate at asking questions to get to the truth. I was wrong about Alaric. Who's to say I'm not wrong about my father, too?

He has a tremendous rage. He always has. When he's furious, he gets so red, it always terrified me as a child, even if he never touched us in anger. But we're his children. Does he show the same restraint with people he doesn't love?

I don't like the turn my thoughts have taken. I don't like them at all. "You'd sold it. Why not just use that money to repay him?"

"It went elsewhere."

I frown. "What do you mean, it went elsewhere? What did you spend it on?" Alaric has worked for Hades for nearly eight years. He's paid off most of the debt and he still had a quarter million left to go. How could he have possibly spent it before my father got to him?

His expression is closed to me. But then, it always was, even when it appeared open. I can't trust anything he says, but this whole story has a ring of truth to it.

Or maybe I'm just a fool who hasn't learned my lesson.

"Where did it go?" I ask again.

He exhales slowly and closes his eyes. "Did you know I'm originally from Sabine Valley?"

I blink. "No, I didn't know that." I'd just assumed either Carver City or, more likely, Olympus.

"I spent most of my time growing up in Olympus, but my uncle and cousins used to run a territory in Sabine. They were betrayed. My uncle was killed and my cousins were forced to flee for their lives. They needed the money. We weren't exactly close, but family is family. It seemed a small enough price to pay. It was only one job to ensure they were able to have enough money to disappear and stay safe."

I search his face. Is this the truth or more lies? I thought I could tell the difference, but I'm doubting myself now. I don't know if I'll ever trust my instincts again. "If that's the case—"

"It is."

"Why not tell my father? Surely he would—"

Alaric snorts. "Your father doesn't give a fuck about me. He doesn't give a fuck about the people who are hurt in Olympus by the drugs that come in. He doesn't give a fuck about anything but maintaining the status quo and lining his pockets with money and power."

He paints such a horrible picture of my father. I don't—I can't believe it. "So you fled to Hades."

"He has a dearth of male submissives. He was willing to

loan me the money in exchange for my working in the Underworld while I repaid it."

"You exchanged money for sex."

His lips quirk. "Let's not throw stones from glass houses."

He's right, of course, but I'm not judging him. If he's telling the truth, he was in an impossible situation. And the money went to help his family, though if they ruled one-third of Sabine Valley, they aren't good people. No territory leaders are.

That includes Ursa.

I can't afford to forget that.

"Why does Ursa want revenge against my father?" I press my lips together. "I know what he says." A tale of betrayal and evil and a man who did what was required for the greater good. But that man and the man Alaric describes can't be the same person. It doesn't make sense. One has to be true and the other false. Maybe if I knew more, I could figure things out. "But I don't know her side of the story."

"That's something you're going to have to ask her. It's not my story to tell."

Which means I'll have to find the courage to ask her myself or go on without knowing. No matter where I'll land, it won't be tonight.

I settle down in the bed, suddenly aware that I can feel the heat coming off Alaric's body. The mattress is king-size, but it's nowhere near large enough. I consider grabbing some of the pillows from the floor to create a barrier between us, but that feels like admitting just how bothered I am by this situation. It feels like weakness.

Instead I close my eyes and force my body to relax, muscle by muscle. I resent the way his breathing evens out almost immediately. Of course Alaric would have no problem sleeping next to me. Why should he? I was only ever a means to an end.

Maybe that's how I should be looking at things. Alaric is a means to an end, even if that end is only pleasure. *Ursa* is a means to an end.

I don't know if I'm capable of making that shift, but I'm going to try. Better to try and fail than to just submit and be swept along without any agency of my own. At the end of this week, I will walk out of here with enough money to be truly independent for the first time in my life. If I play my cards right, I'll also walk out sexually experienced and understanding what it is I truly want.

A big *if*, but it gives me something to strive toward.

It will be enough.

It has to be enough.

CHAPTER 15

ALARIC

J wake up with Zuri on top of me. She's snuggled up around me like the sexiest teddy bear, hugging me tight. I lie perfectly still as she shifts against me. If she wakes up like this, she's going to be pissed. If she wakes up like this and I have a cockstand, I'm definitely getting yelled at, and it's too early for that shit.

She shifts again and I nearly groan. Whatever dreams Zuri's having, they're filthy ones from the way she starts to grind against my stomach.

I take a slow breath and grab her hips to give her a little shake. "Wake up, Zuri."

She goes still and then buries her face in my neck. "I was sleeping."

"Yeah, I know."

I feel her lips curl. "I'm not sleeping now."

I stare at the ceiling, nearly shaking with the need to urge her down to rub against my cock. "I know that, too."

Zuri presses her hands to my chest and sits up. She looks like some kind of nymph in this moment, naked in my bed with the sunlight streaming in, her auburn hair a mess around her shoulders and covering her breasts. She's still smiling though none of the emotions in her eyes are amusement. "I decided something last night."

"What's that?"

"It's silly to fight this. I agreed to seven days and so I'll do exactly as promised." She looks down at my chest. "Which means I can't have sex with you right now."

My breath catches in my chest. "You've been pretty clear on how much you hate me."

"I do." It stings how easily she agrees with me. Which is ridiculous. Did I expect her to object? To tell me that she's changed her mind and she fancies herself in love with me again? It'll never happen. I've more than ensured that at this point.

"Then what are you saying?"

Zuri's smile goes a little hot, a little mean. "I want to suck your dick. I've never done it before, and now is a perfect time to learn. It's a skill I'll no doubt find useful in the future."

When she sucks someone else's cock.

There it is again, that jealousy I have no right to. Zuri isn't mine. She never has been, and she never will be. If she wants this, it's the least I can do. I release her hips and lace my fingers behind my head. "If you want to, I'm not going to stop you."

She moves down my body without any of the hesitation she showed yesterday. Zuri gives my cock a long look and then wraps her hand around the base. "Tell me how to make it good."

I could lord this over her, but I don't have the heart to. Not when I want her mouth on me more than I want my next breath. My voice comes out strained. "Unless you try to bite it off, not a single person with a cock is going to complain that you're sucking them off."

She gives the cutest little smirk. "Are you *sure* I'm not going to bite you?"

"Zuri, I might like it." When her eyes go wide, I force a laugh. "If you try to hurt my cock, I won't be able to fuck you with it later. Your call."

"You're ridiculous." She gives me a slow stroke and presses her lips together. "Seriously, Alaric. Tell me how."

I finally nod. As much as I hate the idea of her sucking another cock, I also get off on the idea of instructing her. "You start like you are now. Hold the cock steady." Playing teacher and student is just one of my many fantasies, and if I've acted it out in all its variations, it feels different with Zuri. Really different. I lick my lips. "Start with the head. It's sensitive as hell."

She bends down and traces the head of my cock over her lips. It's such a gentle touch, but it feels like a bomb going off inside me. I tense, fighting to stay still. "Now your tongue."

Her tongue darts out and drags a line over my slit. My breath whooshes out, and Zuri takes that as the encouragement it is. She shifts her grip on my cock and licks me from base to tip, like I'm a melting popsicle. "Fuck," I breathe. "Yeah, that works."

"Mmm." She swirls her tongue around the head of my cock. "I didn't think I'd like this, but…I do."

"You hold the power," I grind out. "It's addictive."

"Yes, something like that." She eyes my cock. "I'm not going to be able to take you all."

"Not without practice," I agree. "Take what you can. Go slow."

She eases my cock into her mouth, swallowing it inch by inch. Halfway down, she slows, concentration pulling her eyebrows together. I know I need to say something, but the sight of her lips wrapped around my cock is almost too much. I want to dig my fingers into her hair, to take control of this, but I promised to teach her and that's not how the fantasy plays out. I clear my throat. "It takes time and practice to learn deep throating. Don't worry about that right now. You're mimicking fucking. Up and down. Use your tongue." It takes me a moment to continue as she begins to move, sliding off my cock and then sucking me deep. Fuck, that feels good. "This is one of those times when being messy is an asset."

She meets my gaze, a question lingering in her eyes. I take a breath. "Use your spit as lube for your hand. That way you're incorporating the entire length."

Zuri is a quick learner.

She falls into a comfortable rhythm, bringing her hand up to meet her mouth with each stroke. It feels good. So fucking good, I have to close my eyes to fight for restraint. Except... What am I restraining myself for? She didn't ask for a marathon blowjob session. She asked to be taught.

"My balls," I grit out. "Gently."

Zuri slips her free hand down to cup my balls. Her clever fingers explore me, and she goes still when she strokes my perineum and I moan. Holding my gaze, she repeats the motion.

"You keep doing that, I'm going to come."

Zuri does it again.

"Fuck." I clench my jaw. "Decide right now if you want to swallow or not, Zuri. I'm close."

She hesitates for the briefest second and then picks up her pace, sucking me down even as her clever fingers have me exploding in her mouth. I fist my hands in the comforter, desperate to hold on to something that keeps me from grabbing her head and fucking her mouth like I want to. I come hard, and she drinks me down without hesitation.

Zuri gives my cock one last pull as if she can't resist and

then lifts her head. She drags her thumb over the corner of her mouth. "Like that?"

"Like that," I manage. I can't help reaching for her, can't help cupping her jaw for the few seconds she allows it before she sits up and puts some distance between us. I swallow hard, choking on guilt. Ursa's beating and fucking banished it last night, but it never stays gone for good, no matter how many bruises I sport. It doesn't stop me from trying.

"It seems simple enough," Zuri finally says.

"The secret is enjoying it. If you're enjoying it, your partner will lose their fucking mind. Technique is only a bonus." I sit up. "Zuri, come here."

"No." She shakes her head. "That was a lesson, and it's over."

I open my mouth to argue, but the door opens before I can say anything else. Ursa sweeps into the room, looking as perfectly put together as always. She's got her locs styled almost like a crown and is wearing a dress that makes me think of the sea during a storm, an ombre sort of thing with the fabric fading from black around her chest and torso, down to a light frothy white at the hem.

She takes one look at us and smiles. "Good, you're awake." She snaps her fingers. "Come here. Kneel at my feet, darlings."

Zuri obeys without hesitation, blatantly eager to put distance between us. She walks naked to Ursa and sinks to her knees like she's been playing the part of a submissive for years, instead of for less than twenty-four hours.

I follow more slowly, mostly because my body protests moving after the beating I received last night. I smile at how sore I am. It feels good. Cathartic. Not enough to fully banish the guilt lingering around the edges, but the pain helps. It helps a lot.

I kneel carefully next to Zuri.

Ursa circles us, close enough that her dress brushes against me. "Tell me your safe words."

"Mermaid," I answer at the same time Zuri says, "Hurricane."

"Now that we've got that out of the way." She stops in front of us and crouches down. "What have you two been up to?" Ursa grips my cock, dragging her nails along my length. Despite my earlier orgasm, I start to harden. I'd have to be dead not to want this woman.

She cups Zuri's pussy with her free hand. Ursa hums a little. "So wet. Both of you. Were you fucking?"

"No," I gasp. "No, Mistress."

Zuri gives a little moan. "I, uh, sucked his dick."

"Ah." Ursa keeps stroking me and out of the corner of my eye I can see her rubbing slow circles around Zuri's clit. "Then I suppose I'll have to hold off punishing you and skip right to the reward for being obedient."

Her rewards often come with as many teeth as her punishments. The knowledge thrills me. Ursa gives me one last stroke and stands. "Let's eat. I wouldn't want you to get low blood sugar during our activities today." She turns and sweeps out of the room.

Zuri gives a shaky little sigh. "Is it always like this?"

"Yes." I stand slowly, wincing a little. Maybe practically begging Ursa to beat me last night wasn't the best idea I've ever had. Today is going to be rough. I hold out a hand to help Zuri up, but she ignores it and climbs to her feet on her own.

She glances at me, and her skin darkens in a blush. "I don't suppose we get to put on clothes?"

"Only if you want her to make a show of punishing you while she makes you take them off again."

She sighs. "I thought as much."

I take a step forward, and Zuri gasps. "Your back. It looks terrible."

It feels terrible, but terrible isn't terrible at all. Every time I move, I'm reminded of who owns me, and while there might be a time when that knowledge chafes, right now it just feels as close to peace as I'll ever get. "It's what I want." I walk out of the room and head toward the kitchen.

Ursa's corner penthouse is one of the rare ones without an open-floor concept. Each room is neatly contained, most of them positioned with some kind of massive windows and view of Carver City. The kitchen is all white and grays, marble counters and cabinets that reach the ceiling. I've only been in this room a few times; when I've been here before, it wasn't to cook or eat. I *can't* cook, so it's just as well.

She's pulling a few things from the fridge and setting them out. Eggs and bacon and potatoes and what looks like home-made bread. "Alaric, grate these potatoes. Zuri, take a seat."

It feels very, very strange to wash my hands and move to stand next to Ursa. I begin to shred the potatoes on the large grater she hands me. This isn't fucking. It's downright domestic, for all that I'm naked. I don't know what to think of that. I don't have any frame of reference for it. If I want to have a life with Ursa, it will be filled with small moments like this. The thought warms me even as I obey her.

Ursa pulls a cast iron pan from a low cabinet and sets it on the stove. Then she walks out of the room. When she returns, she's holding a large dildo that's shaped like a tentacle. Ursa sticks it to the counter in front of Zuri. "Darling, get familiar with this. It will be inside you later today."

I nearly laugh at how large Zuri's eyes get as she takes in the purple and blue silicone and suckers. Ursa arches a brow. "I wouldn't look too smug over there, lover. *This* one will be inside *you*, too." She pulls out an even larger dildo and sets it

131

on the counter well out of reach of all the food. This one is also a tentacle, but it's black and glittery and nearly twice the size of the other one.

I stare at it, trying to calculate how the curves and bumps will feel inside me. My cock goes painfully hard at the thought. Good. It's going to be very, very good. "Yes, Mistress."

"Good boy." She takes the cutting board with the shredded potatoes and moves to the stove. "Sit down."

I walk around to the seat next to Zuri and gingerly sink onto the stool. She leans close to whisper, "Why are you not freaking out?"

"I enjoy the hell out of Ursa fucking me."

"But it's *so big* and a *tentacle*." She can't quite take her eyes off the one in front of her. "Why is it a tentacle?"

"Because she wants it to be." It's as simple as that. Ursa gives a command and I follow it. "She's the Sea Witch, after all."

"I thought she's called that because she used to drown her enemies in the ocean."

I shoot her a look. "Yeah, that's where she got the name. But with her submissives, she likes to play into it. You'll see."

CHAPTER 16

I let them simmer in anticipation through breakfast. The dildos stay in plain sight, impossible to avoid, and it amuses me greatly that Zurielle can barely take her eyes off the one meant for her.

It's a simple game, but one I enjoy immensely. The longer it takes me to put these particular toys into place, the more they'll consume her and Alaric's thoughts, until they're ready to beg for it.

"Alaric, clean the dishes." I choose to ignore his sigh and take the seat he vacates. "Zurielle, darling, how are you feeling this morning?" I grab her knee and turn her on the stool so that she's facing me, her legs on either side of mine. She instinctively tries to close them, but I don't allow it. I hold her gaze as I stroke her pussy and urge her to scoot forward a few inches so I can slide two fingers into her. She clenches around me so sweetly. Everything about this girl is sweet. I explore her carefully. "Sore?"

"A little." She has a death grip on the counter with one hand, and she's staring at the sight of my fingers sliding in and out of her.

"Did our Alaric start your day off with an orgasm?" One look at her face gives me my answer. I snort. "Of course not. His cock was in your mouth. He wouldn't be overly concerned with returning the favor. Selfish boy."

"I can hear you," he mutters.

I barely lift my voice. "You're out of practice, so I'll give you this one warning and reminder, lover. Be silent unless I ask you a question. Do you understand me?"

"Yes, Mistress."

I love playing these little dominance games. Silence is such a simple thing to ask for, and significantly less simple to provide. Both Alaric and Zurielle are talkers by nature. It's only a matter of time before one of them forgets themselves and I get to indulge in a punishment.

I keep stroking Zurielle's pussy. Slowly. Building her pleasure layer by layer. It's there in the flush beneath her skin. In the way her lips part. In her chest heaving with each inhale and exhale, her brown nipples pebbled and practically begging to be played with. Exquisite. Every bit of her is exquisite.

She was worth every penny.

No, that's not the proper way to look at things. The revenge was worth every penny. Enjoying her is simply a bonus. To remind myself, I say, "What do you think your father would say if he knew I had my fingers inside you right now?"

Zurielle moans a little. "He wouldn't like it."

"No, he wouldn't like it." A vast understatement. "I'm tempted to take a little video and send it to him. There's no pretending you're anything but a willing victim when you're so wet, my fingers are shining."

She opens her mouth but seems to realize that I didn't ask her a question. Zurielle presses her lips together even as another whimper escapes. Her hips move a little, trying to take my fingers deeper.

"So shameless," I murmur, watching her closely. Oh, this little darling loves being bad. She's getting off on knowing that she shouldn't be enjoying my touch. "Will you come all over your father's enemy's fingers?"

Zurielle gasps. "I came on your face last night."

That surprises a laugh out of me. "So you did. Was that a hint, darling? Would you like my mouth on your pussy?" I don't wait for her answer to slide off the stool and to my knees, turning her so her back is to the counter. A position I don't hold often. It doesn't matter. I don't have the patience right now to relocate us. I want a taste.

She makes that sexy little whimper at the first swipe of my tongue. "You're such a bad girl, Zurielle." I kiss one thigh and then the other. "You know I'm the enemy, but you don't care as long as I make you orgasm. Selfish, wanton girl. What do you have to say for yourself?"

She braces her hands on the counter behind her. The move puts her on full display, and I'm not entirely sure it's on accident. She bites her bottom lip and begs me with those big dewy eyes of hers not to make her answer. When I hold firm, she finally says, "Please don't stop."

As if I have any intention of stopping. There will be time for orgasm deprivation and leaving her on the edge later. Right now, I want my dessert.

I wedge my hands under her ass and pull her to my mouth. I figured out what touch she likes best last night, and I set to it now. I drive her ruthlessly higher and higher, until she's whimpering and thrashing and it takes all my strength to pin her in place.

When she comes, it's with a sharp cry. "*Ursa.*"

I suck her clit and dip down to drag my tongue through her folds once, twice, a third time. Soaking up every bit of her taste. I lean back and lick my lips. "Go to the living room and bend over the arm of the couch."

She stares down at me blankly. Her breath comes so harshly, her breasts shake a bit with each one. "What?"

I slap her thigh, just hard enough to sting. "Do *not* make me repeat myself."

Zurielle stands on blatantly shaking legs and staggers out of the kitchen in the direction of the living room. I push slowly to my feet to find Alaric leaning against the sink with a towel in his hands. I raise my brows. "Would you like to watch?"

"Yes, Mistress."

"Come along." I lead the way into the living room. Zurielle has obeyed beautifully. She's bent over the arm of the couch, her forearms propped on the cushion, her ass in the air. It's such a cute little ass, though she could stand to gain some weight. I move to stand behind her and palm her cheeks. "So. You *can* be obedient. One wouldn't know it with how you flounce in the face of simple orders. If you come again without permission, I won't let you orgasm for a full twenty-four hours." I give her one last squeeze and shift position. "Alaric, kneel here." I point to the spot directly behind Zurielle, but far enough away that I won't have to worry about striking him on accident.

Once he's in position, I deliver a devastating slap to Zurielle's ass. If this wasn't a punishment, I'd warm her up a bit more first, but that's not on the current agenda.

She cries out and jerks forward, but the couch arm stops her from being able to escape the second strike on her other ass cheek. Her skin blooms a delightful pink, and I hit her again, layering the strikes a little and changing up the tempo so she can't anticipate me. I'm not hitting her hard enough to truly bruise, but she'll feel the sting for a bit.

She writhes, her breath sobbing out. I squeeze her ass, both soothing and riling her up. "Tell me how you feel."

"It hurts," she sobs. "It hurts so much."

Disappointment flares, but I shove it down. This is just another reminder that Zurielle isn't for the keeping. "Do not disobey me again." I trace my thumbs down the lower curve of her ass and pause. "Zurielle?"

"Yes, Mistress?"

I stroke my thumbs over her pussy. She's wet. Positively *drenched*. "Is all this from my mouth earlier? Answer honestly."

She hesitates so long, I almost give her another smack. Finally, she speaks in a small voice. "No, it's not just from your mouth."

"Explain." Cruel to demand this of her when she's obviously embarrassed, but I don't care. I *am* cruel when I want to be. Right now is one of those times.

"It hurts." She draws in a shuddering breath, her fingers spasming on the couch cushion. "But it's made my skin feel like it's on fire, and I can feel my heartbeat in my pussy."

"Mmm." Many people have this response to spanking, but I can take nothing for granted. "Do you want me to stop?"

"I…" She buries her face in the cushion, and I almost miss her reply. "No, Mistress."

A fucking *delight*.

I give her clit a sweet little stroke and then go back to spanking her. She's too new to take it much farther than I already have, but I enjoy the cries she makes. Just like I enjoy the heat in Alaric's gaze as he watches us. I give Zurielle's ass one last squeeze and turn to lean against the arm of the couch next to her. I crook my finger at Alaric. "Come here, lover."

Zurielle starts to sit up, but I place my hand on the space between her shoulder blades. "Hold still."

She tenses but manages to stay silent. Good girl. This is a different kind of punishment, one that I plan to enjoy just as much as the first.

Alaric gives me a questioning look and, when I nod, lifts my dress. He peppers kisses up my thighs and then his mouth is on my pussy. He growls against my flesh, the dirty boy. I hold Zurielle down as Alaric licks me. It feels so strangely right to have both of them here, both of them catering to my whims, taking care of both of their needs. I dig the fingers of my free hand into Alaric's hair and guide him up to my clit. "Make me come. You can take your time later."

He makes another growling sound but obeys, licking and sucking me the way I like. I'm already halfway there from playing with Zurielle, and it takes only a few minutes before my breath catches and I grind against Alaric's mouth as my orgasm crashes over me. I let him keep kissing my pussy, enjoying how much he enjoys this. He might be selfish when it comes to having his needs met and pretending not to be guilt-ridden the rest of the time, but when Alaric is on his knees, he gives himself over to being mine entirely. It never stops being a heady feeling.

I nudge Alaric back and fix my dress. "Go get her purse." I don't watch him to ensure he obeys. He will. I turn my attention to Zurielle and help her stand. She weaves a bit on her feet, and I catch her elbow. "I have plans for you, little Zurielle, but one thing has to happen first."

She blinks those big brown eyes at me and opens her mouth, no doubt to pepper me with questions, but remembers herself at last moment and closes it.

Alaric returns to the living room with Zurielle's purse in his hands. It's just as small and cute as she is—and expensive. I nod. "Her phone."

Zurielle tenses as Alaric digs through her purse. I can't

help being amused at how confused he seems when he comes up with item after item—tampons and gum and power bars —from the small space. "Fuck, how much shit can you pack in here?"

I give her a look. "Cis men are always so baffled at the hauling capabilities of purses."

Zurielle gives a little laugh and presses her hands to her mouth like she's surprised at her response. Alaric finally finds the phone and hands it over. I almost hate to wipe her laughter away, but this week isn't all fun and games and fucking.

"Call your father."

"*What?*"

I arch an eyebrow. "I spoke clearly enough." I press the phone into her hands. "Call your father, Zurielle. I'm sure he's beside himself with worry about his favorite daughter being missing."

Mutiny shines on her face. "You want to use me to hurt him."

"That's not a secret, darling." I lean closer. She smells like sex, and it takes more restraint than I anticipate not to drag my mouth over her shoulder and up to her neck. "Do you think he's not looking for you? Imagine how many powerful people he'll make enemies of in the process. He'll endanger himself if he thinks he can bring you home. You don't want that, do you?"

"That's not fair."

"It's also not a lie. You know how your father operates." No matter how naive she is, how sheltered, she can't avoid *that* truth. Triton is a rabid dragon of a man, hoarding the few things he cares about in this world and breathing fire at anyone who gets too close. Surely she's smelled the fire, seen the ash.

Zurielle can't quite meet my gaze. "Yes. I know how he

operates." Her eyes skate to Alaric. He must have told her at least part of the truth, then. Good. Alaric doesn't talk to enough people about what brought him to the Underworld. It's ironic in the extreme that the one time he *wasn't* being selfish to a fault is the time that his actions bit him in the ass hard enough to derail his life. I'm glad for it.

It brought him to me, after all.

I walk to the couch and motion to it. "Sit down and call your father. That's not a suggestion; it's a command."

She hesitates but finally nods. "Yes, Mistress." Zurielle walks to the couch and, after the briefest hesitation, sinks onto it. She barely flinches when I join her on one side and Alaric does the same on the other.

Zurielle takes a deep breath as if to brace herself and clicks her father's contact. The volume is loud enough to hear it ring from this close, and a deep voice answer. She swallows hard. "Hi, Daddy."

CHAPTER 17

ZURIELLE

*T*here's a reason I didn't find the time to call home those two days I was in the Underworld before the auction. And I certainly had no intention of doing it *now*. Too bad I don't have a choice.

My father's voice in my ear is usually a comfort. He's larger than life in a completely different way from Ursa. They both dominate a room, but my father has been the cornerstone of my life. My protector. Sometimes my jailor. The one who lifted me up, but then ensured I didn't fly too far.

If Alaric is to be believed, he's also a very bad man who does very bad things.

I wish I could call Alaric a liar, could dismiss his story out of hand. I can't. There's too many little things that line up with what he's said, things that I've ignored until this point. Things I can't afford to ignore any longer.

And the longer I'm outside of his house, the better I can breathe. Surely that's not normal? I have no doubt my father loves me, but love isn't supposed to constrict around a person until they can't manage a full inhale. It's not supposed to feel like a trap around your leg.

Right?

"Zuri? Are you okay? I've been worried sick."

I open my mouth to assure my father that I'm fine, but that's not what comes out. "Do you kill people, Daddy? I know that you oversee stolen goods and drugs. Do you oversee human trafficking, too? How deep does the rot go?"

He's silent for several beats, his breathing coming down the line. "Where are you? It's time for you to come home."

Anger flares. It's not solely directed at him. A healthy chunk is aimed directly at me, at my willful ignorance. There were so many times over the years when I could have asked questions, could have pushed against the boundaries he built up around me, but I was content to be a bird in a cage. Spoiled to an absurd degree, but trapped all the same. *Trapped.* He kept me all but locked up, yes, but I didn't challenge him once. Not until I met Alaric. Not until I left Olympus.

"I'm not coming home. Not when my father's a liar and a thief and maybe even a murderer."

"Zurielle Ti Rosi, don't you dare take that tone with me."

"Or what, Daddy? Are you going to threaten to break every bone in my body?"

He huffs out a breath, sounding like a bull about to charge. "You're my daughter, and I know what's best for you."

"I notice that you didn't respond to that. Is it because you've made that threat so many times, you can't begin to guess who I've been talking to?" Oh, I'm truly angry now. I didn't even realize *how* angry until this very moment. "How could you? You bully and preach and force me and my sisters into the boxes you think we should fit into, until we're damn near paragons of virtue, until we can't make a single step out of line for fear of your anger and disappointment, and you're leaving the house every day to play the hypocrite."

"That's enough."

"That's nowhere near enough." So much of my life has been a *lie*, and it's because of him. Maybe it isn't love at all. Maybe it's greed and possession. He doesn't want daughters with their own thoughts and feelings and ambitions. He wants pretty dolls to move about at his will. I won't go back to that. I *can't*.

I startle when Ursa touches on my leg. She holds out a hand. I almost ignore that silent command, but I'm furious enough to want to hurt my father. And this will hurt him. I hand her the phone.

Her lips curve. "Good girl." She lifts the phone to her ear. "Hello, Triton. It's been far too long since we last spoke."

I want to listen, to slide closer until I can eavesdrop to both sides of the conversation, but Alaric grabs me and hauls me over to straddle his lap. "What are you doing?" I whisper.

"She's proving a point. Now it's your turn." He kisses me before I can ask more questions, and it's just as well. I don't need to listen to know what my father is saying to Ursa. He's yelling and threatening. He'll be too busy demanding she return me to let any important information about their past drop. Listening will only drive home how thoroughly I've shoved my head into the sand when it comes to who he truly is. What did Ursa say that first night? She's a villain, but she's not a monster.

My father *is* a monster.

I let Alaric kiss me, I let him pull me closer until we're pressing together, skin to skin. No matter how much I hate that he lied to me, hate that he doesn't care about me as much as I thought I cared about him, I can't deny that he makes my body feel good.

That's what I need right now. The physical anchor into

the here and now. For him to touch me and make me stop flogging myself over how long I stayed in my father's house, the willing little doll. Maybe Ursa can even flog me for real later. It seems to help settle Alaric.

Ursa shifts, and I lift my head in time to see her push mute on the phone. "Get a condom if you're going to ride his cock. There's extra in the cabinet next to the couch." Without another word, she unmutes the phone and smiles. "Really, Triton, you should stop yelling. It can't be good for your blood pressure."

I climb off Alaric long enough to rifle through the cabinet Ursa indicated. In addition to being half-filled with condoms, it also contains several bottles of lube, a number of silk ties, and padded handcuffs. "Ursa is prepared for everything."

"You have no idea." Alaric grabs the condom out of my hand and rips it open. I lick my lips as I watch him roll it on. I wouldn't let him near me last night, but that all seems so distant right now. I decided to take the pleasure I could this week, didn't I? That's enough reason not to stop myself from climbing back onto him.

Either that or I'm as much a hypocrite as my father is.

Alaric kisses me again before I can think too hard on that. He skates his hands down my back to grab my ass, and I whimper. I'm still sore from being spanked, and the feeling of his hands there both hurts and feels better than I could have imagined. I press myself fully against him, my breasts rubbing against his chest, the length of his cock creating a delicious friction against my clit.

He lifts me and adjusts his angle, and then he's pressing against my entrance. Alaric hisses out a breath. "You're like a godsdamned vice around my cock. Go slow."

But I don't want to go slow. I want to stop my mental spiraling and the only way to do that is to keep going until I can't string two thoughts together. I already know Alaric can do that for me. I need him to do it now.

I brace my hands on his shoulders and force myself down his cock. He stretches me, but it doesn't sting nearly as much as last time. I just feel...full. So wantonly full.

Alaric curses, but I don't care because I'm already moving, letting my body guide me in a slow rolling motion. His blue eyes have gone dark as he watches me. "You look so fucking good on my cock, Zuri."

"I told you...not to call me that."

"Yeah, you did." He digs one hand into my hair and tows me down until his lips brush against mine, until I can taste his next words. "But no matter how pissed you are at me, we're still friends."

"No, we're not." I slam down on his cock and moan. "I don't even know you."

"Sure you do. Just not all of me." He loops an arm around my waist and lifts me, turning and going to his knees next to the couch and setting me where he was just sitting. The couch is low enough that he barely has to adjust his angle to start fucking me.

I thought he was deep before. It's nothing compared to now, not when he loops his arms under my thighs and spreads me to allow him deeper. Alaric's expression goes stormy as he fucks me hard enough that my breasts shake with each thrust. "Your pussy feels good, Zuri. *You* feel good."

I moan and run my hands up his arms. "Oh gods."

"Stroke that pretty clit of yours. I want to feel you come around my cock again."

I don't know why I look at Ursa. I've been vaguely aware of her still talking in that viciously amused tone of voice this entire time, but I haven't been able to focus on the words.

She smiles at me and reaches out with her free hand to pinch my nipple. The shock of it makes me moan. Loudly.

145

Ursa's damn near grinning. "You've truly pissed off your precious daughter, Triton. Shall I describe exactly how my man is fucking her right now? Shall I describe exactly how I intend to fuck her later? It's inspired enough that I do believe you'd approve if it was anyone other than your favorite daughter about to come all over his cock. Can you hear her, Triton? Those aren't moans of protest. She's enjoying every wicked moment of this." She pinches my nipple again. "Apparently she's not the good girl you worked so hard to make her into. A shame, that."

I can hear him yelling from here, and Ursa laughs and hangs up.

I try to protest, but there isn't enough air. Not with Alaric swiveling his hips and rubbing against something inside me that has me feeling too warm, too desperate. "Oh gods."

"You have permission to come." Ursa shifts her touch to my other nipple, pinching it just as hard as she did the first. "I'd say you earned it after that performance."

If I were stronger, if I were less angry, maybe I'd attempt to resist. I'm not. I'm just me, in over my head and sinking fast. When Alaric moves his hips in that devastating motion again, I come apart around him. I'm still whimpering when Ursa reaches between my legs and wraps her hand around Alaric's cock. "Not you, lover. Not yet."

He grits his teeth and looks almost pained, but he finally eases out of me. Ursa laughs. "Good boy. Now get rid of that condom and clean yourself up."

Again, he hesitates the barest second, looking down at me. Finally, he climbs to his feet and walks away, leaving me sprawled on the couch next to her. Ursa shakes her head when I start to close my legs and presses my thigh back open. "I like looking at you. Don't deny me that." She idly strokes my thigh. "Are you angry at me or at him?"

I answer without pausing to think. "I'm angry at everyone. My father lied to me, and the longer I'm outside his house, the more problematic he seems. You're using me. Alaric lied to me *and* he's using me."

She strokes my thigh. "Darling, do you think you're special?"

I blink. Of all the things I could have anticipated her saying, this wasn't on the list. "What?"

"Your father lied to you, but if you ask him, he'll tell you he had his reasons. Do you think a man who sets himself up like a god to his daughters wants to admit that he's anything but infallible? Of course not. At the end of the day, he's simply a man with sins like anyone else. Pride. Wrath. Greed."

I turn my head to look at her fully. It should seem weird to be having this conversation while I'm naked and she's idly touching me, but it somehow doesn't. "You set this entire thing up to get revenge on him. Why are you defending him now?"

"I'm not." She taps my knee and moves to the other thigh, still stroking me. "I'm saying that a smart person doesn't let rage blind them to the realities of the world. No one is wholly good or wholly bad. If you know their motivations, you can use them to encourage the outcome you desire."

It almost sounds like she's teaching me something. I reach out tentatively and put my hand on her leg. Her dress is silky and slides against her knee at my touch. "My father put me and my sisters in a cage. It might be because he wanted to keep us safe, but it doesn't change the fact that he doesn't care if we suffocate in the process."

"Yes." Her dark eyes gleam. "How would you use that as leverage if he was your enemy?"

I barely have to think about it. "I'd take one or all of them. You can't really undermine his business and standing with Poseidon, but the daughters are an easy target to hurt him.

Which is exactly what you did in drawing me here." Really, Ursa was smarter about it because I left of my own free will. That has to hurt more than if she kidnapped me. I frown. "What is your motivation? Beyond revenge."

"Oh no, we're not talking about me." She laughs and gives my leg a tap. "We're talking about you."

"Me?" I shift a little. "Why me? Out of everyone involved, I'm the simplest to pin down. I wouldn't have been so easy to manipulate otherwise."

Her laugh seems to reach across the sparse distance between us to stroke me right between my legs. "Darling, give yourself a little credit. Your father had you nailed down and penned up. You were so desperate for freedom, you let yourself fall in love with a man you didn't know. There's no shame in that. Even the weakest person will find the motivation for strength if given the right set of variables. And you're not weak."

I don't understand her. Is she comforting me? Setting me up for a bigger let down? I can't begin to guess. "I feel pretty weak, and *very* foolish."

"A weak person wouldn't have gone to the lengths you did." She glances at the doorway, where I can hear Alaric walking back toward the living room. "A foolish person wouldn't be holding their own right now."

I frown up into her beautiful face. "I don't understand you, Ursa. You don't have to be nice to me."

"Darling, I'm not being nice." She smiles kindly and stands. "I'm merely stating the truth as I see it. You are not part of my endgame. It doesn't hamper me any to give you a little boost before I set you free next week."

The reminder that this is only temporary feels like cold water dumped over my head. I have no right to the disappointment that sours my carefully balanced bliss at having Ursa's full attention. Six more days and then I'm free. That should make me happy. This was only ever temporary, and if it's a thousand times more pleasurable than I could have imagined? That should be a relief.

I don't know this woman.

What I *do* know of Alaric is just a fake persona he projected to ensure I danced to the tune he and Ursa set.

I should be happy to leave them behind. Should use them for what they can give me and walk away stronger for it. Isn't that what successful people in this world do? At least I can be assured that Ursa and Alaric are strong enough that nothing *I* can do will harm them. I can afford to be as ruthless as they are without guilt.

Except none of these thoughts gain any traction.

All I can think about as I watch Ursa offer me her hand is that I haven't gotten nearly enough time with this woman. She exhibits a pull stronger than gravity, a slow spiral that tempts me into the deep where I'll surely drown. It sounded like a fate worse than death a few days ago. Now, I'm not so sure.

Who needs air compared to the pleasure of drawing a smile from the Sea Witch?

CHAPTER 18

URSA

$\mathcal{I}$’ve seen infatuation enough times to recognize it on Zurielle’s pretty face when she looks at me. I’m just ruthless enough to use it. She’ll walk away at the end of this week with her heart bruised, but she’ll survive the wound. She’ll be stronger for it. Or that’s what I tell myself as I lead her and Alaric into the secondary living room that I’ve converted to a playroom. It sits in the corner of my penthouse suite, so two of the walls are floor-to-ceiling windows. It pleases me in a perverse little way to know that anyone can look through these windows and see the games I play.

What can I say?

I’m a bit of an exhibitionist at heart.

"Kneel there. Eyes down." I turn and stride back into the kitchen to retrieve the dildos. I have a wide selection of them in a variety of sizes and colors. It amuses me to play into the reputation I earned when I was young and impulsive. The Sea Witch. A woman not to be fucked with, not if one wants to avoid a death steeped in salt and brine. Carver City isn’t a port town, so finding a way to bring the ocean here to make examples of my enemies took some creative problem-solving. Creative enough that I haven't been challenged directly in years now.

The territory is stable. More than stable, really. My people are flourishing. If I sometimes take little bites out of the Belmonte territory for my amusement? Well, I wouldn't be human if I didn't give in to temptation from time to time.

I didn't get this far by letting go of old vendettas.

I pause just outside the door to the playroom, letting the emotions stirred up from my conversation with Triton have their moment before I file them away. I've riled him, and the pure satisfaction that knowledge brings is almost enough to blot out the danger. Triton isn't a loose cannon, no matter how intense his anger.

There was a time when I could have anticipated his next move as if it were my own, but I've changed in the last twenty years. No doubt he's done the same. I can't assume that I'll know what moves he'll make.

More, I can't allow hate to consume me until it's all I see.

I've been a thorn in Triton's side since we were still young enough to think that power came without price. Olympus is a heady drug and answering directly to Poseidon, one of the legacy roles within the Thirteen, is headier yet. I worked *hard* to get to that position, to be seen by Poseidon and the others as someone of value. Something far from the little suburban life I had growing up, safe and wholesome and suffocating me more and more with each day that passed. It was enough for my parents, but I wanted *more*. I wanted to hitch myself to the glowing stars that are the Thirteen.

Securing the job working for Poseidon, stepping into a world that only the lucky, the powerful, the ambitious get to see? It felt like coming home, fulfilling the hole inside me that I'd barely been able to define. Even my rivalry with Triton was part of that feeling. We were friends. Occasionally we were closer than friends, at least before he married

Zurielle's mother. Even so, I should have expected the knife in the back, should have known that it'd be his hand that wielded it. It took me longer than it took Triton to understand how the game worked. The Thirteen might be all but the gods they're named for, but they get their power in the same way everyone else in the world does. Money. Edging the line between legal and illegal. More money.

I let fondness for Triton muddy the waters, and it made me hesitate when I should have been the one to strike first. I didn't realize at the time that it had to be him or me, that Poseidon only wanted one second-in-command. The strongest. The most ruthless. The one willing to do anything for the position. I thought Triton would challenge the order to eliminate each other the same way I did.

He didn't.

Better that he killed me. Exile is a bone in my throat, no matter what I've made of my life in Carver City. I didn't have a choice, can never go home again, and for that he has to pay.

I take a deep breath, and then another. With each exhale, I push away the unwelcome thoughts. No matter what role of Dominant I play, that kind of prickly anger has no place in a scene. If it were just Alaric and me, I could trust him to draw the line. He's experienced as a submissive and can ride the waves of my anger easily. He's done it before.

Zurielle?

I might harm the girl.

No matter what she might think of me, *that* was never part of the plan.

Another breath and I have it locked down. I'm able to smile as I step through the door, and the expression becomes more prominent at the sight of them. Alaric and Zurielle. Different in so many ways, but identical in the only way that matters. They submit to me, and do it beautifully.

I leave them kneeling and allow myself to sink into the

simple enjoyment of preparing the next bit of the scene. There are times when I'd want the action ready to begin the moment we walk through the door, but I enjoy making them wait while I do this. They can hear me, but they're both too obedient to disobey a command and look up.

I strip out of my dress and take my time getting the strap-on fastened and adjusted. The larger tentacle destined for Alaric attaches easily and I take a moment to look at myself in the full-length mirror positioned just so.

Perfect.

I snap my fingers. "Zurielle, on your feet." Pleasure courses through me when she obeys instantly. This girl really is a joy. If I were a different person, if she weren't such an innocent... If, if, if.

There is no keeping her. I'd do well to remember that.

I lead her over to the bench I've positioned carefully. It's long and rectangular, and short enough for her to kneel on the ground. The smaller tentacle is fastened to the center of it. I stroke my hand down her hair, enjoying the way she shivers. "You're going to ride that, darling. And while you do, I'm going to fuck Alaric. Be very good and I'll let him lick your clit while I take his ass."

Her gaze flies to my face before she seems to remember herself and drop it. I give her ass a playful little swat. From her sharp inhale, she's still plenty sore. "Come along, little Zurielle." I nudge her forward and arrange her to my satisfaction, kneeling astride the bench. It's just high enough that once she's taken the dildo deep, she won't be able to escape it. Not without standing.

The look she gives me... Gods. She's intimidated and looking for reassurance from *me* despite the fact that I'm the one responsible for what comes next. I love this part of being a Dominant; the dual nature. Punishment and comfort, all tangled up in a delicious knot. Finding a balance between the two is walking the knife's edge, and each moment thrills me, a challenge I'm only too happy to rise to meet.

I don't intend to kiss her. It's sentimental in the extreme to think that kissing means something when we've been exchanging bodily fluids for hours now, but I can't deny the shock that goes through my body as her tongue tentatively strokes mine. As if asking for permission, even in this.

Gods, what if I *do* keep her?

I tangle my fingers in her hair and pull her closer, letting myself off the leash a little, kissing her the way I crave. Deep and messy and oh so decadent. She tastes like innocence. Like a gift that I'm suddenly certain I'm too selfish to give up.

By the time I manage to lift my head, she's got her arms looped around my neck and she's pressing her body to mine. She's so damn *delicate*. So fragile. So fucking breakable. It simultaneously makes me want to crack her open just to see her cry and protect her from all the harshness the world is only too happy to brandish.

I carefully take her throat and urge her back a step. She's flushed and blinking up at me like I just blew her mind with only a kiss. I can't blame her. The world is a little unsteady beneath my feet, though I'll never admit it aloud. I hold her gaze and cup her pussy. She's soaking wet, and I doubt it's solely from the kiss. No, little Zurielle wants what I'm about to give her, even if she's nervous.

It's enough to make me wonder if she'll approach everything I do to her with the same balance of fear and desire. It's a heady thing, and I have to stop myself from coaxing her to orgasm again purely from the delight she brings me. "On the bench."

I hold her hand as she awkwardly sinks onto the bench a few inches behind the dildo. She looks down at it, that delicious trepidation in those big dark eyes. I give her hand a tug, urging her closer to it. "Grind on it, darling. You know you want to."

She rolls her hips a little, rubbing her pussy against it. Zurielle's eyes go wider yet, and she looks at me. "I don't…"

"Dislike it. Yes, I know." I lean closer. "It feels wicked, doesn't it? Rubbing on it like a wanton little thing while I watch."

"Yes, Mistress." She licks her lips and begins rolling her hips again. This time, she doesn't stop. Her body flushes, and she doesn't quite manage to lower her eyes.

No, she's looking at *my* body while she grinds away against the tentacle. I suppose it's the first time I've been anything close to naked in front of her, and she stares at me like I'm her favorite treat. Her gaze traces my breasts and down my stomach, lingering on the strap-on for several long moments before moving to my legs and back up again.

When I finally manage to speak, my voice has gone husky. "Ride my cock, darling. It's there and waiting for you."

Zurielle takes a deep breath and lifts herself up. The dildo is just large enough that it's an awkward thing to sink onto it, and I have to force myself to plant my feet and not assist her. There's a lesson in here. I'm still not sure who it's for, though.

I hold perfectly still and watch her work herself down the tentacle dildo. It begins narrower at the top, curving a little as it expands to the widest part at the base. She whimpers in that sweet way of hers but finally manages to lower herself completely.

"Good girl. Now wait." I smile. "Do not come until I give you permission."

"Yes, Mistress."

I turn to Alaric. "You've been so patient, lover. Come here."

He rises easily despite having knelt for so long and

crosses to me. Gods, he's beautiful. Maybe one day I'll be able to look at him without my breath disappearing, but today isn't that day. No matter how attractive, he's not entirely happy right now. I know him well enough to recognize that.

I catch his chin and lift his face until he meets my gaze. "The only one allowed to whip you is me."

Alaric blinks those pretty blue eyes at me. "What?"

"You've been mentally whipping yourself since you realized Zurielle was here in Carver City." When he doesn't deny it, I raise my brows. "Are you a god, Alaric?"

"No."

"Hmmm. Are you Zurielle's caretaker? Her guardian? Responsible for her choices? Would you like to play her Daddy and keep her in a pretty cage?"

His jaw sets like he wants to trap his answer behind his teeth. Ultimately, my demand wins out. "No."

"You can let that inconvenient guilt go and enjoy what we're both offering this week, or you can go spend some time in your room alone to sulk. It's your choice." I pause. "Just like it was *her* choice to come here, *her* choice to participate in the auction, and *her* choice to continue to obey my every command." I use my grip to turn his face to where Zurielle is panting a little and shaking with her need to move. "Am I forcing her down on that cock?"

"You gave the order."

I sigh. "You're disappointing me, lover. Answer the question honestly. Am I forcing her?"

He's clenching his jaw so hard, it's a wonder he doesn't damage his teeth. "No."

"That's right. Now, stop wasting all our time and make your choice. Stay or go."

He stares at Zurielle for several long moments. I could push him, but the only way to get through to Alaric is to rub his nose in his ridiculousness. If this situation was playing out between anyone else, he wouldn't blink at what was being done. It's only himself that he holds to such strange standards. The man holds his guilt as close as any lover. Closer, even.

Finally, Alaric sighs. "I'd like to stay, Mistress."

I wait a few beats, giving him the chance to change his mind. We both know he won't do it, but this is another sort of punishment. It's all well and good to blame me for everything, but he's made his own choices. Everyone in this room has.

"Kneel facing Zurielle."

He hesitates for the briefest of moments and then turns to kneel before the bench Zurielle perches on. She's got her hands braced on the leather now, her breasts shaking with each breath that escapes her parted lips.

I walk to the dresser and peruse my lube collection before finally choosing one. Another dominance play, but I don't bother to deny the urge. It's especially rewarding when I turn around to find them staring at each other with their hearts in their eyes. No matter how angry she is, Zurielle still fancies herself in love with Alaric. As for what he feels for her... I suspect it's distinctly more complicated than simple lust. Though, if one's honest, they can admit there's nothing *simple* about lust.

Now all that remains is deciding whether I want to heal the growing thing between Zurielle and Alaric.

Or if I want to shatter it beyond repair.

CHAPTER 19

ALARIC

J can't take my eyes off Zuri. She's riding that tentacle dildo in little circling strokes like she can't help herself. Her bottom lip is particularly pink from her biting it so hard, and she's digging her fingers into the leather of the bench.

She's looking at *me*.

"I'm sorry." I don't mean to say it. I'm not even sure if I mean it, but why the fuck would I be blurting it out if I didn't? The guilt that rises every time I think about what I did, the lies I told, demands addressing. Now isn't the time for it, but apparently that doesn't matter. "I'm sorry," I repeat.

Zuri inhales sharply. "Don't lie to me."

"I'm not."

"And I'm supposed to trust *that?*" Her breath is choppy with desire, but anger bleeds back into her eyes. "You hurt me."

"He'll make it up to you."

I nearly startle. For once, I was so focused on Zuri that I didn't even hear Ursa move from her spot next to the cabinet. She sifts her fingers through my hair and gives it a tug. "He apologized, darling. That's step one."

"I don't have to accept it," Zuri mutters.

"True enough." Ursa uses her hold on my hair to half drag me the last foot to the bench. I close my eyes and let the stinging sensation roll through me. It took me all of a week in the Underworld to realize I'm a little pain slut, but it only feels like absolution under Ursa's hands. She gives my hair one last tug before she releases me. As she moves down my body, she presses her fingers hard to my back. I don't need to see her to know she's tracing the bruises she made last night. "Would you like me to punish him, little Zurielle? Beat him until he's sobbing out his apologies? I'll do it and happily."

I stare at the floor, my breath coming too hard. Even I can't tell if it's dread or anticipation for Zuri's answer.

"That's not what I want," she finally whispers.

"Then let's put it behind us." Ursa squeezes my ass. "Alaric will begin the second round of apologies now." I can hear the smile in her voice. "You have permission to come as many times as you like, darling."

Ursa squeezes my ass again, her fingers digging into a sore spot there. "Not you, love. Balancing the scale is often uncomfortable."

I don't comment on the fact that *she's* not interested in balancing the scales. The guilt I feel is entirely my own, and I have to make my peace with that. Life would be a whole lot easier if I could carve out that part of myself, if I could see things in the same stark contrast Ursa does. Every problem she faces falls into one of two categories. If it helps her and her territory, or if it doesn't. There was no good or bad or room for regret.

Cool lube hits my ass and then Ursa starts working the strap-on into me in slow, teasing strokes. We've played with a variety of toys before, but the tentacle never stops feeling strange. Curved and textured and, *fuck*, okay, yeah, it feels good.

"Are you forgetting your task, lover? Zuri's clit looks neglected."

I surge forward and lick Zuri's clit. She whimpers, and Ursa sinks another inch deeper into my ass, which only drives me on. I wish I could say I tease orgasm after orgasm out of Zuri, coaxing her into considering my apology. An artful, intentional seduction.

It's not the truth.

I lick and suck and go after her pussy like a wild thing. With every inch Ursa sinks into me, filling me obscenely, another lock on my control snaps. Until there's nothing left. I break down to my base parts, to pure need.

Zuri cries out above me as she comes, but I'm not stopping. I'm not capable of stopping. It feels like frenzy. It feels like ascendance. It's almost enough to ignore my own body's desperate need. My cock is so hard, it's painful, and every slow thrust of Ursa's hips has *her* cock rubbing against parts of me that have me in danger of exploding. I press my forehead to Zuri's stomach, panting. "Mistress, I'm close."

"Too bad. Hold." Her fingertips press hard to my back, tracing my constellation of bruises. Little pinpricks of pain that light me up just as much as the way she fills me does. "Make her come again, lover. She's so pretty when ecstasy overtakes her."

Another punishment here. Being denied the sight of Zuri coming stings exactly the way she intends it. A reminder that Ursa is the conductor of this scene. Zuri and I are merely her playthings, dealt and denied pleasure as she wills it.

Zuri cries out over my head as she comes again. She's slippery and soft against my mouth, her thighs surprisingly strong where I clasp her. Fuck, I could do this all day.

Except I can't. Because, damn it, I'm about to disobey

Ursa's order. I grit my teeth and try to muscle back the pleasure she deals in rolling waves. "Mistress, please."

"Not. Yet." She pulls out of me so suddenly, I can't help but cry out. Ursa slaps my ass. "On your back, Alaric."

The new position means I have to stop sucking on Zuri's clit. I give her pussy one last kiss and then obey, easing onto my back on the floor. I watch Ursa divest herself of the strap-on and then she's standing over me, gloriously naked. Her body is all curves and dips and soft and strong at the same time. I could spend hours worshiping her large breasts, her soft stomach, her muscled thighs and perfect pussy. I have. I will again.

She flicks her locs over her shoulder. "Do you need a cock ring?"

Probably, but admitting as much feels like admitting failure. "No, Mistress."

She arches her brows. "If you come before I give you permission, you'll be punished. Are you sure?"

Anticipation curls through me. I don't get off on playing the brat, but there's something addictive about pitting my will against Ursa's. Testing. "Yes, Mistress. I'm sure."

She laughs, the sound curling through me in an almost physical way. Fuck, I love this woman. Something I haven't admitted out loud, something I might walk back on when she's not straddling me and sliding my aching cock into her tight pussy. Ursa sinks down slowly, her attention narrowed on my face. "You have little Zurielle all over your mouth." She leans down and kisses me, pressing her body against mine. I should stay still, should submit, but I can't help running my hands up her thighs and over her sides, desperate to touch as much of her as she'll allow. Moments like these, I can't believe how fucking lucky I am. I have *this* woman dominating me, *this* woman riding my cock, *this* woman naked and trusting my hands on her body.

161

She grabs my hands and guides them up to the legs of the bench Zuri's on. "Keep them here."

I grit my teeth as she rolls her hips, fighting against the pressure building in my balls. "Please, Mistress. I want to touch you." I barely register that I'm begging. It doesn't matter. The only thing that matters is getting my hands back on her body.

"No." She presses her hands to my chest and begins to ride me. Her gaze tracks up to Zuri. "Come here, darling."

Zuri moans as she eases off the dildo and stands. I watch her take Ursa's hand and let the other woman pull her closer. Ursa smiles up at her. "I don't think Alaric got near enough of you, little Zurielle. Give him another taste."

Oh fuck.

I lie there as Ursa arranges Zuri to her liking, having her straddle my face, looking down my body. She sinks that last inch and then she's close enough for me to kiss her pussy. Fuck, she tastes good. Too good. With her on my tongue and Ursa on my cock, I'm not going to last. I tense, fighting against my body, but it's no use.

I come hard, growling against Zuri's clit. Ursa rides me in slow strokes even as I empty myself inside her. And then Zuri's grinding down my mouth, her sweet voice hoarse. "Oh gods, oh gods, I'm going to go again."

"It's all right, darling. I've got you." A soft sound. A kiss. Ursa is kissing Zuri, and fuck if that doesn't somehow make this so much better.

I finally collapse the last inch onto the floor. "I'm sorry."

"You seem to be saying that a lot today, love." Ursa climbs off me and then Zuri is lifted from my face. Ursa wraps her arms around the smaller woman and looks at me over her shoulder. Her dark eyes are kind even as her voice goes cold. "You've disappointed me, Alaric."

I lick my lips, tasting Zuri there. "I'm sorry, Mistress."

"You will be." She smiles down at me. "The table. Don't make me wait."

This. This is what I need. I might not have intentionally sought it out, but Ursa's always been able to read me better than most. I obey her command as she arranges Zuri on the couch—the only piece of normal furniture in the room—and drapes a throw blanket over her shoulders. It's a shock of color, bright pink and orange and white and red, all thrown together in a busy pattern that's purely Ursa. She presses a kiss to Zuri's temple. "You're still angry."

Zuri opens her mouth, seems to reconsider, and finally says, "It's complicated."

"Love often is." She ignores the other woman's shocked look and walks toward me. The table I lie on is multipurpose. It can be bent and shortened and there are straps on all four corners that can bind a person in place. Ursa taps my hip. "Do I need to tie you down?" Her tone suggests there's only one right answer.

I swallow hard. "No, Mistress."

She laughs. "We'll see." Ursa walks to her cabinet of many things and takes her time sorting through it. Anticipation and dread spiral through me, an intoxicating mix that I can't get enough of. She turns around, a cane in her hand.

My stomach drops. I crave canings the same way I crave so many other things she does to me, but this is a punishment and in my current position, there's only so many spots she can safely beat me with a cane. "Mistress—"

"Hush." She traces the cane down the front of my body, lightly dragging it over my skin in a way that can only be perceived as a threat. "Last night, I flogged our Alaric." It takes me a moment to realize she's not speaking to me. She's talking to Zuri. Ursa pauses to give my cock a light stroke with the cane. "I used a heavier flogger, which is why he's bruised today, but it's a tool designed to create a wide, dispersed pattern." She taps my thigh. "This is a cane. It will deliver a deeper bruise, and a lot of Dominants like to stripe various parts of their submissives' bodies. Anywhere meaty is safe enough." She stops near the end of the table. "It's particularly excruciating on the bottom of one's feet."

Zuri's voice is so soft, I can barely hear her response. "Why are you telling me this?"

"Alaric needs penance to get over feeling guilty about misrepresenting himself to you. You need him to suffer before you can forgive him."

"What makes you think *this* is how I want him to suffer?" I can't see her because Ursa's standing in the way, but she sounds incredulous.

Ursa laughs. "Lie to yourself if you must, but don't lie to me. He hurt you. I will hurt him in return. It balances things out nicely, don't you think?"

"I'm not going to forgive him just because you beat him."

"I suppose we'll see, won't we?" That's all the warning I get before she brings the cane across the bottom of my foot. There's a beat almost like shock and then pain bows my back and I groan. Even though I trust Ursa not to do true damage to me, caning the bottom of the feet is agonizing. She stripes down my left foot before moving to the right.

I stop worrying about not deserving Zuri's forgiveness. I stop worrying about what the future will bring for me and Ursa. The pain washes everything away, leaving me to float in a curious numbness that always comes once a pain-based scene reaches a certain point. This is what I crave. I sink into it gratefully, wholeheartedly.

Awareness of the room comes back in waves. Ursa standing at my feet, idly rubbing her thumbs over the cane stripes, her expression hot enough to make my body respond on instinct. I start to sit up, but she presses her nail to the arch of my foot. A tiny pain, but enough to make me remember myself.

Zuri?

She's sitting exactly where Ursa left her, tears running down her face. Tears…for me?

Maybe she does still care, after all.

CHAPTER 20

ZURIELLE

*F*orgiveness isn't a simple thing. It's fluid and imprecise and often beyond me. But then, I've never been in a position where my forgiveness was required for something more serious than a petty fight with one of my sisters. Growing up as the youngest of five meant that I was constantly being railroaded by my older sisters. If I had something they wanted, it ceased to be mine and became theirs instead. Sometimes one of the many nannies we went through during my childhood would step in. Giving forgiveness in those cases was easy. No matter how we fight, I love my sisters.

Maybe it really is that easy this time, too.

I thought my feelings were simple once I learned the truth. Now I'm not so sure.

I stare down at Alaric laid out naked on the table. A fine sheen of sweat covers his skin and he's panting as if he just ran a long distance. What Ursa did hurt him, but there's no denying he liked it. I've never seen his expression so relaxed as it is now.

Not to mention his cock. It's hard and curved against his stomach, and has been since the first strike.

"What are you thinking, darling?"

I drag my gaze away from Alaric and look at Ursa. She's fastened her locs at the top of her head, keeping them out of her way, and the hairstyle leaves her gorgeous face on full display. I could spend hours kneeling at her feet, just looking at her. She's worn clothes most of the time we've been together, and it feels like this is the first time I'm really getting to appreciate her fully.

She's extremely curvy. Breasts and hips and ass and thighs, her stomach soft in a way that makes me fist my hands to keep from reaching for her. Her medium-brown skin glistens with sweat, but I get the impression that she could spend all night beating Alaric without pause. That's how strong she is. Something deep inside me quivers at the thought of having all the formidable dominance directed at me while she holds a method of delivering pain in her hand.

Ursa chuckles a little. "I asked you a question, Zurielle."

I clear my throat, my gaze dropping to her breasts before I force myself to meet her eyes. "I'm sorry, Mistress. I can't remember the question."

She laughs again. "I suppose I can't be too mad since it's the sight of me that gave you temporary amnesia."

"You're beautiful." I'm not supposed to speak out of turn, but I find I can't go another minute without telling her exactly how much I want her. "I would like to make you come again."

Her lips curve. "I know. And you will." She snaps her fingers. "Now. What were you thinking while you watched me beat Alaric?"

I don't want to answer. I really don't. But the glint in her dark eyes tells me that she won't allow me to change the subject or dodge the question. I pull the blanket more firmly around my shoulders and stare at the floor. "I was thinking that there are a multitude of sins I will forgive a person if I love them." It feels like she's ripped open a deep wound, and I can't help finishing bitterly. "It seems to be a character flaw of mine."

"Is it?"

I can hear Ursa moving, but I only get a glimpse of her out of the corner of my eye. I swallow hard. "Yes, Mistress. It's impossible to see it as anything but that."

"Darling, you're hurt and looking at this through a bitter shade of glass." She stops next to me and sifts her fingers through my hair. I close my eyes, my body relaxing into her touch even as I wonder when it became such an instant response for me. Ursa keeps stroking me. "You're soft. Others might see that as a sin, but it's not. It's an asset. Cling to that as long as you possibly can, because you'll lose part of yourself when you let the world make you hard."

I don't mean to argue, but then I don't mean to do a lot of things where this woman is concerned. "How can you say that? You run your own territory. You have to be hard in order to accomplish what you have."

"Do I?" She tugs my hair until I look up at her. Gods, the way she looks at me. Like I'm a present wrapped up just for her. Like I truly am *hers*. "You haven't been paying close enough attention." She gives my hair one last tug and releases me. Ursa walks to the table and urges a still-dazed Alaric up. She kisses him, deep and thorough, and leans back. "You're forgiven, lover. Don't disappoint me again."

"I won't, Mistress."

She helps him ease off the table, and I don't miss the cruel little edge to her smile as he winces with each step. Ursa eases him down next to me and pulls another brightly colored blanket out from the basket next to the couch. She drapes it around Alaric's shoulders. "Scoot."

We instantly obey, parting like the Red Sea to allow her a spot between us. She settles down onto the couch in the vacated space and draws us back to her. Ursa tucks me under her arm and guides Alaric down to lay his head on her thigh.

I don't mean to close my eyes, but the events of the last few days are catching up with me and Ursa feels so gloriously solid against my body. It might be because I can't see her, but I hear her slow exhale as she relaxes against us. As if she's setting down a burden she's been carrying for a while.

She's so strong all the time. Does she allow herself to lean on anyone? It's not my right to ask—to demand that—not when I won't be here after this week, but I hope she lets Alaric in, at least. I stroke her thigh in slow motions, giving comfort in the only way I think she'll allow from me. A soft touch. A gentle slide of my skin against hers.

Ursa sifts her fingers through my hair slowly, soothingly. This whole moment settles something in my chest even more than the sex has. I'm *enjoying* my time with them. I don't want it to stop. Any of it.

Time passes slowly, the strange cocktail of adrenaline and lust wearing off and leaving me aching and strangely sated. My ass still stings and my pussy is sore in a delicious kind of way, but it's my soul that feels the most exhausted. The highs have been too high. The lows, too low. I don't know which way is up any longer. I'm a deep sea diver that's gotten confused and lost. I have a fifty-fifty chance of swimming for the surface. An equal chance to descend to depths I'll never return from.

I should be more scared.

I know that, rationally. I am in the home of a territory leader in Carver City, one who's already stated that she wants revenge against my father. Just because she's kind to me doesn't mean she won't enjoy me for this week and then dump my body on his doorstep at the end of it. I *know* that,

169

but I can't get the fear to stick. There's some bone-deep belief that Ursa won't harm me, and I can't seem to reason my way past it.

It's too late, anyway. I'm here and I've agreed to uphold my part of the contract. If she's going to turn on me at the end of it, if taking my virginity wasn't enough to capture her revenge… There's little I can do about it.

Or maybe that's just what I tell myself so I don't have to think about escaping. Maybe I'm just so weak that I am only too happy to cuddle up next to my father's enemy because she showed me a little bit of kindness. Because she talks sweetly to me and touches me like I might be precious to her.

It's a lie. It has to be.

I've already been sucked in once by Alaric. Surely I'm smart enough not to make the same mistake with Ursa?

The thought makes me open my eyes and sit up. I don't look at her. I can't, or I'll be enraptured by her again and forget about the distance I desperately need to maintain. I clear my throat. "I, uh, I need a shower."

"In a moment." She takes my wrist in a gentle but immovable grip. "You tensed up, darling. Thinking dark thoughts?"

Again, honesty pours forth despite my best efforts. "Are you going to kill me and dump me on my father's doorstep at the end of this?"

"*What?*" She sounds so genuinely shocked, I forget myself and look at her. She masks the shock quickly, but I know what I see. Ursa shakes her head. "What motivation could I possibly have to go through all this only to kill you?"

"You hate my father. I still don't know your side of what happened, but you went through such lengths to get revenge. Surely you're not going to stop with giving me orgasms."

Now Alaric sits up, though he's moving a little gingerly. "Ursa isn't going to kill you."

"She's right," Ursa says slowly, almost as if she's contemplating it. "A life for a life, so to speak."

Alaric shoots her a sharp look. "Stop it. She doesn't know you're just fucking with her."

"Am I?"

"*Ursa.*"

"Oh, fine." She clasps his chin and gives him a quick kiss before turning to me. "My goal is to cause your father pain—not start a war between Olympus and Carver City. If you die, he'll do everything in his power to make me pay, even if he has to raze both cities to accomplish it."

I stare. "The way you say that makes me think you actually considered killing me at one point."

"*Barely* considered, darling. As I said, it served no one in the end." Ursa glances at Alaric, seems to take in his tense look, and sighs. "Fucking you is as good as killing you. You consented to this, consented to it from beginning to end and with eyes wide open. You knew Alaric and I wanted to cause your father pain, and you went forward with it anyway. There wasn't complete honesty, but there also weren't truly lies, either. You knew who we were to him." She shrugs. "Your father will never forgive you."

Pain lances through me. It's the truth. I know it's the truth even as part of me wants to deny it, to claim that love will conquer all. Really, I'm not *that* naive. "You can't know that."

"Can't I?" Ursa arches a brow. "Go ahead. Call him now and see if he picks up for his traitorous slut of a daughter." The words have no heat, not until I imagine my father saying the same words in anger.

I flinch. "So you'll use me and discard me."

"Darling, you're walking with over half a million dollars. You can go anywhere, can decide to be whoever you'd like. I'm leaving you better than I found you."

I can decide to be whoever I like. The thought brings

171

another on its heels, one that I'll never voice, no matter how addicting it is to tell Ursa the truth.

I want to be yours.

I'm not hers. Not in the way Alaric obviously is. Wanting that is about as effective as wishing on stars. It will never happen, not when she looks at me and sees her revenge against my father instead of a person. If she's kind enough while doing it? That changes nothing.

Ursa takes a slow breath. "Come on, darlings. Let's get you cleaned and rested for tonight."

I almost don't ask, but I'm desperate for something else to focus on beyond my realization of how far in over my head I am. "What's tonight?"

Ursa rises and waits for us to join her on our feet. "Tonight, we're going to the Underworld and playing a little game."

A little game. Because that's all this is to her—a game. She only chose me so she could punish my father, not because she actually wants me. I bite down my disappointment and follow her down the halls and through her bedroom to the master bath. The tub is more hot tub than bath, a deeply recessed area with jets and seating for four. She leans over, giving me an excellent view of her ass, and turns the taps on. "It will be a moment. Stay here." Then she walks away, leaving me and Alaric alone.

"I'm sorry."

I look at him and my heart gives an uncomfortable thump. Things would be so much simpler if I could just turn off my feelings for him. For both of them. It doesn't seem to matter how angry I am, how clear the evidence that he lied… I still care.

But that doesn't mean I can let go of what he did.

I sigh. "You're not sorry. Not really. You feel guilty, but

that's not the same thing. You wouldn't do anything differently if you had a chance to go back."

He starts to argue but finally shakes his head. "Maybe I'd tell you the truth from the beginning."

"It wouldn't work." It pains me to admit it, but this strange addiction to honesty continues even when Ursa isn't around. "If you told me what my father was while I still lived in his house, I don't know if I'd believe you. Even if I did, I can't guarantee that I'd agree to help you hurt him."

"Zuri, you didn't agree to help us hurt him," he says it gently, as if trying to reassure me.

"Don't do that." I shove my hair back from my face. "Don't give me an out. You might have helped manipulate me into making that choice, but ultimately it *was* my choice. Just like it was my choice to fuck you while Ursa was on the phone with him."

Alaric holds perfectly still, watching me with those clear blue eyes. "You're going to have to clarify what you're getting at because I don't understand."

I take a deep breath. "What I'm saying is that I understand why you did what you did. I'm not giving you a free pass, but I get it. If I were in your position, I can't say with any confidence that I wouldn't do exactly the same thing. It wasn't personal."

"Zuri."

I really should remind him that he's not a friend and only my friends call me that. It feels like a lie, though. I turn, and Alaric catches my hands. He's still moving stiffly, but his grip isn't weak. He gives me a light squeeze. "If I'd known you, I never would have agreed to play things out this way. I *like* you, and you deserve better than to play the part of a pawn."

"Yes, I do." I look down at our joined hands. "I'm still very angry, but it's all mixed up in other feelings. It's confusing."

"Welcome to spending time with Ursa." He chuckles. "It will be okay. It's only tonight and another five days."

The reminder feels like it's weighing down my entire body. "Right. Five days." Only a fool would beg to stay beyond that. As Ursa said, she's leaving me better off than she found me. At least materially.

It doesn't change the fact that I've sacrificed *everything* for people who will move on with their lives together and forget that I ever existed.

CHAPTER 21

ALARIC

I'm doing a shit job of comforting Zuri. It's like following the steps to a dance I've never heard of, and I'm fumbling it. I take a deep breath. "Look, I'm not good at this."

"I never would have guessed." She arches one of those perfectly shaped brows. "Though you're going to have to be more specific about what you mean this time."

That startles a chuckle out of me. "You know, you always surprise me when you slide in the knife like that."

Zuri blinks those big dark eyes. "I'm sure I have no idea what you're talking about."

I almost let it go, but there's still something brittle in her that I can't leave alone. "I've been on my own since I was a teenager. My mom was…" How to describe Maura Paine. "She's one of those people that shouldn't have had kids. She was driven out of Sabine Valley when she chose my father over her family, and then the bastard barely stuck around long enough to knock her up. He left her alone to raise me in a city that wasn't hers."

"I'm sorry."

I wave that away. "I don't want your pity. I'm just trying to explain. I was on my own a lot growing up, and I learned that the best person to look out for what I wanted was *me*. I made my way well enough, but when she asked me to do this one thing that might make her happy, that might get her back in with her family..." I shrug. "I did it, even though it was reckless and dangerous. I didn't look for another way to make that money. I wanted the task complete and her out of my life, so I went the fastest route to the money. And I paid the price."

She wraps her arms around herself. We're standing here shivering in the bathroom while the tub fills. This is ridiculous. I hold out a hand. "Come here, Zuri."

I don't really expect her to obey. She's told me she hates me more times in the last two days than I want to count. She won't forgive me, and I can't really claim I deserve her forgiveness. Why the hell would she accept this from *me*?

But Zuri finally slips her hand into mine and lets me tug her close and wrap my arms around her. We're naked and I can't quite stifle my physical response, but this isn't about sex right now. "I'm an asshole, Zuri. I'm never *not* going to be an asshole. But I regret that you got hurt in the process, and that's the truth."

She carefully lays her cheek against my chest. "I'm still angry, but I can't pretend it's just because you lied." She gives a shuddery little sigh that's too close to a sob for my liking. "I'm just a little overwhelmed."

I rest my chin on her head. "I don't think Ursa plans to just kick you to the curb without helping you out a little. Even if she does, *I'll* make sure you land on your feet." It hurts to say the words. It's only been two days with this woman, but I feel like we've shown each other more truths in the last forty-eight hours than we did the entire time we were dancing around that bullshit back in Olympus. Zuri isn't only a sweet, biddable daughter, wreathed in innocence. She's strong and a little mean and rolls with the punches better than I could have imagined. I *like* her.

I like her more than I could have anticipated.

Ursa walks back into the room, her hair hidden beneath a floral head wrap and a silky purple robe tied around her body. She arches an eyebrow at me. "The tub's half full. Get in, darlings."

I guide Zuri up the few steps and into the tub. The water is hot enough to make my breath hiss out, but after the first shock of it, it feels amazing. Maybe I should let go of her, but I pull her down into my lap as I settle. I half expect Zuri to tell me where to shove it, but she settles back against me with a little sigh.

Ursa gives us a long look. "You were both very serious when I came back in here."

Zuri tenses, but I answer first. "I told her that we wouldn't just kick her to the curb as soon as the seventh day is finished. Even with all that money, she's in a new city where she doesn't know anyone. The very least we can do is make sure she gets where she's going or help her find a place in Carver City if she's staying here." I can't quite stop myself from holding Zuri closer. Fuck, I'm not ready to let her go.

Five days. Really, more than five days because we still have tonight. In the past, a week has been more than enough time for me to get anyone out of my system. Working at the Underworld, having my deal with Hades, it was like heaven the first few years. I loved the work, loved scening and fucking the most powerful and beautiful people in Carver City. It wasn't until later that the novelty started to wear thin. I have no qualms with playing the delightful toy, but that's all I was to them. That's all I'd ever be.

Until Ursa. It started off as simply sex with her, just like with everyone else, but somewhere along the way we both forgot to maintain a careful distance. Somewhere along the way, we fell for each other.

Something strange passes over Ursa's face, but she finally nods. "Of course we'll see Zurielle safely to wherever she's landing. It's no hardship."

"Thank you." I don't have to see Zuri's face to know that she's speaking through her teeth. At a faint nod from Ursa, I move Zuri, shifting her around until she's straddling me. She allows it, but she's frowning as she settles back onto my lap. "What are you doing?"

"You're unhappy."

"Thank you for telling me how I feel."

I kind of enjoy the fact that she saves this tartness just for me. Ursa gets the sweet and I get the sour, and I like Zuri's duality on that note a whole hell of a lot. I lean back a little against the jets and rest my hands on her hips. "Last night, you couldn't wait for this week to be over and for you to be free of us. Now you tense up every time we bring it up."

"Stop it, Alaric."

"I haven't done anything."

She presses her hands to my chest but doesn't put any force behind it. Still, there's something akin to panic written across her features. "You have my body for the next five and a half days. Be content with that."

"Zuri—"

"That's enough, lover."

Zuri wiggles out of my hold and practically launches herself from the bath. She accepts the towel Ursa wraps around her and then dodges *her* touch, too. "I'm going to take a shower in the spare room."

"Wait, I—" I bite back the rest of my words at Ursa's sharp look. We both watch Zuri stride out of the bathroom in silence. I start to stand, but Ursa motions me back down.

"You need a longer soak or you're going to be even stiffer

later." She props her hip on the counter and looks down at me. "What was that?"

"What was what?"

"Don't play coy with me. Last night, you couldn't get away from her fast enough and now you're practically begging for this to extend past the week. She didn't change her feelings on this. *You* did. I was never going to let the girl drown once we were done with her and you know it."

Yeah, I did know it. Ursa can be cruel and manipulative and downright vicious when the situation calls for it, but she doesn't harm innocents for the sake of doing it. What we've done to Zuri can be called harm, though, so I don't know where her line is any more. "I wanted you to say it. I know you'll keep your word."

"Do you?" She crosses her arms under her breasts. "I think you're not being honest with yourself."

"I'm always honest with myself." Even to my ears, my protest sounds weak as hell.

"Tell me what you want, Alaric." She says it quietly, a request more than a command.

Because of that, I'm helpless to resist. "I want you." I swallow hard. "And I want to keep her."

Ursa shakes her head, looking tired in a way I've never seen before. Tired in a way she's never *let* me see. "You're asking for the moon, lover. She might enjoy what we do, but she's not for keeping. Not for people like us."

My heart aches. I hold out my hand. "Join me?"

For a moment, I think she might say no, but she finally shrugs out of the robe and climbs into the bath with me, settling astride my lap. I draw her down for a kiss, and she allows it for a few beats before she leans back, kisses my forehead, and moves to the seat across from me. "Some things you can't charm your way out of—or into. This situation is one of them."

I want to fire back an argument, but I make myself slow down enough to consider her words. To consider what she has and hasn't said. "You want to keep her, too."

For the first time since I met her, Ursa won't quite meet my eyes. "I meant what I said. That girl has been protected and cosseted her entire life. Even Triton knew enough to shield her from the darker aspects of what he does. She'd hate it here if we tried to keep her. She'd hate *us*."

"You can't know that."

"I do know that." She gives a smile that's a shadow of her normal one. "There are two kinds of people in this world. Those that flourish in the shadows—and those that suffocate in them. We're the former. That girl is the latter. Trying to keep her would be cruel and selfish, and I may be ruthless to a fault, but even I have to draw the line somewhere. She'll walk from this with a good story about her dance on the dark side, and then she'll return to the light and marry some nice normal person who doesn't have an earned reputation for drowning her victims." She looks at me. "And one who doesn't lie, cheat, and steal in order to further his own goals."

"Ouch."

"I don't say it to hurt you. I say it because it's truth—for both of us."

She's not wrong, but... "That's not the full story, though." I lean forward and stroke her knees under the water. "If she were that sunny, she wouldn't happily step to every line we draw in the sand. She's fierce, Ursa. Fiercer than I could have imagined."

She gives me a long look, something vulnerable lingering in her dark eyes. "Are you sure you aren't saying *you* want to keep her, rather than *we* want to?"

I sit back abruptly. In all the time I've known Ursa, she's never once shied away from what she wants, whether it's people, possessions, or territory. She's bold and ruthless, and if she dresses it up in a kind exterior, that just makes her better at accomplishing her goals. Why is she balking *now?* "You want her." I say it slowly. "I see the way you look at her."

"We're not talking about me. You're the one that follows her around with hearts in your eyes."

I push down my instinctive urge to defend myself. No matter if I want to admit it or not, my feelings for Zurielle are complicated in the extreme. Realizing that she's fiercer than I could have dreamed only makes them more complicated. Before, I felt bad for dragging a near-innocent into this mess, daughter of Triton or no. Now? She could be one of us. I know it, and if I know it, then Ursa's already considered it. I don't understand her hesitation.

"Surely you can see that she worships the ground you walk on." I keep pressing, even when the set of Ursa's shoulders warns me off. We *have* to talk about this. We have to talk about *something* beyond fucking. "She wants to stay, Ursa. What's so wrong with letting this extend past a week?"

"That's your problem, Alaric." She stands abruptly, water cascading down her breasts and stomach and hips. She looks like Aphrodite emerging from the sea, and my body responds despite the fact that we're in the middle of a careful non-argument. Even now, she's holding me at a distance. The only change is that I am painfully aware of the space remaining between us. Will she ever let me in? I had assumed we'd slip into something resembling a normal relationship once I was free. Now I'm not so sure.

Ursa's expression is that careful smile that doesn't reach her eyes. "You let selfish wants motivate you without thinking things through. You want her. You don't care about her wants or needs in this situation, only yours. That's always been your problem."

I flinch. She's not wrong, but in all my time of knowing her, she's never cut me down verbally quite so neatly. Again,

I can't help pushing. I *am* as selfish as she claims, but she's also dodging her feelings on this whole subject. She's shutting me out and I hate it. "I never expected you to be a coward."

Ursa steps out of the tub and dries off with one of her oversized fluffy towels. She doesn't look at me as she takes her time rubbing lotion into her skin. It's not until she's shrugged back into her robe that she gives me her attention, as if she needs that little bit of barrier between us. It doesn't make a damn bit of sense to me.

I'm *right here*. "Ursa, talk to me. Let me in." I don't really mean to blurt out the words, but I have the sudden fear that if she walks out of this conversation right now, it will harm something fragile in our fledgling relationship. "Please."

She shakes her head slowly. "That girl isn't for us." She turns and walks to the door, pausing to look over her shoulder. I've never seen her look so closed down. "But if you want her that badly, you're more than free to go when she goes."

CHAPTER 22

URSA

*M*aybe I am the coward Alaric names me. It's hard to argue with it when I dress quickly and slip out of my penthouse. I haven't snuck out of *anywhere* since I was a teenager, and it didn't go well the single time I tried.

I stop short at the elevator and have to force myself to push the button. I haven't thought about when I was a young for a long time. There's no point. I was a happy child of a happy couple, and my parents supported and loved me— even if they didn't understand my need for *more*. They were content in the little house that always made me feel like the walls were closing in. They enjoyed their normal jobs that didn't require anything more of them than showing up for work Monday to Friday. They enjoyed their perfectly normal marriage.

At least they did until their unexpected deaths when I was still working for Poseidon. They never lived to see my exile, certainly never to see what I've become.

I try not to contemplate what they'd think of me now.

Would they still love their precious daughter knowing I've taken a life? Many lives?

Impossible to say. Better not to ask.

I *hate* that I'm thinking about this now. I don't falter. I haven't since I set myself on this path, one that puts me at the top. It means getting my hands dirty from time to time, but I have to take those measures less now because I set a precedent early on. As much as I pretend it's a happy side effect, it *matters* to me that the people in my territory are better off than they were under the last leader.

The elevator takes me down to the garage, and I waste no time sending Malone a text.

Me: Are you home?

Malone: Yes, why?

Me: I'll be there in twenty.

I step out of the elevator and find Monica waiting for me. From the faint sheen of sweat on her dark brown skin, she ran here from the main security hub. She gives me a long look. "I *know* you weren't about to leave without a driver or security or even talking to me."

I'd been about to do exactly that. "I won't need a driver for this." And Monica is one of the few people close enough to me to call me on my shit, something I'm not too eager to experience. Not when I'm still so raw from the conversation with Alaric.

"Yeah, no. That Domme lady tone doesn't work with me." She crosses her arms over her chest. "Get in the car. If I'm not satisfied you're in your right mind by the end of the drive, we're turning around and coming straight back here."

Frustration bubbles up in my chest. "You do realize that *you* work for *me*, correct?"

Monica arches a brow. "You pay me, sure, but right now you look like you need a friend more than you need your head of security. Get in the car."

There's no point of arguing with her. She's right, after all.

I'm running and knowing that still isn't enough for my pride to kick in and send me back up to my penthouse. Let Alaric and Zurielle comfort each other if that's what they need. Alaric can handle Zurielle's needs while I'm gone.

He shouldn't have to. I should be there to take care of things.

Instead I'm climbing into the back of my town car, about to have yet another uncomfortable conversation I would rather avoid. Monica doesn't make me wait long. We're barely out of the parking garage before she meets my gaze in the rearview mirror. "You're going to Malone's."

"Yes."

She shakes her head. "She's going to tell you the same thing I'm about to: you're being ridiculous."

I bite back a sigh. Monica's never parsed her words with me, which is something I value in a head of security. The person in the position needs to be self-assured enough to speak up to ensure my safety and the safety of the people within my care. In the years that Monica's held the position, we've become friends. Most of the time I enjoy her upfront attitude.

Most of the time, she's not directing it at me like this, though.

"I'm not being ridiculous."

"Oh, I see." She nods slowly. "That's why you're running halfway across town to get away from those two up in your apartment. Because you're *not* being ridiculous. Makes perfect sense to me."

I glare. "You wouldn't understand."

"It's literally my job to have all the information required to keep you safe. I probably understand better than you do. Alaric's not happy in the little box you put him in, and he's rattling his cage, which is rattling *you*." Her gaze softens the

185

tiniest bit. "You didn't really consider what it'd be like once he's free, huh?"

"Alaric and I are fine," I say stiffly.

"Ursa." Now her tone has gone soft, too. "That man worships the ground you walk on. You should be firmly in the honeymoon stage right now, not *fine*."

"I can't trust him. Not completely. Not where Zurielle is concerned." The words spring free despite my best efforts to keep them internal. "Letting him too close right now is a mistake."

Monica's silent for several blocks. "What if it isn't, though? Have you thought about that?"

Yes. Of course I have. The temptation to dismantle my walls and lean on him is almost too much to bear. I've stood alone for *so long*, and I am so incredibly tired. Alaric might not understand the sheer amount I carry, but he wouldn't think less of me for wanting to set it down for a little while. He even seems to crave that intimacy.

It scares the shit out of me.

I can't say this to Monica, though. Not unless I want another lecture about how good Alaric could be for me if I'd just get out of my own way. She's liked him from the moment she met him during his first overnight at my place. Hardly an impartial party. "I'll give it some more thought."

"As long as there's some *action* involved with all that thinking."

"There will be." Just not yet. Not tonight.

We make the drive to Malone's place in thirty minutes. Like most of the other territory leaders, she makes her home in one of the skyscrapers in her territory. Unlike the rest of us, she's actually CEO of the perfectly aboveboard company that runs out of this place. That's what makes Malone so formidable. She's one of the most powerful people in Carver City on both sides of the law. But then, she's an Amazon, so of course she is. Those women all like to have their fingers in both legal and illegal businesses.

Her head of security, Sara, meets me at the front door. They're a large Maori non-binary person with long black hair braided away from their strong face. They nod at me and step aside. "She's waiting for you. Monica can wait here." They smile. "Good to see you again."

"You, too." Monica grins back. "Love what you've done with your hair."

"Thanks."

"You two behave yourselves while I'm up there."

Sara snorts. "We always do. Poker?"

"Definitely." Monica makes a shooing motion. "Go talk to Malone. Maybe you'll listen to *her* advice."

"I listen to yours." I sound like I'm protesting, and the look Monica gives me says she notices. There's nothing to do but stage a studied retreat. "I'll leave you to it."

Malone and I come and go from each other's residences often enough that our teams have become friendly—though that would go up in smoke in a second if we ever went to war. Private security can make a person's life a living hell if they aren't careful, no matter what their boss says. I know for a fact that Malone sends gifts to my main team on their birthdays, the crafty bitch. I've made a habit of doing the same for her people.

I find her in her living room. Her penthouse is much like the woman herself; stark and beautiful and more than a little cold. I frown at the pristine white couch she lounges on. "Is that new?"

"Rogue took exception to the last one."

"You're the only person I know who is willing to spend obscene amounts of money on furniture just for your cat to demolish it."

"Everyone needs a hobby."

I glance around the room. "Where is the little demon?"

"He's around. I'm sure he'll make his presence known at some point." She motions an elegant hand to the couch. "Sit. You look frazzled."

"I look nothing of the sort." I sit despite my protest. Malone is dressed in a variation of her usual outfit, black slacks and a deep red blouse. It's a little more professional and a little less sexy than what she normally wears to the Underworld. She must have been working when I called. "I interrupted your day."

"It's nothing." She waves that away. "I was done with my meetings for the day. You saved me from a few hours of going over tedious reports."

Tedious reports she'll no doubt circle right back to the second I leave. I sigh. I should know better than to run to Malone, just like I should know better than to try to get around Monica to do it. I never show up like this, so of course she dropped everything in response. If I were wiser, I'd keep my own counsel, but I can't help the messy feelings bubbling up inside me. "You've never lost your mind over a sub."

She pauses, green eyes narrowed. "I know you didn't come here to rib me about Aurora. I hardly call my reluctance to play with her the same thing as losing my mind."

"That's not what I meant. If I wanted to give you shit about her, I'm more than capable of doing it over the phone." I stifle the urge to do exactly that. Malone is so icy with most people that it's jaw-dropping to see someone get under her skin. Especially Aurora, who's one of the sweetest and most unassuming subs in the Underworld. Oh, she's gained some teeth and claws since taking over as Megaera's second-in-command, but she's still a nice girl. "What *are* you going to do about her?"

"Ursa." Malone glares. "The only time you work this

hard not to talk about something is if it's really bothering you. What's going on? Is it Alaric?" She tenses. "Shall I handle it?"

"Darling, I'm more than capable of handling my own problems."

"And yet you're here, talking to me instead of doing exactly that."

She has me there and we both know it. I settle back against the couch with a sigh. "I have done unforgivable things to grasp and maintain power. I've had to work harder and be more vicious when I'm challenged than a white man would in my position. You understand that."

"Yes," Malone says slowly. "I fail to see what that has to do with anything. You haven't gone and developed a conscience on me, have you?"

"No, of course not." Except when I think of a conscience, it's Zurielle's face that appears in my mind. No matter what Alaric thinks, she's got a moral center that we would damage if we tried to keep it. Trying to force the three of us to fit in a permanent way will only result in ruin. Why can't he see that?

Why can't he stop pushing until I'm ready to let him in?

"Ursa." Malone's tone goes as gentle as she's capable of. "Tell me what's going on."

"Alaric wants to keep Zurielle."

"He can fuck off, then." Malone folds her hands on her knee. "He's a wonderful submissive, but he's a fuck boy and I've never understood what you saw in him that convinced you to go so far as dating him."

I roll my eyes, a reluctant smile pulling at the edges of my lips. "Really, darling, don't hold back on my account." *No one* is holding back on my account today.

"Yes, yes, you have feelings for him." She shakes her head as if she can't understand it. One day Malone will be knocked fully off balance by someone, and I'll enjoy every moment of watching it happen.

"He doesn't want to leave me for her." Things would be simpler if that were the case. He was never truly mine, not in full. Easier to lose him before I really had him… Or that's what I try to tell myself. It doesn't feel like the truth. "He wants *us* to keep her."

"Oh." Malone pauses. "So keep her."

"Not you, too." I slump back on the couch. "It's not that simple."

"It's exactly that simple." She's looking at me like she's never seen me before. "You have never had a problem taking what you want, Ursa. Even the girl; you had a plan to acquire her and so you did. I don't understand why this is bothering you."

I don't entirely understand it, either. What do I care if staying with me damages Zurielle's innocence? The world isn't kind to the innocent. Only the strong survive, and she'd survive longer with me than without.

Except…

I sigh. "I care about her. I don't want her to be damaged by being with me."

Of all the responses, I don't expect Malone to burst out laughing. She starts to speak and then erupts into laughter again, until she's bent over and clutching her stomach.

It makes me want to shove her right off the couch. "I don't see what's so funny, you bitch."

"*You* are so funny." She gasps in a breath and manages to reclaim her normal icy calm…mostly. "Oh, gods, you are too much. I never thought I'd see the day where you get so twisted up over some little thing. Her pussy must be down-right magical. You've only had her for two days."

"Malone, be serious."

"I *am* being serious." She carefully wipes at the edges of

her eyes with her black-tipped nails. "I'm sorry. You surprised me."

"You don't have to enjoy it so much." I sound grumpy and out of sorts, nothing like my normal calculated tone of amusement, but my careful mask has fractured in the last twenty-four hours and I can't quite manage to reclaim it despite my best efforts. "She's just so *good*."

"*Is* she?"

"*Malone.*"

"Yes, yes, apologies again." She doesn't sound any sorrier this time than she did earlier. "Ursa, if I didn't know better, I'd say that you're scared."

"I'm not scared." I protest too quickly, making a liar of myself.

"Are you sure? Because you're sitting in my living room instead of having a conversation with your two submissives."

How can I explain it to her in a way that makes sense when I can barely make sense of it myself? "In all the years I've been working my way toward power, toward this position of holding an entire territory, the one line I haven't crossed is harming an innocent. The single line, Malone. If I keep her, I'll harm her by virtue of the life I live."

Malone studies me for a long time. "She auctioned off her virginity and lost her entire life back in Olympus in the process. Even *I* know that Triton is horribly backwards about that sort of thing. Explain to me how that isn't harm?"

"She chose it." It sounds weak when I say it, but it's the only defense I have.

"And if she chooses to stay?"

I open my mouth, but it's too neat a trap. "It's different."

"It's really not." Malone doesn't touch me—that's not her way—but she gives me a sympathetic look. "So tell me again that you're not scared."

"You're twisting my words, darling. It's not that simple

and you know it. We can't do what we want for the sake of doing what we want, especially when it comes to having a partner." It's a double standard for the ages. The men who run territories can take partners and no one blinks, no one thinks that they're no longer in charge. But a woman does it? Things become infinitely more complicated. A *Black* woman? I already have to be ten times better than anyone else just to be taken seriously. It's exhausting, and I'm so incredibly tired.

I've convinced myself it's worth it. I have the power I always dreamed of. I'm at the top of the hierarchy. Above the corrupt politicians who pretend they have any say in the things that truly matter. Above the laws that have been wielded against the people who can defend themselves the least. The only law that matters is *mine*.

"Then why aren't you worried about it with Alaric?"

I am. I push to my feet. "That's different."

"Is it?"

"Yes." That, I believe, no matter how fledgling this relationship is in some ways. We've been fucking for years, but the intimacy is still developing in other areas. All that said, I *do* know him. Alaric wants to be kept. He's been fighting and clawing his way through the world since he was born. He wants to let someone else take the lead, and he's more than happy to kneel at my feet. "He has no interest in the rest of it. He just wants me." *All* of me. I'll give him everything. I will. I'm just...afraid.

"What's to say this girl doesn't just want you, too? Really, Ursa, you're making this more complicated than it needs to be. Even if you decide to marry one of them, *you're* the one running the territory and everyone knows it."

She makes it all sound so reasonable, which makes me feel dramatic and ridiculous. "You know, I came here for a friendly chat where you confirm that I'm making the right

THE SEA WITCH

choice, not for you to systematically pick apart my argument."

"Sometimes friends should play support, sometimes they should shine a light on hard truths." She re-crosses her legs. "I support whatever you choose to do, of course. I simply think it's silly for you not to take what you obviously want because of some outdated sense of right and wrong." Malone smiles, cold as a winter day. "Might makes right, Ursa. And you have all the might in both your territory and these relationships. If you want the little princess, then keep her until you're tired of her."

I look at my friend for a long time. I've mostly held my tongue about her strange dancing around Aurora, but if we're dishing out hard truths, then there's no reason for me not to participate. And I'm petty enough to want her to feel a sliver of the discomfort that I currently do. "You should live by your own advice, darling. If you want Aurora, take her. A little time with her on her knees for you might put you in a better mood."

Malone narrows her eyes. "*If* I decide I want Aurora again, then that's exactly what I'll do. Now, get back to your submissives so I can get back to my reports."

"Your pep talk skills need work."

"Do they? Because you look steadier on your feet than when you walked through my door."

Damn her, but she's right. I shake my head, a true smile pulling at my lips. Our brand of comfort might not work for everyone, but it works for us. "Come to the Underworld tonight and have a drink with me."

Her smile warms a few degrees. "I'll see you there."

Monica manages to hold her peace until we're in the car again. "Are we going home or do you have more procrastinating to do?"

"Gods save me from supportive friends." I press my

fingers to my temples. I could come up with half a dozen errands that need running, but the truth is that both Monica and Malone are right. I won't figure this out by avoiding it. "No, take us home."

"Yes, boss."

"You're such an asshole."

"You love it." She grins at me in the rearview mirror. "That's why you pay me the big bucks."

"That and the fact you're the best head of security in Carver City."

"And the best shot."

I smile. "And the best friend. I don't deserve you."

"Don't go getting sentimental on me, Ms. Sea Witch. You'll make me ruin my makeup."

We fall into an easy conversation the rest of the way back to my building. Monica has instituted a few personnel changes. She likes to rotate people through various positions to keep them from getting complacent or worse—bored. So far the process is working out wonderfully.

All the while I'm thinking about what my friends have said. And the fact that every one of my arguments has holes large enough to drive a semi through. It all boils down to one question—what's *truly* stopping me from keeping Zurielle and letting Alaric in?

I walk into my penthouse and pause, listening. A sliver of unease courses through me when all I hear is silence. Surely Alaric didn't take me at my word and run with Zurielle? The thought has me moving quickly to the spare bedroom, and I stop short in the doorway.

They're on the bed together.

Sleeping.

Zurielle is on her side, her legs drawn up into fetal position as if she can make her already small body smaller. Alaric is at her back, a careful six inches between them, but there's no missing the way he curls his body around hers protectively.

I watch them for a long moment, measuring the rise and fall of their chests, the way *my* chest feels just from observing the tableau they create. I have never once had a problem taking what I want up this point. Why am I so hesitant to take Zurielle in a permanent way?

I want Zurielle. That much is true. I take a deep breath and turn to walk down the hall and into my bedroom. I have been so incredibly careful to keep everyone at a distance, and these two are like a whirlpool pulling me in, a force I can no longer fight. I demand vulnerability and trust from my submissives—from Alaric and Zurielle—but maybe it's time I gave a little trust in return. The thought has my chest tightening in response, but I carefully breathe through it. I can do this. It might feel like the hardest thing I've ever tried, but rationally I know it's not true. If this blows up in my face, it's only my heart that will bear the pain. No matter what else is true, neither Alaric nor Zurielle want me dead.

No one has ever died of a broken heart.

Surely I won't be the first.

CHAPTER 23

ZURIELLE

J didn't mean to fall asleep, but the last few days keep catching up with me and knocking me on my ass. When I closed my eyes on the massive bed in the spare bedroom, I was alone. I'm not alone any longer. A male body is pressed against my back, his heavy arms wrapped around me like I'm his favorite teddy bear. Alaric. The steady rise and fall of his chest tells me that he's sleeping still. Of *course* he's here again, and of course we found each other in our sleep. Again. No matter how conflicted my heart is when it comes to this man, my body doesn't have the same reservations.

I open my eyes to find Ursa lounging on the bed just out of reach, a laptop on her thighs and a pair of bright turquoise square glasses perched on her nose. She glances at me and keeps typing. "Good, you're awake. You have a little time before we need to get ready."

I shift, and Alaric's arms tighten as if even in sleep he wants to keep me with him. "You left."

"I needed to clear my head." She clicks a few things on the laptop and shuts it carefully. "You left first, little Zurielle."

Her dark eyes take me in as if she can see right down to the very heart of me. "You don't like the idea of what happens after this week is over."

She says it like she already knows the answer, but what little pride I have left demands I not roll over for her. At least not in this. "I've only known you a few days. It would be very ill-advised if I wanted more than this week with you."

"With both of us." Again, Ursa states it as fact instead of a question. She reaches out and sifts her fingers through my hair. "If I kept you, it would change you, Zurielle. There's no avoiding it."

I stare up at her, fighting not to arch into her touch like a cat begging for pets. "Ursa." I clear my throat and force myself to continue, to take courage from this quiet moment. "I'm already changed from the last two days." When she glances away, I continue. "But I was going to change regardless. No one stays the same their entire lives. It's just not how things work."

"There are changes, and there are *changes*." She sighs. "At the end of the day, my operations aren't that much different than your father's. Carver City appears to have the function of a normal city, but the territory leaders are the ones who rule in truth. And they don't do it with kindness and charm. Power demands sacrifices, and I will continue to make those offerings while I hold this seat. I am not a good woman, not by any definition. But the people in my territory are safe from a number of threats because of the power I wield. I won't give that up, not for anyone."

I'm not sure if she's arguing with me or just being really insistent that I go into this with eyes wide open. "My father lied to me. I won't pretend that I'm thrilled to be part of a criminal empire, whether in Olympus or here, but that's the crux of it—I was already participating and benefiting from a number of illegal activities, even if I wasn't aware of it at the time."

"I would point out that you not being aware of it makes it a very different situation." She examines her nails, but the tension in her body gives lie to the absentminded motion. "And you have options beyond choosing between your father and myself."

"My father isn't an option at all." Not because he wouldn't take me back at this point. He wouldn't. But it ultimately doesn't matter what *he* thinks because I refuse to return to living that half life in his household. No matter what the future holds, Olympus isn't an option for me any longer.

"Alaric cares for you."

I blink at the apparent change of subject. "That's up for debate." He's still relaxed at my back, which amuses me despite myself. Apparently Alaric is a heavy sleeper.

"No. It's not." Ursa finally looks up from her nails. "He would leave with you if you asked."

I frown. I thought she was changing her mind about letting me stay, but this seems like it's just a continuation of our earlier conversation. Like she's feeling me out for what would be my best option forward in walking away.

Disappointment sinks its claws into me, and my voice wobbles a little when I finally manage to speak. "You already said that you're not keeping me. You don't have to be cruel." When she raises her eyebrows, I keep talking. "Alaric loves you. He's never leaving you. Not for me. Not for anyone else. You don't have to stick that knife in and twist it. You couldn't be clearer that you don't want me. You don't have to forcibly remind me that he doesn't want me, either."

Her expression softens. "Little Zurielle." She cups my face with one hand and draws her thumb across my cheek and down my face. "Whether it's wise or not, I intend to keep you."

My breath stalls in my lungs. "What?"

She continues as if I haven't spoken. "But the fact remains that I am not in the business of permanent captivity, no matter how fun it is to dabble in. A week is one thing. Long term is entirely another. If you stay, you will have to compromise some of those sterling traits you cling to so tightly."

"What sterling traits?"

"Your innocence." She traces my bottom lip. "Your righteous anger at everything your father's business is. As I said, our businesses are not so different—then or now. Being a hypocrite isn't a charming look."

She's being serious, so I give her words serious thought. What *am* I willing to compromise on? "Do you deal in human trafficking?"

Ursa makes a face. "No. It's an untoward business on multiple levels, and I won't have it in my territory." She tilts her head to the side. "Actually, now that I think of it, all of the current territory leaders feel the same. How novel."

That's a relief. "And everything else?"

She shrugs. "I am not a saint. I've never lied and said otherwise."

I can accept this and we can try, or I can refuse to and be done at the end of this week. If I were the good person I pretend to be, I would leave. I would start a new life and find someone normal and mundane to love. The thought leaves me cold.

Really, there's no choice at all, and that tells me all I need to know. I am just as selfish and complicated as my father. It's not enough for me to forgive him for all the lies and for him trying to control every part of my life, but a small part of me understands him. The high pedestal he put me on isn't one *I* choose. I don't know where I stand on so many things, because I haven't had a chance to figure it out for myself. Not while I lived in my father's gilded cage.

I might as well start now.

I want Ursa. I want her more than I have right to. From the moment I first saw her sitting in the back of that town car, I felt a connection I still can't quite put into words. It's stronger than ever now, thrumming between us so blatantly, it's a wonder I can't see it disturb the air. But there's one thing I need to know before I say the words trying to fling themselves from my mouth. "What happened with you and my father?"

She's silent for a long moment, and I think maybe she won't tell me. But finally Ursa sighs. "That's a fair enough question." She sets her laptop aside. " I was freshly out of college and very green when I took the position at the shipyard working for Poseidon. Your father was in an identical position and we became friends. He'd worked for the company longer and showed me the ropes." Her dark gaze is distant, focused on what happened decades in the past. "We were friends."

Friends.

I don't know why that surprises me. Of course their enmity flares crueler because there was genuine caring before things went sideways.

Ursa takes a breath and continues. "Several years later, Poseidon's eldest son came of age and he wanted the boy in one of the positions held by us. We both knew too much about the operations to be fired so he lay down a challenge of sorts. Only one left standing."

Easy enough to read between the lines. I tense. "So you tried to kill my father."

She laughs bitterly. "No. I thought we could find another way. I naively assumed Triton felt the same, so when he said he wanted to meet me at the docks after hours, I thought nothing of it. He pulled a gun on me and offered me a choice —a bullet or exile."

I frown. "That explains why you hate him. It doesn't explain why he loathes you."

"Yes, well." Her lips curve in a self-satisfied smile. "I might not have thought he'd kill me, but I wasn't a complete fool. I cleaned out several of his secret accounts, the ones he didn't believe anyone knew about. It was more than enough money to pave my way to Carver City and stage a coup for this territory."

"Ah. That would do it." I study her expression, thinking it over. "Would you have killed him if you knew he was willing to be that ruthless?" She'd killed others, after all. It's how she got her nickname.

She opens her mouth, but pauses. "I don't know. Maybe. I was very young and much softer than I am now. I don't believe I had the capacity to pull the trigger on a friend in cold blood."

"Thank you for telling me."

"I have to be stronger and more ruthless than other people who hold territory leader positions because of who I am. That won't change, not as long as I live. But..." Another of those careful pauses, as if she's arguing with herself. "But I can try to be open with you and Alaric. If you stay."

I take a deep breath. "If I say I want to stay, what happens then?"

"So cautious." Her lips quirk, some of the amusement returning to her dark eyes. "Then you stay. We see if we can find a proper balance with the three of us. If it works, then it works. If it doesn't, then you're more than capable of walking at any time with my blessing." She glances over my shoulder, and that's when I notice that Alaric has gone perfectly still behind me. "But we're a package deal, darling.

KATEE ROBERT

If you can't forgive Alaric for what he's done, then you shouldn't be able to forgive me, either."

I open my mouth, but she presses a finger to my lips. "Don't decide now. I'll ask you again at the end of the week. Until then, we'll enjoy each other."

She says it as if it's so simple. Maybe it is. Haven't I decided to do exactly that? Enjoy everything they give me this week? I didn't expect it to be so complicated. That was naive of me. I swallow hard. "Okay."

"Good. Let's get ready. We'll need to leave before too long for the Underworld." She smiles at me and then climbs off the bed and walks out of the room.

Leaving me alone with Alaric.

I should turn to face him, but my courage fails me. "You heard that."

"I heard it."

He starts to shift away, but I grab his arms, keeping them wrapped around me. It's easier to speak without looking at him, to admit how foolish I was that I let him close enough to cause me pain. "You hurt me badly when I realized that it was all a lie."

"It wasn't all a lie."

"Alaric, you're not the man you pretended to be. You're not a nice guy who made a mistake. You're not a devil, but you're not an innocent, either."

"You're right." He huffs out a breath. "But that doesn't change the fact that I *did* enjoy my time with you in Olympus. And I've enjoyed my time with you here, too."

I smile despite everything. "We've spent most of the time fucking or fighting."

"What can I say? I have a bit of a masochistic streak." He chuckles. "I won't pretend that we both didn't say some hurtful shit, but verbally sparring with you? I like it."

I finally force myself to turn in his arms so I can see his face. "It's that simple for you."

"Yeah." He shrugs as much as he can in his current position. This is the first time I've seen his blue eyes unshielded without some kind of kink involved. He looks almost... earnest. "I like you, Zuri. I liked you in Olympus. I like you even better now." I open my mouth, but he cuts me off before I have a chance to respond. "Don't you fucking dare tell me it's because I like your pussy. I, of all people, can keep sex and messy emotions separate. I've been doing it for years."

It's really, really none of my business but I can't help asking, "Do you think you'll miss it?"

He blinks. "Miss what?"

"Working at the Underworld. Having sex with so many different people. All of it."

I half expect him to answer quickly, but he takes the time to really think it over. "I don't know. I haven't really considered it because I've been so focused on getting free of Hades's leash and moving my relationship forward with Ursa. Maybe I'll miss it. Maybe I won't. However I feel, I'll talk it through with Ursa, and we'll figure it out."

Somehow, his words reassure me more than if he rushed to tell me that he would never, ever miss the sex work. He's being honest, rather than telling a soothing lie. Nothing in this world is so cut and dried, and Alaric might have chosen to make a deal with Hades, but he also chose the method of his repayment. I know enough to know that. "Okay."

Alaric studies me. "Does that bother you?"

"I don't know." It's the honest answer, if an unsatisfying one. I don't know what I'm feeling right now, only that I'm swinging madly from one emotion to another. Elation that Ursa wants me. Fear of what the future might bring. Confusion on how this could possibly *work*. "You and Ursa haven't even had a chance to figure out your relationship now that your debt is paid. You don't have a problem with her inviting me to stay?"

Alaric's smile is surprisingly tentative. "I'd like you to stay, too."

I can't fault him for being an asshole last night, not when I was more than a little bit of an asshole on my own. "What if we can't make it work?"

"Then we can't make it work." He sits up, bringing me with him. "No relationship is guaranteed, Zuri. Not even the happy ones. We might fall in love and fall out of it again. I might be hit by a truck tomorrow. A meteor could destroy the world."

I blink. "That is an exceedingly dark way of looking at it."

"Not really." He shrugs. "Knowing that it could end only makes it sweeter while you have the good stuff. Life is hard. Really fucking hard. Hell, you know that. You haven't been untouched by death."

He means my mother.

"That's not the same thing. I barely remember her." Is it possible to miss someone you only have the faintest smudge of memories of? I don't know. I've never been able to figure out if I miss her or just the fantasy of the mother my sisters say she was. Kind and strong and fierce at times. My father always says I looked the most like her, *was* the most like her, but how can I live up to the memory of a woman I only remember as a soft hug that smells faintly of orange blossoms?

"It counts." Alaric smooths my hair back, his touch gentle. "Look, I won't pressure you one way or another. But I'm willing to talk through this shit if you are."

I glance at the door. "Maybe later? I get the feeling Ursa doesn't like to be kept waiting."

He grins, his seriousness falling away so quickly, I have to wonder if he's as relieved to set this conversation aside for the time being as I am. "That's the damn truth." Alaric climbs off the bed and holds out his hand. "Come on, Zuri. Let's show you how good the Underworld can be when you're *really* indulging."

He sounds so happy, so full of anticipation, that I allow myself to smile and take his hand. "I can't wait."

CHAPTER 24

ALARIC

I'm still reeling from Ursa's offer when we finally arrive at the Underworld. It's late enough that the lounge is filled when we follow Ursa through the door, flanking her on either side. Zuri drifts a little closer to her, the only sign that she's overwhelmed, though she keeps shooting glances at the people gathered. Maybe she's trying to pick out the people who bid on her. Or maybe she's just finally getting a good look at the sheer amount of beauty and power packed into this club every weekend. Everyone in the room has one or the other; most have both. It's surreal in the extreme, and working here for eight years still hasn't quite worn off the shine of it.

It's strange, though.

Strange to be back here as a patron. Strange to be fully dressed when usually I was wearing some kind of costume or kink gear. Strange to miss the Underworld a little, even if it's a place that felt so much like a cage for the last few years.

Our outfits coordinate, something I've found amusing when others did it in the past. It doesn't feel amusing tonight. It feels like a public declaration that we belong to

Ursa, that we're part of her household. That we're sharing her bed.

She's wearing one of my favorite dresses of hers, a black wrap dress that hugs her generous curves and is deceptively see-through. Every step she takes gives hints to the purple lingerie she wears beneath it, little glimpses that make my mouth water. I'm wearing black slacks and a purple button-down in the exact same shade. Zuri has on a matching purple dress that is short enough to almost be indecent, her heels making her lean legs look even longer. The dress hugs her body, leaving as little to the imagination as Ursa's clothing does, but in a very different way. Her only accessory is her mother's necklace.

Fuck, but I'm a lucky man.

Ursa leads the way to a booth that's been her customary one for as long as I've lived in Carver City. She motions Zuri to precede us into the booth and I follow her in, sliding until we're pressed together from knee to shoulder. It's only touching her like this that I can feel Zuri tremble, just a little. None of those nerves show on her face, her expression a calm mask as she surveys the room.

Ursa slides in from the other side, so that we're bracketing Zuri. Like most everything she does, this is intentional. She picked up on Zuri's unease, too. Ursa is too careful with her public image to openly comfort Zuri when gazes around the room focus on us, but I don't miss the fact that she gives the other woman's bare knee a quick squeeze under the table.

Aurora appears next to our table as if by magic. She winks at me and gives Ursa a wide grin. "I see that you're enjoying your auction prize."

"You have no idea." Ursa's smile is just as wide, just as practiced. "You look delightful tonight, Aurora."

Delightful and *different*. Her blue hair is a shade darker

than it was a few days ago, edging toward a deep indigo, and she's wearing *red*. On anyone else, the complicated lingerie set would be hot and it would end there. But in eight years, I haven't seen Aurora in anything but white. Her whole thing has been playing to type—the innocent virginal submissive who just wants to kneel at her dominant's feet and give them whatever they desire.

I catch a glimpse of metal beneath the red lace. "Did you pierce your nipples?"

"A lady never tells." She gives me a dazzling smile. "But she might show you." She reaches down and tugs both lace cups away from her breasts and shows us that she has, indeed, gained two new piercings. The silver shines against her brown nipples, pretty little additions.

I glance over to find Zuri watching Aurora with interest. I didn't see the show they put on for the auction—Hades hadn't wanted anyone circulating the room and distracting bidders—but I'd heard about it afterward.

Zuri catches me looking and blushes. "I like them."

Ursa shifts, and I catch her trailing her hand up Zuri's thigh, stopping just short of the hem. "There are a number of places to be pierced, darling. I think you'd enjoy quite a few of them."

If anything, Zuri blushes harder. "Maybe."

I have to focus on *not* thinking about Zuri adorned with jewelry through her nipples and clitoral hood. Of how I could drive her wild toying with them with my tongue. Except focusing isn't working because I can't stop picturing it. I groan. "Damn it, Aurora. Now you've gone and done it."

"Sorry." She flashes a quick grin at me. "Not sorry." She turns back to Ursa. "I'll get those drinks started. It was nice to see you again, Zuri." She's a professional, so there isn't even a hint of question there about what we're all doing here together, dressed as if this is permanent and not just a week-long assignation.

"Would you like to play with Aurora again, darling?"

Zuri shifts, but we're both pressed against her so there's nowhere for her to go. I watch her face carefully. It's a simple enough question, but there's nothing simple in her expression. She finally looks at Ursa. "I don't know."

"Elaborate."

"I enjoyed what we did on stage."

Ursa watches her just as closely as I am. "Mmhmm."

Zuri shifts again, pressing back against me. I respond to the silent ask and drape my arm around her waist and pull her into my lap. She exhales slowly. "If it's something you want, I'll obey."

"That wasn't what I asked you. I know what *I* want already. I asked what *you* want." She edges closer, her hand drifting up Zuri's thigh again. It makes Zuri squirm, which is hell on *my* control because she's squirming against my cock. Ursa's hand disappears beneath her dress, and I know the exact moment she penetrates Zuri because she goes soft and all but melts back against my chest.

Ursa's hand moves beneath her dress. "I'll ask again and this time, answer honestly. Would you like to play with Aurora again?"

"No." The word shudders out. Zuri clutches my arms so tightly, there are bound to be imprints of her fingernails long after she's let go. "I just want you…" She whimpers a little. "Both of you."

"There now. Was that so hard?"

Zuri lets her head drop back to rest on my shoulder. "No, Mistress." Her voice is barely above a whisper.

"Come quietly, love. You don't want everyone in this room to know that I have my fingers in your pretty pussy, do you?" Ursa's gaze is intent on Zuri's face. Not just intent.

Intense. I wait for a wave of jealousy in response to the possessive look I've only ever seen directed at me. It doesn't come. Having Zuri with us just feels right. Maybe it's because I want her, too. Maybe it's because her softness and her steel perfectly complement us, perfectly rounds out our relationship. I don't know. There's no point in questioning it. It simply is.

Ursa works Zuri to orgasm right there in the booth. With every roll of her hips, I have to grit my teeth harder to keep myself under control. There will be pleasure aplenty later. I don't need to blow my wad at the table from a little dry humping. Or that's what I tell myself as I hang by a fucking thread.

Zuri comes with a near-silent moan, shuddering in my lap. Ursa smiles, her entire expression going both warm and soft for a fleeting moment before she packs it away and all that remains is a cool smile. "Good girl." She shifts her attention to me. "And you, lover. You've shown excellent restraint." She withdraws her fingers, wet with Zuri's orgasm, and presses them to my lips. "Taste how good she is."

I take her fingers into my mouth eagerly, sucking and flicking my tongue over her skin. Zuri tastes sweet, but I keep it up long after I've licked Ursa clean.

She slowly pulls her fingers out of my mouth and shakes her head. "You're such a handful."

"That's what you enjoy about me."

"One of the many things." She turns her attention back to the room. As suspected, we have a bit of an audience. No one has moved from their respective booths or seats at the bar, but a good portion of the people here just watched that little show.

Historically, Ursa doesn't play in public often. I think I can count on one hand how many times she's done it, and all were special occasions for one reason or another.

I guess tonight is a special occasion, too.

Malone walks through the door, and her entrance is like a rock thrown into a placid pool of water. Ripples of people turning back to their drinks or conversations as she passes. She ignores the bar and comes straight for us, looking as perfectly put together as always. She's wearing fitted black pants, suspenders and a gray silk blouse. And, of course, her customary heels. With her icy blond hair swept back from her face, her beauty is on full display.

She's one of the few power players in Carver City that I haven't played with—her tastes run more to the feminine persuasion—but I've seen the way Underworld submissives go all starry eyed after they've participated in one of her scenes. Her reputation is more than earned.

Malone casts a slow look over us before finally settling on Ursa. "Smitten."

"Sometimes I *do* take the advice of my friends." Ursa shrugs. "Have a drink with me."

Malone curves dark red lips. "You have two pretty submissives practically panting after you right now, and you want to have a drink with me?"

"It's good for them to learn patience." Ursa cuts a look in my direction. "Alaric, take Zurielle and go find out where our drinks went. Bring a gin and tonic for Malone."

"Yes, Mistress."

It's awkward to slide out of the booth with Zuri in my lap, but she's still a little loopy from the orgasm. I carefully edge past Malone where she stands by the table and set Zuri on her feet, keeping my hands on her hips in case she sways. I should know better by now. She's steady enough, but she gives me a small smile like she appreciates the thought. Or maybe I'm just projecting, hoping that this might really work.

I want her to stay.

I want her to forgive me, even though I sure as fuck don't deserve it. Especially because, deep down in my soul, I know I wouldn't do a single thing different. Not when my actions brought Zuri into my life—into *our* life.

I take her hand and head slowly toward the bar. The surreal feeling from before is back. How many times did I spend the first part of the night in this lounge, carting drinks to and from tables? More than I can count. I played bartender for the first year after I sealed my bargain with Hades, while I was still in training to learn to play both submissive and Dominant. Though I didn't do nearly the former nearly as much as I did the latter. Not that I minded. I didn't hate my time here.

I just hated not being my own person.

"This place feels so larger than life."

Looking around, I try to see it like Zuri does. The entire Underworld drips in understated elegance, trending toward cool neutrals and expensive fabrics. The lounge is no different. Each of the circular booths tucked against the walls were handmade and have the leather seats changed out with different subtle patterns whenever Meg gets an itch. Or I guess Hercules, since he's the one who took over that part of running the club.

The bar is a masterpiece. It surrounds a large sculpture that manages to depict an orgy without crossing over into vulgar, and the lighting was installed intentionally to spotlight it. The bar is always lit, no matter what time of night, and the drinks are all top shelf. Even the wood floor beneath our feet shines as if dirt wouldn't dare touch it.

Yeah, larger than life about sums it right up.

We stop next to the bar, and I sling my arm around her waist simply because I can. The large Dominican woman behind the bar smiles at me. "Back so soon, Alaric? I knew you'd miss us."

"Only you, Tis." I give her my charming grin right back. "This is Zuri."

"We met briefly." Tis gives her an equally warm smile. She might be a badass with the patrons, but she's always had plenty of warmth for those of us who work at the Underworld. Or, at least, those who used to. I resent the pang in my chest at the thought. I fought so hard to get free. Why the hell does part of me *miss* this place?

Zuri holds out her hand, a proper princess. "It's nice to see you again."

Tis shoots a look at me as she takes Zuri's hand. "Is she always this polite?"

"No." I chuckle. "She's on her best behavior right now because she's overwhelmed."

"Alaric." Zuri glares at me. "Stop it."

I give her a reprieve and change the subject. "We came to collect our drinks and add a gin and tonic for Malone."

"Ah." Tis moves a few feet down the bar and nudges a round tray with three drinks on it over to me. "Give me a second for the fourth."

The glasses have condensation beading the outside of them. "Did something happen to Aurora?"

"She was called away." Her careful reply tells me everything I need to know. Aurora saw Malone and decided to find somewhere else to be. I've seen the disappearing act enough times, but I've never been able to get to the bottom of it. Aurora might submit prettily and cry easily, but she's a vault when it comes to things she doesn't want to talk about. Malone lands firmly in that category.

"I'll run the drinks back to our table when Ursa is ready for us."

"Thanks." Tis sets the fourth drink on the tray and moves to the next person waiting.

Zuri leans against me a little. "Is there a reason we're waiting?"

"Ursa will motion us back when she wants us there." At Zuri's questioning look, I elaborate. "She and Malone are both territory leaders. That means sometimes they're talking as friends, and sometimes they're talking business. When they're friends, Ursa doesn't care if we hang around. Business is different."

Zuri frowns. "But if you're her partner, shouldn't you be looped in?"

I almost laugh. Only the fact that it's an earnest question makes me wrestle back the impulse. "Zuri, honey, I don't know if you've noticed, but my track record shows that I am shit when it comes to being in charge of my own life, let alone any others'. I have things I'm good at, but playing official second-in-command to a territory leader isn't one of them."

The line between her brows makes me want to smooth it away with my thumb. "So you want to be a…kept man?"

"Something like that." Truth be told, we're still figuring out the dynamics of our relationship, and this week hasn't allowed for much in the way of talking about it. But I know where I stand. "Ursa has stood alone for decades at this point. She's kept people at a distance because she can't afford to let anyone close who might undermine her. If I can help create a safe space for her to let down her hair and actually relax, that's worth a whole hell of a lot, don't you think?" She's still frowning, so I give in to the urge to press my thumb to the line between her brows. "If you choose to stay, that doesn't mean you have to do the same thing, Zuri. There's room to find your feet, too."

She smiles at me, but it's obvious she's still mulling over my words. "There's still a lot I don't understand, but I don't think I want to hold the same kind of position you do."

"You have time to figure out what you want." But even as I say it, I'm reminded of the fact that there might not be much time left at all. A few measly days. If we don't convince Zuri to give us a chance, she'll walk and that will be that.

I'll be happy with Ursa. Fucking deliriously happy.

But I can't help feeling that, without Zuri, our relationship will be missing a vital piece.

CHAPTER 25

"My drink's getting warm while you're playing games with your submissives."

I raise my brows at Malone. "Someone's in a mood tonight." I suspected as much the second she walked through the door. I'm not sure what happened between when we spoke earlier and now, but Malone's entire body is practically vibrating with tension. I lean forward and lower my voice. "What's wrong?"

"Nothing you can help with."

"Darling, it's not always about helping. It's about being there for you." When she doesn't respond, I keep prodding. "That's what a few decades' worth of friendship is for. Tell me."

She finally turns those cold green eyes on me. "There's trouble back in Sabine Valley. Even with all my resources, I can't help, and it's aggravating in the extreme."

"Trouble…" Malone isn't the sentimental sort, so she doesn't talk overmuch about the city she grew up in. I have my own sources of information, though. I know Sabine Valley is run by three factions. One of the factions used to be

Alaric's cousins before they were run out of town and his uncle was killed. One of the others is run by Malone's older sister. The Amazons are matriarchal, and since she wasn't the heir and wouldn't inherit, Malone came to Carver City and took over her own territory. "Is your family well?"

"They're alive." Malone looks away. "Due to the folly of my sister, two of my nieces have paid a high price. I don't know what happens next."

Alive is a relief, but we both know all too well the harm that can be caused while a person still breathes. "I'm sorry."

"Me, too." She gives herself a shake. "I'll know more in the morning, but tonight I needed the distraction." Her mouth twists. "I'm doing a hell of a job with it."

"You're allowed to buckle from time to time."

Malone gives an elegant snort. "Really? Do tell me how that weakness has worked out for you?"

She's got me there. When I buckle from the pressure, I do it alone and behind locked doors. Even being territory leader for as long as I have, there are no guarantees. I'm only as strong as my weakest day, which means I can't have a weak day. It's only recently that I've admitted that I *want* to stop being so damn strong when I'm home with the people I care about. I'm still not entirely comfortable with the idea, but I'm warming up to it. "We're not talking about me."

"Mmhmm." She makes a show of looking at the bar, where Alaric and Zuri linger. A flicker of appreciation ignites in my chest. Alaric's been around the block to know how things work without me having to hold his hand and walk him through it. This one small action of anticipating my needs before I voice them feels... It doesn't feel small at all. It feels like another sign that we can really make this work.

Malone leans back against the seat. "I take it you've made a decision."

No point in playing coy. "I'm going to keep them." If Zuri

decides to stay. No matter how willing I am to bathe my hands in blood, I won't keep that woman with me if she doesn't want to be there. There have to be lines, thin though they are. Nonexistent, some might argue.

"Good. You deserve some happiness."

I turn back to Malone. "Careful, darling. That was almost tender."

"Missteps are known to happen." Her smile is knife-sharp. "Now, if you'll excuse me, I'm going to return the favor and take your advice."

I watch her stand. "Do tell."

"I've got to see a man about a bratty little submissive." She waves an elegant hand and walks away before her words have fully penetrated; no doubt to prevent me from having the last word. I watch her go and hope I haven't made a mistake. It's easy to give advice from the outside, but the truth is that I don't actually know why Malone has avoided Aurora all these years. It's too late to go back and change words, and I'm not entirely sure this *is* a mistake. Only time will tell.

I catch Alaric's eye and motion him to return. He keeps one hand laced with Zurielle's as he heads in my direction, the drink tray expertly balanced on the other.

It's only been a few days since he was employed here, but he already moves differently. Lighter. Even with the frown on his face, he's definitely benefiting from being his own man. Regardless of whether being his own man means he's mine or not.

Perhaps I should remind him that he's free to leave. Perhaps. But I don't want to. I finally have him all to myself, and I'm loath to do anything to make Alaric look to the horizon instead of to me. It might happen anyway. I care about him, but I'm not naive about the kind of man he is.

There may come a day when I won't be enough. But as he smiles at me, I have a hard time remembering that.

The future will bring what it will bring. I have him now, and it's enough.

I have them both.

Alaric releases Zurielle so she can climb into the booth and then he sets the drinks in front of us. "Just a minute." Then he's gone, striding back to the bar.

Zuri reaches for her drink. "I don't know if I can do what he does."

My chest gives a pang, but I smother it. She hasn't made a choice. She's simply asking a question without asking a question. "Elaborate, darling."

She takes a big sip of her drink as if she needs the courage. "Alaric can be a jerk, but he's happy to be submissive to you all the time."

There still wasn't a question in there. "Yes." I touch her wrist when she starts to lift the glass to her lips. "Speak your mind, little Zurielle. You don't need the liquid courage for it."

"I have been *kept* my entire life." Her mouth twists. "I think I understand why it's a comfortable place for Alaric, but that doesn't mean I want the same thing." She lifts her chin, finally meeting my gaze. "I want more."

For the first time, it strikes me to wonder what she might become if the people around her stop trying to attach stones to her waist to keep her with them in the depths. I want to reach out, to touch her, but I'm acutely aware of the power dynamics of the moment. If I want this woman to choose me —to choose *us*—then I need her to do it on her own. If I try to tip the scales, she'll resent me the same way she resented her father. "As I said—elaborate."

She deflates a little. "I don't know. Right now, I don't know what I want; I just know what I don't want." Zurielle looks at her glass. "That sounds ridiculous, doesn't it? How can I not know what I want?"

"You haven't had the opportunity to figure it out for yourself." I understand Triton's desire to keep his daughters locked away and safe. The world is not a kind place even in the most mundane of lives. Moving through the worlds we do? It's even crueler. A handful of days in Carver City and Zurielle has already lost a little of her shine. She's seen a tiny bit of what people are capable of and it's cracked her rose-tinted glasses. "You have plenty of time now."

"Do I?" She sets her glass on the table. "Five days isn't much time."

"Darling, you don't have to know all the answers by the end of the week." I should leave it at that. I know all too well what comes from letting my emotions get the better of me and grasping for things just beyond reach. Pain. Disappointment. The kind of loss that burrows down deep and leaves scars in its wake. Astounding that this girl is able to dredge up these old fears in me, but I'm old enough to see situations for what they are, rather than what I wish them to be. I take a slow breath. "If you stay, we'll figure it out. Together."

"As simple as that."

"As simple—and as complicated—as that." I reach out before I can think of all the reasons not to, and place my hand over hers. "You're not in this alone, Zurielle."

"Ursa?"

"Yes?"

She licks her lips. "My friends. Uh, the people who care about me. They call me Zuri."

"Zuri." I say it slowly, testing it out. I know Alaric calls her that, but I chose to keep the distance between us. This is a small step toward something more, a step I have to force myself to take at a measured pace. "It suits you."

Alaric returns, his blue gaze jumping from me to her and back again. "You both look incredibly serious right now."

"Nothing to worry about, lover." I slide out of the booth and hold out my hand to Zuri. "Let's have some fun." It wasn't necessarily what I had in mind when I decided to bring them to the Underworld tonight, but it's glaringly clear that it's what we all need. A release. A break from navigating treacherous waters.

I lead them toward the door back into the public and private playrooms, smiling when I recognize the Black woman leaning casually against the wall. "Allecto."

"Ursa." Her lips curve, though her gaze stays cool and professional. "Going to get into trouble tonight?"

"Of course not, darling." I smile at her. "I don't suppose tonight is the night you'll finally take me up on my offer?" I've been trying to tempt her away from Hades since I first met her—ever since Monica met her and demanded I find a way to bring Allecto onboard. It's a lost cause—she's one of Hades's Furies, one of the three women who answer directly to him and keep this place running—but I still get a perverse amount of enjoyment in trying. Allecto is the head of security at the Underworld, and anyone who can run a tight ship and keep all the powerful people here in line is someone I want on my staff. Granted, one of the very things that makes her such an asset it the very thing keeping her from ever accepting my offer. She's too loyal. It's a shame, but I enjoy ribbing her lightly about it.

"The answer's never going to change, Ursa." Allecto shakes her head. Like every other person Hades employs, she's beautiful, all dark-brown skin, long black braids, and a strong body that could kill anyone in this room in half a dozen different ways. Really, she's a gift.

"It can't hurt to keep asking. You never know when circumstances might shift."

She rolls her eyes and motions to the door. "Go play with your submissives and get out of my hair. Don't cause any trouble tonight."

"I never do." I save my troublemaking for other places. The Underworld is too valuable a hub to risk its doors being closed to me. I might enjoy irritating Hades when I get the opportunity, but I obey the rules of neutral territory just like everyone else. The benefits far outweigh any inconvenience.

I can feel Alaric and Zuri at my back, and the thrill of knowing they're both mine has me fighting not to pick up my pace. I feel...possessive. Like I want to strip them down and play with them where everyone can see, stamp my mark all over their bodies so everyone in this city knows who they belong to.

I almost veer off toward one of the empty sitting areas in the room. Almost give into that impulse. Almost.

But in the end, they aren't quite mine. Not in truth. Until we figure out the finer details, there will always be some doubt there, and while there's doubt, I won't let my impulses get the best of me. It's not safe. Not for my territory. Not for my heart.

Instead, I lead them through the halls that contain the private themed rooms. Given enough time, I'll plumb Zuri's fantasies and enact them one by one, but for now I chose a simpler route. I open the designated door and walk through, holding it so they can follow.

It amuses me entirely too much to watch the confusion flicker over Zuri's face as she surveys the room. It's set up with a small stage against one wall and three couches arranged in a half circle around it. Simple, yes, but effective. There's a wardrobe tucked back in the corner that holds a number of toys and tools to utilize, but I'll get to it later. For now, this is about recreating something I *know* Zuri enjoyed.

Something I know Alaric will enjoy just as much.

I shut the door and give them both a long look. "Your safe words."

"Hurricane." Zuri immediately drops her gaze and folds her hands in front of her.

Alaric gives me a quick grin before he lowers his eyes. "Mermaid."

I circle them slowly, letting the click of my heels on the hardwood floor increase their tension. Zuri is practically shaking already and I've barely done anything. By the time I move back to stand in front of them, Alaric's cock is a hard bulge at the front of his slacks.

"I'm in a mood, lovers." I smile. "A mood for a show."

a show.

At Ursa's command, Alaric and I move to the stage. He gives me a hand up even though it's barely two feet off the ground. I enjoy the contact, though. I enjoy the way his touch steadies me even more. Anticipation curls through me as we once again face Ursa.

She walks to the center couch and leans a hip against it, watching us closely. "You enjoyed being on stage, little Zuri. You liked being on display for the entire room of people."

It's not quite a question, so I press my lips together to keep from breaking my silence. The truth is that I *did* enjoy it. I would have enjoyed it more if I'd known the ultimate outcome, if there was no fear of who might win the bidding involved. Even with that... Yes. Enjoyed doesn't begin to cover it.

"Alaric."

"Yes, Mistress."

"I would like to see what my money won." She still sounds warm, but I've learned all too well how that kindness can shield cruelty beyond imagining. Maybe I shouldn't like it so much, the bite that comes with a kiss, but I can't help myself.

Alaric takes my hand and guides it over my head, spinning me slowly as if we're dancing. When I'm once again facing front, Ursa holds up a hand. "She's very pretty."

"Yes, Mistress."

I don't dare look at him, but there's a hunger in his tone that I can't help but respond to. I can't help but respond to *all* of this. Except... Why fight it? Why worry about my response? Ursa is fully in control of this scene, which means I don't have to be. I take a slow breath and let go of all my trepidation. I like what she does to me, what they both do to me. That's all that matters right now.

"Tiny little thing," Ursa murmurs. "Practically bird-boned. Do you think we'll break her, lover?"

He chuckles. "Only way to find out."

"All in good time." She moves to sit on the couch and crosses her legs, looking completely at ease. "Let's see the rest of her. Slowly."

He steps behind me and guides my arms up and lace my fingers at the back of my head. Then he runs his hands over the front of my body, as if trying to smooth the dress even closer to my skin. It's as if the last few days haven't happened, as if *this* is what happened after the auction.

Ursa laughs. "Now you're just teasing me. Come now, lover. You know what I want."

"Yes, Mistress." He hooks his thumbs at the top of my dress and tugs it down to my ribs, baring my breasts. "Pretty little things," Alaric murmurs. He cups them as if offering them up for her inspection. "Small and perfectly shaped." He plucks at my nipples and hisses out a breath when I moan. "Sensitive."

"Show me exactly how sensitive they are." Her voice has

gone a little raspy in a way that's so fucking sexy, I can barely stand it. "With your tongue."

It would be hot for Alaric to touch me like this, to bend back over his arm and close his mouth around my nipple. Having Ursa command us every step of the way? It's exponentially *more*. More of everything.

He licks and nibbles and sucks hard on first one nipple and then the other, until I'm shaking and whimpering and on the verge of begging one of them to touch me where my pulse pounds between my thighs. I barely manage to keep my silence, barely manage to keep up the thin veil of fantasy that I'm truly the prize they're examining.

Alaric finally straightens and guides me back to lean against his chest. "Very, very sensitive." His voice is lower than normal, nearly growling. "She tastes sweet."

"That was just a tease." Ursa re-crosses her legs. "The dress. Don't rush."

He peels the dress off my body slowly, inch by inch until I'm quivering from the sensation of cloth dragging over my sensitive skin. To my waist, over my hips, and finally down my legs, until I can feel him kneeling behind me. I carefully step out of the circle of fabric, standing there naked except for my heels.

Alaric rises and brackets my hips with his hands. "She's shaking."

"It's not fear." Ursa leans forward. "Is it, little Zuri?"

"No, Mistress." I lick my lips. "It's not fear."

She nods as if she expected nothing else and sits back. "Now the rest. Show me what I purchased."

My face flames as Alaric guides me to turn around and kneel on the cool wooden platform. He kneels next to me and nudges my knees wide. I'm still trying to find my balance when he places a broad hand on the center of my back, inexorably pushing me down until my cheek presses against the stage. The position leaves my ass in the air and with my legs spread so wide, there's no doubt that Ursa can see *everything*.

Alaric drags his hand up my spine, guiding me to arch my back a little. "There," he murmurs. "Look how pretty she is."

"You can do better than that, lover."

He skims his hands over my ass and down to pull my legs wider yet. And then he's pulling my cheeks apart and giving a low sound of appreciation. "Will you take her ass, Mistress?"

"All in good time."

That isn't a no.

I try not to tense, but I can't tell if I like the idea of her *taking my ass* or not. Especially considering the way I saw her take Alaric's. But then... the tentacle was weird, but it *felt* really, really good in my pussy. Maybe it'd feel good in my ass, too.

I close my eyes as Alaric's hands move down to my pussy and part my folds. "She's wet." He strokes a single finger through me and I don't have to look to know he's showing Ursa. "Practically dripping."

"Little Zuri likes to be put on display. She likes to be a toy for us to play with." Ursa sounds almost like she's musing, but I know her well enough now to recognize that she's already thought this out. Planned this out. "Continue."

He presses a single blunt finger into me. "She's so wet, Mistress." He pumps slowly. "Tight, too. She's clamping around my finger with every stroke."

"Give her two." She lifts her voice a little. "Zuri, you don't have permission to come. Don't disappoint me."

I press my hands flat to the stage. "Yes, Mistress." Surely I can hold out. Surely. I want a reward more than I want a punishment right now. I hiss out a breath as Alaric wedges a second finger into me. It feels good, but it's more than him penetrating me. It's that I'm in this obscene position, my pussy and ass on full display, while Alaric and Ursa talk about me like I'm a new toy for them to play with. It's like I'm less than a person but also cherished beyond measure. The conflicting feelings only make the entire situation hotter.

"Now her clit."

He withdraws his fingers and uses his other hand to urge my back to arch more. He slides his fingers up my slit and parts me farther. "Just as pretty as the rest of her."

"Mmm. That is the truth." Does she sound closer? I can't tell.

And then Ursa's mouth closes around my clit and I squeak. I think I jolt, but Alaric's hand on my back holds me in place as she explores me with her tongue. She's gone before the orgasm brewing deep inside me gets out of control. "You're right, lover. She's so incredibly sweet."

"May I?" Alaric's so hoarse, his words are barely above a whisper.

"Just a taste."

He shifts and then it's *his* mouth on my pussy. He licks me as if trying to gather up all my taste. "Fuck, Mistress. You're right. She's even sweeter here."

"Mmm." A soft sound and I know without a shadow of a doubt that they're kissing, passing my taste back and forth between them. I want to look, to see, but I don't want to disobey, either. It's agony. Sexy, titillating agony. Finally, I can't stand it any longer. I twist to look.

Ursa breaks the kiss as if she was just waiting for me to waver. "Disobedient little thing, aren't you?"

I try to go back to my former position, but it's too late. She grabs my hair, holding me in place. "Alaric, go to the wardrobe and get the vibrator. The one that's both internal and external." We both watch him obey, and when he returns, he's got a U-shaped toy in his hand that's wider on one side than the other.

Ursa guides me to turn around and sit on the edge of the stage. She takes the toy and eases it into me. I whimper and shift, trying to adjust to the foreign feeling, but she doesn't give me a chance to. She snaps her fingers at Alaric and that's when I notice that he's got a remote in his hand. He passes it over. Ursa takes my hand and moves it to hold the vibrator in place. "Do not move it. Do not come. Do you understand me?"

"Yes, Mistress," I whisper.

"If you want to watch, little Zuri. Then you'll watch." She moves back to sit on the couch and smiles at Alaric. "You've been so very good, lover. Would you like a taste?"

He's already moving, kneeling between her thighs and lifting her dress. He doesn't bother to take off her panties, merely tugs them to the side and lowers his head to her pussy.

The picture they make. I could come from watching them alone.

Ursa reclines against the couch, her legs spread, looking like nothing more than a queen on her throne. Alaric's head moves between her thighs, his hands moving up to clutch at her hips even as he moans against her.

That's when the toy inside me buzzes to life. I jolt, but there's no escaping it. It vibrates against my clit, a pulsing motion that has me biting my lip. The part inside me is moving, too, a rolling motion remarkably like a fingertip flicking against my G-spot.

I can't help it. I moan. "Oh gods."

"It's not the gods in control of your pussy right now." Ursa is a little breathless. "It's me. Your pleasure is in *my* hands."

I shift, trying to flee how good it feels. "I…" I'm gasping, and I can't look away from where she laces her free hand through Alaric's hair, lifting her hips to grind against his mouth. "I'm going to come."

Instantly, the vibrations change. It's not enough to pull me back from the edge, but it keeps me from coming. I sob out a breath. I'm not sure if this is a gift or further punishment. "Mistress, please."

"You have your command." She holds my gaze as she sets the remote down and then drops her other hand to Alaric's hair. Ursa closes her eyes and leans her head back against the couch, effectively dismissing me.

It stings.

It only makes this hotter.

"Use those clever hands of yours, lover," she murmurs.

Alaric instantly obeys, shifting enough to push two fingers into her. I can see it perfectly from where I sit, the way he spreads her, how her desire coats his fingers, the flick of his tongue against her clit even as he fucks her with his fingers.

All the while, the toy in my pussy pushes me closer to coming.

Ursa orgasms, and I lose it. I cry out, writhing even as I try to keep my eyes open because I don't want to miss a moment of this. The vibration of the toy shifts again, and now I'm sobbing because it's too much but I don't want it to stop. "Please, Mistress!"

"So disobedient." She sounds only slightly out of breath. By the time I get my eyes open, she's rearranged her dress and Alaric kneels at her feet. She touches the remote, and the vibrations finally stop. "Come here, Zuri."

Every time she says my name, it feels like an intimate caress. I carefully scoot off the stage and stagger the few feet to her. She catches my hand and reaches between my legs to ease the toy out of me. "I'm disappointed."

Against all reason, tears prick my eyes. "I'm sorry, Mistress. I tried."

"Our Alaric was putting on a good show for you and you missed the culmination of his hard work."

"Doesn't feel like work," he murmurs without looking up.

Ursa's lips twitch, and she shakes her head. "You'll have to make it up to him. Come. Sit." She tugs me into her lap. I tense for half a second, but Ursa is having none of it. She sits forward until her breasts press against my back and arranges me the way she wants me to be, my legs on either side of hers, my hands at the small of my back, pressed against her stomach. She crooks a finger at Alaric. "Up, lover."

He rises and that's when I realize where this is going. Ursa wraps a fist around his cock and uses that hold to pull him closer, until he's standing between our spread legs. "Fuck her mouth." She lowers her voice. "If this gets to be too much, tap my leg with your foot. Do you understand?"

"Yes, Mistress," I whisper. Alaric isn't small, though it's not as if I have a lot of material to compare him to. Even so, giving him a blowjob in bed when I'm on top is very different from this. From him fucking my mouth. Maybe I should be intimidated, but all I feel is a frantic buzz of antici- pation. I want this. I want everything the three of us do together.

I tilt my head back a little and part my lips.

CHAPTER 27

ALARIC

*I*f ever there was a moment that I want to snapshot and keep forever, it's this one. Ursa's hand around the base of my cock. Zuri's mouth closing around the head. The two of them so close together. For the first time since this all started, I'm completely at peace. It didn't even take Ursa beating me to get me there. The background buzz of my thoughts and guilt eases with each inch Zuri takes.

I meet Ursa's eyes and, fuck, I almost blow right then and there.

She looks happy, too. Yeah, she's got her Domme face on and her grip is unyielding even as Zuri sucks more of me into her mouth, but there's something soft in Ursa's eyes that I've never seen before. Like she's let down a layer of wall that I've been fighting to get over for so long, I'd lost all hope of it.

I reach down and cup her face. "I love you."

She raises her brows. "Zuri must be doing something right if you're talking like that."

I shake my head. "Don't do that." It's an effort to push the pleasure away, to speak through the need to move. "I mean what I say, Ursa. I love you."

She parts her lips like she's going to keep arguing but finally smiles a little. "Show me. Fuck her mouth."

I try not to let disappointment take hold. Of course she didn't say it back. She might be quickly becoming my world, she might care about me enough to let me into her home, but I'm still the guy she fucked on the side while living her life alone. It'll take time to let me in.

And Zuri?

I look down at her big brown eyes and, fuck it, I'm already putting all my shit out there. No reason to stop now. "I love you, too, Zuri." I thrust a little when she starts to retreat. "Don't argue with me. Just suck my cock like Ursa told you to."

She glares a little, but there's no heat behind it. Especially when Ursa gathers her long dark-red hair back into her fist and holds her immobile. "Now, Alaric."

I start slow. Slow enough that Ursa glares, a silent command to stop dicking around. I stroke Zuri's jaw, urging her to relax into it, and then I pick up my pace, sliding into her mouth nearly far enough to gag her before retreating. Over and over again. It feels so fucking good, too fucking good for me to last even with all my training. No one undoes me like these two women. "Mistress, I'm close."

"Then stop holding back." Ursa leans forward, bringing Zuri with her, urging her down my cock until she gags. She lets the other woman retreat, pulling her off my cock. "You can take it, can't you, love?"

Zuri licks her lips, tears streaming from her eyes. "Yes, Mistress." She sounds halfway to subspace and we've barely done anything yet.

"Now."

I stop holding back.

It's rough and dirty and Zuri is moaning and crying and, fuck, it's so hot that I'm fighting not to release. I almost manage to hold out. Until I look down and realize that Ursa has her fingers in Zuri's pussy. The sight of it shoves me over the edge. I come hard, hard enough to buckle my knees, and Zuri drinks down every bit. And then she keeps sucking my cock, interspersed with little licks that have me moaning and easing back. "Jesus."

"He has nothing to do with it." Ursa pulls me down onto the couch next to them, though she doesn't stop playing with Zuri's pussy. "Lean back, love."

I settle in next to them and watch Zuri relax back against Ursa, submitting to everything she's doing to her without question. This is how it could be with us. How it *will* be. The rest of it will figure itself out. We have the foundation.

It might be a foundation built on a lot of bullshit, but the bones are good. It wouldn't be this easy for the three of us to be together if that weren't the case. Even as the effects of my orgasm fade, the feeling in my chest only gets stronger. Ursa will say that my declaration was because Zuri had her mouth around my cock, but it's not the truth.

I love them.

I don't give a shit about timelines or what's reasonable or all the other things Ursa will try to bring up to prove that I don't really feel what I feel. It doesn't change the truth. They wouldn't twist me up the way they do in their own individual ways if I didn't love them. Love is messy and beautiful and claws through me harsher than hate ever has. Infatuation isn't anywhere near as intense, no matter what it feels like in the first throes of it. This is love. I *know* this is love.

Ursa kisses Zuri's neck. "Come, love. You earned it this time."

I watch as she winds Zuri tighter and tighter, until her expression morphs into a bliss that looks almost like pain and she shudders. Ursa angles her back and kisses her. Despite my coming recently, the sight has my cock hardening again. Fuck, but they're beautiful. So different, and so flawless in their own ways.

Ursa breaks the kiss and looks at me. "Sometime soon, I would like to put on a show in here." Her lips curve. "You and Zuri on that stage."

"Yes."

Zuri shivers. "I think I'd like that."

"I know you would." Ursa gives her another kiss and breaks it reluctantly. "I had further plans tonight, but…" She seems to steel herself. "I would like us to go home and sleep together."

Zuri goes perfectly still, her eyes widening. Even in such a short time, she understands how rare this is. Since she doesn't seem eager to break the ensuing silence, I do it for us. "In your bed."

"In my bed."

I'm already pushing to my feet. "Let's go."

Ursa blinks at me, looking surprised. "You're awfully eager, lover."

"No shit, I'm eager. I want to sleep next to you. Both of you." I love fucking them. *Love* it. But Ursa is offering an intimacy I've been denied until now. I'm not going to give her a chance to change her mind.

I help Zuri climb to her feet. She still looks a little dazed. We guide her back into her dress and she submits, though it's obvious from her face that she's thinking really hard about something. I want to press her. Both Ursa and I have made huge strides tonight, and I want Zuri there with us. That's not how shit works, though. She'll either bridge the last distance between us when she's ready...or she won't. Either way, neither Ursa nor I have any real control over what her final decision is.

We leave the room and head back down the hallway to the public playroom. Ursa slows and stops, and I follow her gaze to the public scene going on right now. I instantly recognize Gaeton and Isabelle Belmonte, youngest of the Belmonte sisters who rule to territory bordering Ursa's to the north-west. Gaeton has Isabelle bent over one of the couches, and her face is in the lap of their third, Beast, sucking his cock like her life depends on it.

"Perhaps we'll stay to watch the rest of the show."

I snort. "You just want to fuck with them when they look up and see you there."

Her smile is downright wicked. "Power plays, lover. They're not just for the bedroom. Come." She strides to an empty couch facing where the three are doing their public scene and sinks onto it, motioning for me to sit next to her and then guiding Zuri onto my lap. "You've both pleased me tonight. You may play until they're finished. Don't forget the condom."

I look at Zuri. "Do you want to watch?"

She kisses me. Which is an answer itself. I shift down to lie across the couch with my head resting in Ursa's lap. She raises her eyebrows at me, and I grin. "It's a better angle."

Ursa rolls her eyes and leans back against the couch, turning her attention to the scene playing out in the center of the room. But she sifts her fingers through my hair, lightly dragging her nails over my scalp.

I dig out a condom from my pocket, and Zuri rushes to free my cock, her expression intent. We've already teased enough tonight; I want inside her as much as she seems to want me there. I roll the condom on and she barely lets me get my hand out of the way before she sinks onto my cock, working herself down my length until it's sheathed to the hilt. She braces her hands on my chest and starts to move, rolling her hips as she rides me.

I've played publicly in the Underworld more times than I can count, usually submitting to one Dominant or another. I've been beaten, tormented, fucked until I'm damn near unconscious, and I've loved every second of it.

None of it compares to this moment. Of Zuri riding my cock with her dress bunched up around her waist, with me on my back and mostly dressed, with Ursa commanding the entire experience without saying a word.

Without taking her eyes off the other scene, Ursa reaches over and presses her free hand to Zuri's lower stomach, circling her clit with her thumb. Zuri moans and picks up her pace.

"Slow," Ursa murmurs. "Enjoy yourself, love. Gaeton can last a very long time; no need to rush."

I turn my head enough to see them. Isabelle is relatively new to the club, but she's jumped in like a fish to water. Both Gaeton and Beast have been regulars for a long time. I've scened with both of them, though Gaeton more than Beast. And yeah, Gaeton can last for hours when he's feeling particularly motivated. He drives into Isabelle from behind, and I can see how red her ass is even from this angle. He squeezes her cheeks with every thrust, and she's writhing and moaning around Beast's cock.

It's hot as fuck.

Even hotter to be watching while engaged in our own little scene.

Zuri obeys Ursa's command, slowing down until she's barely moving. The little circles she makes with her hips have me gripping her, though even I can't tell if I'm hanging on or trying to guide her movements. It doesn't matter. Ursa has things well in hand.

"We have an audience." She speaks softly, just for us, even as she keeps stroking Zuri's clit. "She doesn't fuck you like a little virgin, does she, Alaric?" She keeps speaking, obviously not requiring a response. "No, she fucks you like a little slut."

There's something about us having sex, my head on Ursa's thigh, while she plays with Zuri's clit, all without looking at either of us… It threatens to incinerate me. It's like we're an afterthought, like us rutting right here, the wet sound of Zuri's pussy taking my cock doesn't matter in the least. Like it's barely worth noting.

Because we're hers.

I grit my teeth. "I'm close."

"No, you're not." She tugs on my hair and finally looks down at me. "Zuri will ride you until she's finished and you will not come until I give permission. Do you understand?"

I stare up into her face, enraptured. "Yes, Mistress."

"You say 'yes, Mistress' and then you disappoint me. Don't do it tonight." She gives my hair a sharper tug. "Hold still, Alaric. Let her use you. That's what you need, isn't it? You love playing the toy just as much as our Zuri does. Little sluts, both of you. So ready to fuck where anyone can watch." Ursa sighs as if she's losing her patience. "Might as well make it worth everyone's while." She reaches up and yanks Zuri's dress down, baring her breasts, and then goes back to playing with her clit.

Zuri slows down even further, the little tease. She arches back and braces her hands on my thighs, putting her full body on display. I knew she was an exhibitionist, but this is just further confirmation. She gets off on knowing people are watching, on knowing that they *want* her.

"That was an invitation, lover. You know how she loves her breasts played with."

I skate my hands up Zuri's sides and cup her breasts. I'm rougher than I mean to be, but Zuri grinds down on my cock and moans loudly. A reminder that our girl appreciates a little hurt. I pinch her nipples, testing her. Harder and harder, as her strokes become more frantic, her head tilting back and her long fall of hair moving over my thighs.

Ursa pinches Zuri's clit and then she's coming, loud and messy enough to turn heads. Ursa shifts her hand down to grip my cock around the base. "Now you may come."

I drive up, fucking Ursa's hand, fucking Zuri's pussy. Again and again, until I can't hold back any longer. I come, pulling Zuri down onto my length, onto Ursa's hand, as I empty myself into the condom.

I drag Zuri down for a kiss, losing myself in the taste of her. She finally eases off my cock and rises up to kiss Ursa, too. Then she grimaces. "I'd like to clean up before we leave."

"Of course." Ursa motions to the doorway on the other side of the room. "There are bathrooms and the like through there. Don't tarry."

"Yes, Mistress." She presses another quick kiss to Ursa's lips and then climbs off me.

I get up long enough to dispose of the condom and then rejoin Ursa on the couch. She has a pensive look on her face. I take her hand and lace my fingers through hers. "I meant it."

"Alaric—"

"I meant it," I repeat. "I *mean* it. I love you."

She exhales slowly, studying my face. "I...love you, too." The words sound jagged, as if she's forced them out. "It's not easy admitting it, but it's the truth."

"I know." It's there in every touch, in the way she takes care of me, in her offer to share her bed tonight and in the future. I lean in and kiss her. "I'm keeping you, Ursa. I'm yours and you're mine. No matter what else happens."

When I lean back, she has a vulnerable look in her dark eyes. For the first time since I've met her she doesn't immediately mask it with a careful smile. She just lets me witness it. Ursa cups my face in her hands. "You're a gift, Alaric. No matter what else you believe about yourself, believe that. You're priceless to me."

In that moment, I believe her.

Completely. Truly. Without reservation.

CHAPTER 28

ZURIELLE

*I*t doesn't take long to right myself and clean up in the bathroom. I linger a few extra minutes, trying to catch my breath. I can appreciate how even the *bathrooms* in the Underworld are all understated elegance and somehow sexy. I walk through the door and nearly run over Hercules. "Oh. I'm sorry. I didn't see you."

Hercules glances in the direction of the public playroom and then looks at me. "Come with me." He takes my arm and turns me in the opposite direction, moving quickly enough that I have to skip every few steps to keep up.

"Hercules, what are you doing?" I try to get a good look at his face. He doesn't seem angry or scary at all; just really intent. But that doesn't change the fact that he's practically dragging me in the opposite direction of where I want to go. "Let me go."

"There's someone you need to see." He stops at a door at the end of the hallway and looks up. I follow his gaze to a security camera tucked up in the shadows of the corner. The lock on the door flashes green and he pushes through, taking me with him.

I hadn't been in this part of the Underworld when I was here before, but I saw behind the scenes enough to recognize an employee hallway. It's plainer than the public hallways, with dark-gray walls and equally dark-gray tiled floors. Hercules turns us to the right, and I dig in my heels and say the one thing guaranteed to make him listen. "Hercules, you're scaring me."

He slows and huffs out a breath. "I'm sorry. I just didn't think I'd get a chance to get you alone and then there you were, so I had to hurry before someone saw us."

He gives me another tug, but I refuse to budge. "That is not an explanation."

Hercules moves closer and lowers his voice. "Your sisters are here."

Of all the words I expected to come out of his mouth, *those* didn't number among them. I blink. "What?"

"Zuri, Hades is going to kick my ass for this. Can we please talk while we move?"

I finally nod. If this were anyone else, I'd expect a trap of some sort, but Hercules has no more love for Olympus than I do. And he's so *good*. Good enough that my father never worried about us spending time together when we were teenagers, back before Hercules was driven out of the city by Zeus. I shiver and try to keep pace with his longer strides.

He leads me to a set of stairs that go down to a floor I *do* recognize. The employee suites, which is where I stayed the night when I was here earlier this week. Sure enough, Hercules stops in front of the very door I was in before and opens it, all but shoving me in.

I narrow my eyes. "How much trouble are you going to get in because of this?"

He smiles so suddenly, I almost back up a step. "Oh, Hades will flog the shit out of me, or maybe have Meg do it. I can handle it." If the look on his face is any indication, he's anticipating it. A week ago, I'd be worried for him, but I've seen firsthand how pain can ignite into pleasure for some people. For me, even, though I'm still dipping my toes into that particular pool.

I'm stalling. I know I'm stalling.

I take a deep breath and turn to face the room. Not all my sisters have come, which is a relief of sorts. It's only Aya and Jael, the two sisters closest in age to me. Looking at them, someone not familiar with our family might not think they were even related. Aya is like me in that she favors our mother. Short, petite, straight dark hair, and warm beige skin. Jael is very much our father's daughter. She's tall with an athletic build, wavy red hair, and the kind of pale skin that immediately burns on contact with sunlight. They wear identical expressions of worry, though.

Hercules releases my hand. "You don't have long, but I'll give you some privacy." He steps out the door and closes it softly behind him.

Jael rushes forward. "Thank the gods you're here." She grabs my shoulders and eyes me. "You're a mess."

"*Jael.*" Aya smacks her hands. "Stop manhandling her." She turns to me. "Zuri, we're here to save you."

I blink. "Save me?"

"I don't know what the Sea Witch said to trick you, and it doesn't matter."

"Father is furious, but he'll get over it once you're home safely. He's just worried about you." Jael clears her throat. "He's threatening to bring his people to Carver City and rescue you himself."

"We thought this would be a better option." Aya takes my hands. "Are you okay?"

Am I okay?

Such a simple question, with no simple answers. I look from Aya to Jael. "What are you doing *here?*"

Aya worries her bottom lip. "Hercules reached out. He knew we'd want to know you were safe."

I'm going to throttle him when I get a chance. I had every intention of talking to my sisters. *After*. After the auction, after this week, after I figured out what I'm doing with my life. They want answers, and I have none for them. Not yet. "So you came for me."

"You're our sister. Of course we came for you." Jael glances at the door. "He said we don't have much time. Come home with us. Once you're back in Olympus, there's nothing the Sea Witch can do. Father won't let her."

I shake my head, trying to clear my circling thoughts. "You said Father is organizing his men?"

"Yes." Aya's watching me with dark eyes so much like my own. "Zuri, what's going on here? We thought you were captive, but you don't *look* like a captive." She hesitates. "You look…happy."

Because I am happy.

The thought, so mundane on its surface, is anything but. I'm *happy* here in Carver City with Ursa and Alaric. We still have things to work out, but that doesn't change the fact that they make me happy. That I care about them.

That I…love them.

Alaric shocked me when he said the same. I wanted to brush it off, to ignore it, to not look too closely at the way my feelings mirror his. But standing here with my sisters, there's no hiding from the truth. I've gone and given my fool heart to both Ursa and Alaric.

And now my father will bring his men and try to take me back.

Even though he attempted to keep us from his business, Father always maintained security at the house and any time we ventured outside those four walls. I'd have to be particularly naive not to recognize those people as the killers they are, especially in hindsight. It's there in the eyes, an emptiness that scared me even though Father acted like they were part of the scenery.

If they come for me, they'll hurt Ursa. They might even kill her. And now that Father knows Alaric played a part in this, they'll do the same to him.

Ursa is a leader of a territory. She has security and scary people that answer to her, too, but the only one I've seen is her head of security, Monica. I can only make decisions based on the facts I know.

Ursa and Alaric are in danger.

My father isn't going to let me go; he's going to try to take me back.

My sisters offer an opportunity to dodge the coming conflict.

I hold up my hands. "Give me a second. I need to think."

Jael shifts from foot to foot. "You don't have long. Hercules said he could get us ten minutes and we're coming up on that fast."

"Give her a second," Aya murmurs.

If I stay, Father will come. If I go, I'll hurt Ursa and Alaric, possibly beyond measure. I'll hurt *myself* beyond measure. I don't want to leave them, don't want to walk away from what might be my chance at a real happily ever after. Not one that I imagined while wearing my rose-tinted glasses, falling for the fantasy of someone instead of the real person. I *see* them. I love them. I want a life with them.

If I leave, they'll still be alive.

That's worth more than everything. More than happiness. More than love.

My throat feels tight and hot, but I manage to say, "Okay." I try to think. "Just give me a second to—"

"There's no time." Jael starts for the door. "If she knows you're leaving, she'll try to stop you."

She might not, but Alaric certainly will. The thought of walking away without saying anything is a horrible one, but what's the alternative? Letting them convince me to stay and one of them being hurt because I didn't move quickly enough to hold off my father?

No, Jael's right. We have to go now.

Aya shakes her head, still watching me closely. "Are you okay? You don't look happy to be going home."

Because I'm not, though I'm not sure I can explain it to either of my sisters. We've been taught to hate and fear the Sea Witch our entire lives. How can they understand that I've fallen in love with her? "I have to stop father."

Aya frowns. "If you're sure…"

"She's sure. Let's go." Jael grabs both our arms and muscles us toward the door. "I don't know about you, but I'd rather get out of here before our window closes and the Sea Witch has three captives instead of one."

"This is neutral territory." I let her tow me to the door and open it. "Hades rules here."

"Yeah, well, I don't expect *he'll* be happy to lose out on his percentage of your auction fee." Jael glances at me, taking in my shocked look. "Yeah, we know about the auction." Her determination flickers, replaced by guilt. "I'm sorry we weren't there to save you from it."

"It was my choice."

But she's not listening. She opens the door and pulls us out into the hallway. Hercules is waiting for us there and though he's perfectly still, there's an impatient tension in his body. He looks at us. "Well?"

"She's coming with us."

Just like that, I am back to being the little sister. The follower. The innocent one in need of protecting. The one incapable of standing on her own. I dig in my heels for a moment. "Promise me that no matter what happens to the money, Alaric's debt remains paid."

He hesitates but finally nods. "I promise I'll make sure he stays out of Hades's debt."

"Okay." There's nothing left to do but go. I let my sisters all but drag me from the building and down to the street where a nondescript gray sedan waits for us, it feels like they're shoving me back into a skin that no longer fits. One I've outgrown at some point in the last week.

Half a dozen times, I open my mouth to tell them no, that I've changed my mind, and half a dozen times, I stay silent. What price can I put on Ursa and Alaric's lives? I can't. The cost of losing them is too high.

It doesn't matter if it feels like my heart is shattering into half a million pieces. They're alive. I don't have to live in a world where they no longer exist, even if they're no longer in *my* world.

Jael slouches back against the seat and exhales. "That went so much smoother than I expected." She drums her fingers on her thigh. "Though I'll admit I'm kind of disappointed we didn't get a look at her."

"Jael, hush." Aya takes my hands. "Zuri, you look sick. Are you okay?"

I'm not okay. I'm not sure I'll ever be okay again. I should try to smile, should fall back into my practiced way of ensuring my sisters don't worry about me, but the mask feels cracked beyond repair. But how can I tell them the truth? I swallow hard. "I'll be fine." Even that lukewarm statement feels like a lie.

Aya finally nods and turns to Jael. "We have to be careful sneaking back in. Father's going to be furious."

"He'll get over it." Jael sounds so unconcerned, but then she's always been fearless. Even with him. Especially with him. She takes after Father in more than just her features and hair color. She's got his temper and brashness, too. It means they clash more than he does with any of my other sisters, but somehow she gets away with whatever she wants to despite that. Or maybe because of it.

Aya lowers her voice. "We have to talk about how to broach the subject of Zuri being back."

At this, I stir. "I'll take care of it."

"Zuri—"

"I said I'll take care of it." I look at my sisters. "I chose to leave. I'll talk to Father myself when we get back." It only gives me a couple hours to figure out what to say, how to handle the coming confrontation, but it will have to be enough.

We pass beyond the Carver City limits, and I close my eyes, the last of my shock fading away. Anger takes its place, a deeper, darker rage than I've ever known. He couldn't just let me go. Couldn't let the Sea Witch come out on top. No, he had to be right, to win, to regain his possession. Even if I find a way through this, it's too late now.

Ursa and Alaric will never forgive me for making the choice I have tonight.

I've lost them.

CHAPTER 29

URSA

*Z*uri's been gone longer than she should be. I try to be patient, because as tame as tonight has been compared to some of the things we've done, it's still a significant jump forward in our relationship. I'm feeling a little unsteady, so it stands to reason that she and Alaric are as well. I suspect our progress forward will be all fits and starts, but it *will* be progress.

Gaeton and Beast finish with Isabelle a short time later, and that's about as long as I'm willing to wait. I nudge Alaric up. "Let's go find our little Zuri."

He frowns. "She couldn't have gotten lost. It's a straight shot from here to the bathroom."

"Maybe she needed some time to collect herself." We've thrown a lot at her in a short time, and Alaric compounded it tonight with his declaration.

He loves me.

I admitted that I love him, too.

And the sky didn't fall. We're still standing, still looking at a future that's hopeful and filled with something just for me. Some*one* just for me. Two someones.

I find I'm smiling as we make our way to the hall that houses the bathrooms. I give Alaric's hand a squeeze. "Go get her."

He returns a few seconds later, a frown pulling his brows together. "The bathroom's empty."

Alarm bells peal through my mind. Sometimes it's easy to forget that we're rubbing shoulders with enemies in the Underworld because it's neutral territory, but really it's only the threat of Hades that stops people from making moves here. If someone took her…

She could be hurt right now. Scared. She could be fucking *dead*.

I shove the thoughts down. There's no reason to worry. Maybe those things would be a risk somewhere else, but not here. This is the Underworld. Hades rules here with an iron fist. There is absolutely no chance that she's come to harm within this building, no matter what my fears are clamoring.

But I still gather up my dress so I can take longer strides as I head back into the public playroom. Zuri couldn't have come back this way without us seeing her. Even knowing that, I pause and survey the room. It's crowded enough that it takes a few moments to confirm what I already know. She's not here.

I glance at Alaric. His worry comes off him in waves, but I can't reassure him because I don't know for sure that it's not warranted. Hades rarely spends time on the floor these days, preferring to let his partners and employees run the night to night operations. "It will be quicker to figure out where she is if we have access to the security cameras." Something I can't demand on my own, no matter my status. I have to request it, and nicely, or Hades will deny me out of spite. Though he's gone a little soft in his honeymoon stage with Hercules. He might simply help. I can't bargain Zuri's potential safety on it, though. Better to play this softer.

I lead the way out of the room. Thankfully, Allecto is still on duty. I pause. "Has Zuri come this way?"

Allecto shakes her head. "No. I haven't seen her."

I suspected as much—she'd have to have come through the public playroom to get through this door—but it bears asking all the same. I take a deep breath, trying to smother the flutter of panic in my stomach. "I seem to have misplaced my submissive."

She pushes off the wall, the slouch disappearing from her posture. "Give me two minutes."

It's two minutes longer than I'd like, but I nod. This isn't my territory. I have to take my lead from Hades's people.

Alaric is practically vibrating at my side as we watch Allecto pull out her phone and type out something. He turns to me. "Something's wrong."

Something is definitely wrong, but I can't help trying to comfort him. To comfort myself. "We don't know that."

"Yes, we fucking do."

Allecto looks up. "Hades will meet you in his office. You know the way."

"Thank you." I turn and stride through the lounge, not caring that I am moving too fast, that I'm giving myself away. Alaric's right. Something *is* wrong.

I have to stop outside Hades's office and collect myself. No matter how rattled I am right now, I cannot let my emotions get the better of me. He is another territory leader and appearances are everything. I take a slow breath, all too aware of Alaric's impatience. "Okay."

He opens the door and moves aside to let me precede him into the room. Hades leans against his desk instead of occupying his customary position behind it, which might be enough to give me pause if I hadn't already muscled all my messy feelings down deep. "Where is Zurielle?"

Hades crosses his arms over his chest and waits for Alaric to close the door. "I am formally apologizing."

Oh no. No, no, no, no. I keep my spine straight through sheer force of will. "You're going to have to explain what you're apologizing *for* first."

He motions at the chairs in front of him. "Sit."

"I don't think I will."

Hades sighs. "Zurielle is gone."

For one horrific moment, I think he means she's dead. "*What?*" I've never seen Hades look so uncomfortable, but I can't bring myself to enjoy the experience; not when he's dragging this out. I clench my fists. "Where the hell is she, Hades?"

At last he shakes his head. "Her sisters came for her. I was not informed of this fact, and Hercules took it upon himself to spirit her out of the building before anyone knew it was happening." He lifts his head and stares me straight in the eyes. "I promise you that punishment will be delivered accordingly, but under no circumstances will I hand him over."

The words are all in the correct order, but they barely penetrate. "I…" Alaric moves up and takes my hand. He's still behind me, offering silent support even though I can feel him shaking. I clear my throat. "She still had several days left on her contract."

"I am aware." Another sigh. "Of course, all the money will be returned to you." He flicks a glance at Alaric. "I'm willing to lift the prohibition for a Carver City resident paying the balance of his debt since Zurielle obviously intended for a portion of the money to be paid there."

"I don't want it. Pay off Alaric's debt and ensure she gets the rest." The words are out before I can think them through, but thinking is something that's incredibly difficult right now. Zuri *left*. She wasn't taken. Hercules might have "spirited her out" but he's too much a puppy dog to abduct her. No, she chose this.

She chose to leave us.

Every breath feels like knives in my lungs, but my voice is remarkably normal when I find it. "She pleased me well. See that she gets her money."

Hades lifts his brows, but finally nods. "As for Hercules—"

"I trust you to take care of it." I have to get out of here. I can feel my composure cracking. I can't be in the Underworld when I lose control. I manage a smile. "If that's all?"

He's watching me so closely, I know I'm not convincing him, but Hades finally nods. "As I said, you have my utmost apologies. This happened under my watch and it shouldn't have."

"You're right. It shouldn't have. I expect recompense beyond you playing with your boyfriend." I turn and stalk out the door, every step making the pain in my chest spike higher.

I don't remember what happens next. I should remember. I am the one in control, the one that my people lean on. I can't afford to buckle, no matter how much it hurts to know that someone I care about deeply left me.

It seems like one moment we're in the entranceway to the Underworld and the next we're back at my apartment. Alaric leads me through the door, keeping a firm hold on my hand. I stare down at our interlaced fingers. "You should go, too."

He stops short and looks at me. "What?"

I try to stifle the words, try to keep control, but I can't seem to stop myself. "You love her. She'll have you without me in the picture. You should go. Be happy. Have babies and the white picket fence you won't admit you want."

Alaric takes my shoulder, gripping me nearly hard enough to hurt. "Ursa."

"What?"

"Shut the fuck up."

I blink at him. "What did you just say to me?"

"You heard me." He glares down at me. "You don't think that I'm hurting because she left? I fucking am. But Zuri made her choice, and I made mine the second I fell in love with you. *This* is the life I want, and hell yes, I want her in it, but I want you. Full stop. With or without her in it, I want a life with you."

To my horror, my lower lip quivers. "I wanted her with us."

His expression softens. "I know. I did, too." Slowly, as if he's expecting me to reject him, Alaric pulls me to his chest and wraps his arms around me. "But we don't know for sure that she left of her own will. We could—"

"No." I speak against his chest. I can't quite bring myself to lift my head. "No. If she was taken, Hades wouldn't apologize like he did. He would have mobilized his people to get her back in order to preserve his reputation."

Alaric is so tense, he might as well be made of stone. "You're right. I fucking hate that you're right."

"She left." It hurts to say the words. I fight to be so hard, so untouchable, and this slip of a girl knocked me astray in the course of a few days. I've seen it happen to others, of course, but I never thought I'd be struck down by something as mundane as love. "We will respect her choice."

"But—"

"No." I finally lift my head. "No, Alaric. She made her choice, and we will respect it."

He holds me tighter. "What about your revenge?"

Funny, but I hadn't even thought about my revenge until now. I wanted to make Triton twist and squirm and feel even a portion of the agony he put me through. It all feels so fucking hollow right now. "I don't know." I reach up and cup his face. "I'm sorry. I should be strong for you and—"

"No." He pulls me closer yet, holding me as if he's afraid I might shatter into a million pieces if he lets go. I'm not sure he's wrong. "No," Alaric repeats. "You've been my rock for as long as I've known you. You don't have to be strong right now. I can be strong for both of us."

I don't know how to let go, but I don't seem to have a choice right now. "I just met her. I shouldn't be this twisted up over a near-stranger."

"Zuri has a way of getting beneath a person's skin." His smile holds no joy. "Let's go to bed. Maybe things will look different in the morning."

They won't, though. When the sun rises, the facts will remain the same. Zuri chose to walk away before the contract was up rather than be with us another minute. I thought she was truly considering a future with us, but obviously something changed. Or perhaps I never had a good read on her to begin with. I don't know. I won't find any answers tonight, though.

It feels strange to get ready for bed with Alaric beside me. To brush our teeth and undress. To wrap my hair and climb into bed with another person. I lie there, hurting and raw and unable to vocalize what I need. Somehow, he knows.

Alaric tucks me against his chest and wraps his arms around me. He holds me close, using his body to brace mine. "I have you, Ursa. I love you."

For the first time in as long as I can remember, my walls crumble away to dust. The first tear catches me by surprise, but more quickly follow. I don't say a word. I don't think I can.

Through it all, Alaric holds me and strokes my back with a hand. He seems to know that I can't take any verbal reassurance right now, that I'm already well past my comfort zone with showing him this breakdown. He just...holds me.

255

Just weathers the storm of my emotions even though he's in the midst of his own hurt.

He loves her, too.

I give a weak, wet laugh. "I love her."

"I know," he murmurs against my temple. "I know."

We stay like that for a long time, sharing a kind of comfort that has nothing to do with sex. The world still hasn't steadied when my tears finally dry, a hollow feeling taking up residence in my chest. If the circumstances were any different, I would take my people and go after Zuri and bring her back. I would fight Triton for her. I would fight the entire world for her.

If not for the fact that Zuri made the choice to walk away.

I love her enough to respect that choice, to not chase after her and try to influence it.

But, gods, it hurts so much to stand back and let her flee the life we could have had.

CHAPTER 30

ZURIELLE

I don't sleep.

I can't stop thinking about how Ursa and Alaric must have felt when they realized I was gone, how much I hurt them. If I could have left a note... But doing anything except walking away was just asking for Ursa and Alaric to try and follow. To put themselves in danger for me. I couldn't risk it. I need them safe, and this was the only way to guarantee it.

I pace around my room. It's been mine since birth. It never felt so claustrophobic as it does now. The walls are too close, the weight of my father's will pressing down on me despite not having seen him yet. My sisters tried to cluster when we arrived back in Olympus, but I can't deal with them on top of my own guilt.

My resolve, on the other hand, remains strong. I will do anything to save those I love. Anything.

Another circle paced around the room does nothing to quell the restless feeling in my chest. The sun has long since risen. Father will have already eaten breakfast and convened with his head of security to go over the plan for the day. He'll know I'm back. The fact that he hasn't summoned me to him is a power play, a punishment.

I'm tired of waiting on the whims of others.

I dress carefully, pulling out a pair of tailored slacks and a green blouse. Clothing is as intentional as anything, and these are items that I've worn maybe once or twice, preferring dresses. There's nothing wrong with dresses, but I need every weapon in my arsenal for what comes next. I style my hair into a sleek ponytail and apply my makeup with a stronger hand than I normally would. When I pick my lipstick, it's a bright red that makes me think of Ursa.

The thought brings a pang in my chest. What must she think of me now? No doubt that I betrayed her, that I left with no intention of returning. If things work out like I hope and I'm able to travel back to Carver City... Will she even have me? She's a woman with many walls and just as many spikes, though they're clothed in sweetness. It took a lot for her to open up to me, to let me in, and she'll see this as a betrayal of the highest order.

And Alaric? He finally showed me his true self, told me he loved me, and I immediately turned around and disappeared back to Olympus. Impossible to see that as anything other than a slap in the face, especially considering they're unlikely to know what my sisters said to me. He won't see this as me trying to protect them. No, he'll view this as much of a betrayal as Ursa will.

I close my eyes and focus on steadying my breathing. Even if neither of them ever forgives me, they'll be safe from my father.

But my time of going with the flow in order not to make waves is over.

I open my eyes and place my mother's necklace around my neck. Its heavy weight feels like the last bit of armor sliding into place. I don't know what she'd think of this entire situation, but I feel stronger just wearing it.

I take one last fortifying breath and stride out of my room, my heels clicking on the tile floors. As expected, I find my father in his office; another fifteen minutes and I'd have missed him as he headed out to the shipyards.

He looks older than the last time I saw him, which seems absurd. It's been a little more than a week. People don't age so quickly. But I could swear there's more silver in his red hair and more lines around his gray eyes. He's a large man, nearly as tall as me even while sitting down, and this is the first time in my life that I've really acknowledged how strength hasn't only been used to protect our family.

It's been used to hurt people.

It's been used to keep me and my sisters caged. To control us.

I plant my feet and try to steel my spine. This won't be easy. "Father."

He doesn't look up from his computer. "I am not ready to see your traitorous face, Zurielle."

I embrace the flare of anger. It gives me the strength to ignore the anger in his voice and shut the door. "I don't care what you want."

"You made the abundantly clear when you ran off to Carver City and fucked my enemies." He sits back and levels a look at me. Faced with the same expression, a younger me would have fled the room until he calmed down. A *cowardly* me. My father looks me over, something brittle in his gaze. "I'll admit I didn't expect to see you again whole. The Sea Witch doesn't often leave her victims so intact."

"She has a name." I swallow hard. "And I'm not Ursa's victim."

"How would you know? She's manipulative and vindictive." He sighs and shakes his head. "You're an innocent, Zurielle. She had no business laying hands on you."

I was prepared for his anger. I was not prepared for him to try to shove me right back into my old self the same way my sisters did. I reach up and grip my necklace, letting the edges of the jewels press hard against my palm. I'm so angry, it leaves me breathless. "She did a whole lot more than lay hands on me."

His jaw tightens. "That's enough."

"No, it's not." I glare. "When are you going to admit that I am more than capable of thinking for myself?"

"When you prove that you can make decisions like a fucking adult!" He slams his hands on the desk and shoots to his feet. "I have driven myself crazy with worry about you, and you acted like a selfish little brat."

"You *lied* to me." I take a step forward, refusing to back down in the face of his anger. "You have hurt just as many people as she has. Don't act like it's not the truth."

"Anything I've done, I've done for this family."

I laugh. "That's rich. It's noble when you do it, but when she does it, it's evil. You keep pretending like she betrayed you, but *you* are the one who drove her out of Olympus so you could play second-in-command to Poseidon without competition. You are a hypocrite."

His face darkens to a deep red color. "Did you come home to lob insults at me? How mature. If you're going to act like a child, you can go to your fucking room like a child."

He's not going to listen to me. He's acting like he has every other time one of us has done something he doesn't like. My father becomes a rage-filled steamroller and annihilates any form of resistance. The impulse to retreat nearly sends me fleeing the room. I don't want to do this. I don't want to fight, to spit these hateful words at each other.

But if I don't stand up to him now, I'll never get a chance to do it again.

"No." I take a breath.

"What the hell did you just say to me?"

"No," I repeat. "I am not a child. I am not a rebellious teenager. I'm sure as hell not a princess locked in a tower. You are my father, but I'm no longer accepting you as my jailer."

He laughs, harsh and cruel. "Now I know she's put words in your mouth. I'm not your jailer. I'm your father. I only want what's best for you, and if you can't see that, you're not ready to have this conversation."

It would be so easy to slip back into that old skin, to stop fighting. I have twenty-three years of learned behavior, all that experience clamoring for me to stop arguing and leave the room until he's less angry. Instead, I plant my feet and straighten my spine. "I am an adult and you keep me locked up in this house, unable to go anywhere without an armed guard, unable to talk to anyone who isn't approved by you. You keep me from getting a job, from having access to my own money. From *everything*. Tell me what that is if not a jailer?"

"I—"

But I'm not interested in whatever he's about to yell at me. I keep going. "I only came home in order to tell you that I'm done. You have to let me go."

He blinks. "What?"

"You have to let me go," I repeat. "Do you think that I've learned nothing from you? Do you really think that I'm so much of a fool that I don't know my own heart?"

He leans back a little. "What are you saying?"

"I'm saying that I'm moving out." I measure each word carefully, all too aware that rushing through this will give him further ammunition not to take me seriously. To say that

I'm too emotional to be rational right now. "I am starting my own life and making my own decisions while doing it." I watch him closely. "I would like you to be a part of it, but if you can't support me, then you won't be welcome in my new home."

"Your new home," he echoes. Father sinks back into his seat, all the red rushing from his face and leaving him pale. "You're going back to her."

"You will stop any plans to take your people to Carver City."

"Or what?"

I hoped it wouldn't come to this, but I'll do what I have to. I can't afford to waver right now. I only have one chance to make this stick, to protect the people I love and ensure my freedom. "Or I'll tell Poseidon that you're utilizing his resources to attack another city and potentially drag all of Olympus into a war. Because of your pride. Because you don't trust your daughter to make her own way."

He pauses for a long moment, and finally says, "What makes you think he'll care?"

"I'm sure he can do basic math. We have a line of supplies that go straight into Carver City for what I imagine is a large amount of revenue. A war would cut that off, in addition to costing both sides a fortune in supplies and lives lost."

Something like pride flickers through his eyes. "It would seem you have me over a barrel."

"Father... Daddy..." I sigh. "I love you. I've been blind to your faults for too long and let you keep me in this cage because of that love. It's over now. Either let me fly or get out of my way."

He surprises me by chuckling. "You're so much like your mother."

My chest pangs, but I refuse to soften. Not until I have his agreement. "Give me your word that no harm comes to anyone in Carver City."

"Including the Sea Witch."

"Including the Sea Witch," I confirm.

"If she harms you…"

"She won't." I don't know if I'm lying or not. If she turns away from me when I go back to Carver City… Well, I don't know what happens next. I've sacrificed the money earned for the auction. I trust Hercules's promise that Alaric's debt remains paid, but the extra money no longer belongs to me. I'll be in a city I barely know, with no money or resources of my own. But at least I'll be free.

I have to risk it.

I have to *try*.

My father is silent for so long, I have to quell the urge to fidget. Finally, he sighs. "There will be no turning you from this, will there?"

"No."

"If I lock you in your room, you won't be able to go running to Poseidon with stories." He almost sounds like he's musing. "I could send a team of my best men and finally remove the blight of the Sea Witch from my life."

My chest tries to close in on itself, but I refuse to quake. "If you do that, I'll never forgive you. I'll spend the rest of my life doing whatever it takes to bring you down and make you pay for it."

He nods as if he expects no less. "She's been my enemy for a very long time, Zurielle. Decades."

"Is your revenge worth more than my happiness?" I stare at him, willing him to see reason. "Is your hate for her greater than your love for me?"

My father looks at me like he's never seen me before. "She makes you happy."

263

"Yes." I hesitate. "She will if we're given half a chance to see what we might become."

This time, when Father sighs, he sounds defeated. "So be it. I give you my word. With the understanding that if she harms you, I will burn that entire city to the ground, Poseidon's disapproval or no." His lips pull up into a half smile. "I guess you really have grown up."

No point in reminding him that I fucked Alaric while he was on the phone with Ursa. Or in pointing out how beyond out of line his actions have been since the beginning. Not with this fledgling peace blossoming before my eyes, not when I am nearly free. "I love you, Daddy."

"I love you, too." He scrubs a hand over his face. "I've got to get to work. Be careful."

Careful is the last thing I'm going to be. Not when my heart is beating so hard, I feel a little light-headed. This worked. I can't believe this worked. "I promise."

He rises and walks around the desk to pull me into a hug. "Call me when you get there so I know you're safe."

"Okay." It's the very least I can do, a concession in response to a larger concession.

He walks out of his office without another word.

It worked. I can barely believe it. I walk back to my room in a haze. I have to pack, but as I look around, the handful of things I can't live without are already in Carver City. I hear footsteps behind me and turn to see Aya. She looks at me and looks at my room. "You're leaving again, aren't you?"

There's no point in denying it. "Yes."

Aya nods as if it's nothing more than she expected. "You care about her, don't you? The Sea Witch."

"Her name is Ursa." I take a deep breath. "I love her. I love both of them."

Aya's brows rise. "Why didn't you say something last night? Tell us that you wanted to stay?"

"Would you have listened?"

She opens her mouth but seems to reconsider. "I don't know. Being in that place…" She gives a delicate shudder. "It feels like another world. Having you stand here and tell me with clear eyes that you're in love with her—with them— feels more concrete." She shakes her head. "I'm sorry. We should have paid better attention."

"Don't be sorry." I cross to her and give her a quick hug. "I had to come back or Father would have done something unforgivable. You brought me that news, and that's important."

She gives me a trembling smile. "Will you come back to visit?"

No. I don't think so. At least not anytime soon. "Maybe. But you're more than welcome to visit whenever you want." I don't know how it will work, or if I should be making promises like this, but I won't take it back.

"Okay." This time, her smile is far firmer. "I'm happy for you. Truly."

"Thank you." I hitch a breath. "I have to go."

"Be safe."

"I will. I promise." So many promises.

I hope I'm not going to make a liar of myself.

CHAPTER 31

ALARIC

I wake up in Ursa's arms. She's relaxed in sleep, her body pressed against mine. This soft moment, quiet but for the steady sound of our mingled breathing, is something I've wanted for a very long time. To share her bed. To share her *life*.

I didn't anticipate having a half-broken heart while doing it.

Pushing away the hurt Zuri's departure caused doesn't work. It's still there, lingering beneath the surface, all teeth and claws that strike every time my mind veers back to her. To the memory of what we all shared. To the future she threw away without a second glance.

And that's just what I'm feeling. I'm a selfish bastard, but my walls don't have anything on Ursa's. It took me years to get close enough to bring her heart into play. It took Zuri three days.

The strongest woman I know, the most dangerous, cried in my arms last night. As much as I am appreciative of the sign of her trust in me, as happy as I am to be a rock to her for once instead of the other way around, I can't stop the slow ignition of anger in my chest.

Ursa shifts against me, and her breathing changes. "Good morning, Alaric."

"We should go after her."

She lifts her head. "What?"

"Zuri. If she wants to leave us, she can damn well tell us like the adult she wants to be instead of running like a coward." Another thought below that, one more insidious. "And if she didn't leave by choice like Hercules claimed, then *we* left her in the hands of her father overnight because we were too hurt to think clearly."

"Hades wouldn't lie about something like this. His entire reputation rests on *everyone* in the Underworld being safe at all times."

I run my hand down her arm. "Exactly. His *entire reputation*. Hades would lie to protect that. Zuri is nothing to him, and Hercules is one half of everything." The more I think about it, the more foolish I feel for not realizing it last night. "Do you know that when Jafar first staged a coup of the territory Jasmine eventually took over, the security of the Underworld was breached? Ali made it into the private rooms and threatened her."

At that Ursa lifted her head. "You never told me."

"I heard about it later, and it was downplayed. Similar to how Hades downplayed things last night." I huff out a breath. "I'm sorry. I didn't think of it. I—"

"Neither one of us was thinking clearly." She sits up. "But you're right. She's more than capable of telling us she's finished with us to our faces."

My pulse kicks up. "So we'll go after her?"

"Yes, we'll go after her." She rises, and it strikes me that I've never seen Ursa in the morning light. Not like this. She catches me watching her and raises a brow. "Yes?"

"Nothing. Just that you're beautiful and I love you."

Her lips quirk, though it's obvious her thoughts are on the next steps. "I love you, too. Now get dressed."

It doesn't take long to pad to my room and pull on some clothes. I take a few extra minutes to fix my hair, but I don't bother to shave. Even as quick as I am, she beats me to the door, looking as perfectly put together as if she's had several hours to get ready instead of fifteen minutes. She's twisted her locs up into a crown of sorts and is wearing one of my favorite dresses of hers, a black wrap that fades to a deep purple at the hem. She looks me over. "You'll do."

"Thanks," I say drily.

A knock on the door freezes us both. She frowns but moves to it. I hold up a hand. "Wait, shouldn't we—"

"I pay for the best security money can buy, lover. It's one of my people." She opens the door and, sure enough, it's her head of security, Monica. Ursa frowns. "What's going on?"

"I found something of yours on the sidewalk outside." She steps aside to reveal Zuri. "Thought you might want her returned to you."

"Thank you, Monica," Ursa says faintly.

Monica nods at her, and then at me, and then eases out of the room and shuts the door softly behind her. Then there's nothing to look at but Zuri. She's changed since we saw her last, which is to be expected. The slacks and green blouse are almost too severe for her, especially with her hair slicked back. It makes her look like a different person, like she's someone I'm not sure I know.

She smooths her hands down her pants. "I'm sorry."

Ursa hasn't moved since she appeared. "So he didn't take you after all."

"No. He didn't take me." Zuri takes a deep breath, her gaze jumping from me to Ursa. "My father was going to level an attack on you. I took care of it."

"You…took care of it." Ursa exhales a rough laugh. "What in the gods' names made you think such a reckless act would work out?"

"I had no choice." Zuri lifts her chin, a sure sign that she's not going to back down. "I have his word that he won't move against you or anyone in Carver City."

"What makes you believe his word?" I blurt.

She cuts a look to me, her eyes going soft. "Because if he doesn't, I'll inform Poseidon that he's about to bring war between the two cities. The Thirteen won't allow it."

"They might kill him if you do that." I drag my hand through my hair. "He has to know you're bluffing."

"I'm not bluffing." She turns back to Ursa. "I'm sorry. I shouldn't have left like that, and I know it hurt both of you. I knew you would assume I'd made my choice and left, but I still went through with it because I'd rather you were alive to hate me than the alternative."

"You have such faith in your father. He's been trying to kill me for years." Ursa still hasn't moved, every bit of her expression locked down.

"It's only recently that I know what he's been doing outside the house, but I know what his people are capable of. I am less sure of yours. I couldn't risk it." Zuri clenches her hands, her expression resolute. "It may be too soon, but I love you, and I refuse to lose you. So I took care of it. He's not going to welcome us back into the family home anytime soon, but he won't move against you. If making that choice is unforgivable, then I understand and I'll leave. But I'm not sorry I moved to protect you; I'm only sorry that my actions hurt you."

I can barely believe that she's *here*. Safe. Returned to us. Last night hurt, but fuck. I can be angry about her choices and still be grateful that she's come back. That she didn't actually choose to leave in a permanent way.

269

But I'm not the only one in this relationship.

I look at Ursa, waiting for her response. Finally she exhales shakily. "Am I to take this to mean you've made your choice, little Zurielle?"

"Yes." Zuri takes a step forward and then another. "I choose you, Ursa. And I choose you, Alaric." She gives me a quick smile. "I choose this life and the future we build together."

I take the last step to close the distance between the three of us and press my hand against Ursa's back. It's like that touch unfreezes her. Ursa pulls her into her arms and buries her face in Zuri's hair. "I was so *worried* about you."

"I'm sorry."

Ursa grabs me with her other hand and pulls me into the embrace. "Don't you ever do that again, Zuri. Do you hear me? *Ever* again. If there's a problem, you come to us and we figure it out together." She meets my gaze. "That goes for you, too, Alaric."

"Understood," I say faintly. I hug them both tightly, something inside me finally realizing that Zuri is *here*, that we're all safe. That we are actually going to have the thing I want more than anything—the three of us together.

I kiss Ursa. Or maybe she kisses me. I'm not sure how it starts, but one moment we're hugging and the next the three of us are stumbling down the hallway, shedding clothing in our wake. We end up in Ursa's room on her bed, Ursa on my cock and Zuri between our thighs, her mouth on Ursa's clit. It's hard and fast and messy, Ursa riding me to orgasm as I fight to hold my own at bay. It's no use. It's *never* any use, not when I have the two women I love in bed with me.

Ursa tumbles Zuri back onto the bed and then she's fingering her, kissing her like she'll never get another chance to again. I go down on Ursa, needing this connection, needing *everything*.

I never really believed in happily ever after. Not for people like me.

I believe in it now.

I'm *living* it.

* * *

THANK you so much for reading Ursa, Alaric, and Zuri's story. If you enjoyed it, please considering leaving a review! Still craving more of these three? If you sign up for my newsletter, you get a bonus scene featuring them!

THE WICKED VILLAINS series reaches its smoking hot conclusion in QUEEN TAKES ROSE! Aurora and Malone have been circling each other for nearly a decade and it's finally time for them to get each other out of their system… Or that's what Malone thinks. Aurora? She's got darker plans for this queen.

LOOKING for your next sexy read? You can pick up my MMF ménage THEIRS FOR THE NIGHT, my FREE novella that features an exiled prince, his bodyguard, and the bartender they can't quite manage to leave alone.

* * *

KEEP READING for a sneak peek of QUEEN TAKES ROSE!

IT TAKES me three minutes to get to Hades's office. I pause outside his door and take several deep breaths that do absolutely nothing to calm me. It's enough to get my public face in place, though, and I'm smiling as I walk through the door.

A quick glance around the office shows that it's the exact same as it's always been. Hades has a private office, but this is the room where he prefers to handle any club business that arises. The room is done in shades of gray, and careful lighting that always leave the man behind the desk bathed in shadow. It's very dramatic, but I'd never be fool enough to say as much to Hades.

He's the only one in the room.

I almost drop the smile, but I still don't know what this is about. It could be something as simple as planning a surprise scene for Meg, but if that's the case, there's no reason for Malone to be involved. Those two don't play together. Malone is Dominant, and while Meg is a switch, she only submits to Hades.

I clear my throat. "You called for me?"

"Sit."

As I make the short trip across the office to sink into a chair across the desk from him, it strikes me that this might have nothing at all to do with Malone...and everything to do with the pending deadline of my bargain coming up. I clasp my hands in my lap and try to keep my voice even. "Are you going to kick me out the same way you kicked out Tink?"

Even in the shadows, I can see his surprise. "You and Tink are hardly the same, Aurora."

A sentiment I've heard more times than I can count, especially since I took over her position. If Tink wasn't one of my closest friends, it might make me hate her. As it is, she gave me large shoes to fill when she left. I try to still my sudden shaking. "With respect, that's not an answer."

He gives a nearly soundless sigh and leans forward to prop his elbows on his desk. It brings his features into the light. Hades is an attractive older white guy with salt and pepper hair and black square glasses that frame his dark eyes. He's handsome in a scary kind of way, but he's never been anything but kind to me.

Not that he'd label it as such. The man has a reputation to uphold, after all, and if I ever pointed out that he got the raw end of our bargain, he'd deny it. Hades doesn't do *charity*, but in my case, there's no other way to describe it. What other man would give an astronomical amount to a seventeen-year-old girl and then refuse to let her even inside the club until she's twenty-one? Even then, he resisted letting me work as a submissive until I practically begged him.

I clasp my hands in my lap. "Then what is this about?"

"You're more than welcome to stay in the Underworld once your bargain with me expires. This is your home as long as you choose to stay, and once your time is officially up, the negotiated percentage that I take out of your wages will be halved." His lips quirk. "But I'd be remiss if I didn't point out that half of Carver City would happily welcome you into their homes, too."

Into their homes, and into their beds.

But not in a permanent way. I've been here long enough to watch them find their true loves, one by one. They might enjoy scening with me from time to time, but I'll always be on the outside looking into those relationships. No invitation to their homes would be permanent. I'm not naive enough to believe otherwise. "Is that what you called me in here to say?"

"No." He sits back, once again bathed in shadows. "Malone would like to contract you out for two weeks."

"*What?*"

"Yes, it surprised me, too." I can't see his eyes, but I can feel him watching me closely. "I'm inclined to say no, but Malone doesn't demand much and it runs the risk of alienating her. However, considering your history with her, it's a terrible idea."

Hades is the only one who knows who my mother really is. I don't think he's even told Meg or Hercules. Which means he's the only one who can understand why I *need* to do this. "I accept."

"Aurora."

"Hades." I can't quite soften my tone into playfulness. I never talk back to Hades. Never. Partly because I owe him so much, and mostly because of the sheer dominance he exhibits without seeming to try. He's got himself bottled up right now, but the man can send me to my knees with a single look. "This is why I came to you in the first place."

"No, you came to me in the first place because you couldn't stand the thought of pulling the plug on your mother." His quiet words are merciless. "Your need for vengeance rose later."

He's not exactly wrong, but it stings all the same. "Then let me have my vengeance."

"Malone will eat you up and spit you out. She will *harm* you."

I shove to my feet. "There is nothing she'll do that hasn't already been done to me a hundred times over during my time here." I like *everything*. Pain and humiliation and degradation. Soft words and gentle touches and kindness. It all gets me off.

It wasn't like that the single time with Malone.

I shove the thought away. I was younger then. Greener. Still new enough to the BDSM scene that I didn't know my limits as well as I do now. I didn't know how to keep my emotions separate from the physical actions. I know better now.

Hades stands slowly. I don't know how he manages it, but

it feels like his power unfurls through the room. "I would have thought all these years would make you less reckless."

The desire to apologize bubbles up inside me, but I shove it down. I am not weak, and I am not a fool. All those years ago, I came to the Underworld with two goals: to keep my mother alive and to get revenge. I've managed the first. Now it's time for the second. "I'm not reckless."

"You are the very definition of reckless." He sighs. "But you're an adult who knows her own mind. I can keep you from Malone now, but the moment the bargain is done, I suspect you'll be taking that contract."

I will. Now that she's finally made a move on me, I refuse to miss this opportunity. "Better to let me do this while I'm still yours."

He takes off his glasses and pinches the bridge of his nose. "I dislike you attempting to manipulate me, but you do have a point."

I press my lips together. Pushing him now won't guarantee victory, and it might just backfire. So I force myself still and wait while he thinks about it.

Finally, Hades shakes his head. "I'll allow it."

Relief makes me a little dizzy. There's no guarantee that Malone's offer would stand in another few weeks once I'm free of Hades's bargain. I need this, and I need it now. "When do I start?"

"Tonight."

ONE-CLICK QUEEN TAKES ROSE NOW!

ACKNOWLEDGMENTS

Thank you for all the readers who have showed up for this series book after book. It's been one hell of a ride!

Thank you to my amazing editor Man for your comments and suggestions to make this book the best version of itself. Thank you to Lynda for the copy editing!

Big thanks to Jenny and Sarah for your endless support of this series from the conception. Ursa having a collection of tentacle dildos is solely because of that one chat we had for the Wicked Wallflowers Podcast and the book is 110% better for it!

As always, thank you to Piper, Asa, Jenny, and Andie for being one text/chat away and always being ready to help me muddle through my plot snags and tell me that "too bonkers" doesn't exist. Love you all!

Hey Tim. Yes, I know you just opened the book to this page to check for your name. This year has been even more bonkers than my books. Pandemic times. Health stuff. Kids and dogs and me climbing the walls while in quarantine. I can firmly say that I wouldn't have survived without actually following through on my threat to feed the family to wolves if it wasn't for you holding down the fort, let alone actually keep it together enough to write books. Love you like a love song.

ABOUT THE AUTHOR

Katee Robert is a *New York Times* and USA Today bestselling author of contemporary romance and romantic suspense. *Entertainment Weekly* calls her writing "unspeakably hot." Her books have sold over a million copies. She lives in the Pacific Northwest with her husband, children, a cat who thinks he's a dog, and two Great Danes who think they're lap dogs.

Website: www.kateerobert.com